To Russ

MW01146842

"Enjoy the ride

Robert H. Mitchell

Fellow Lawyer
Fellow Board
Member" - The
best of luck!
Thanks
Robert

RIDE THE LIGHTNING

RIDE THE

A Novel by
Robert H. Mitchell

LIGHTNING

University of Oklahoma Press : Norman and London

The most extensive property damage caused by a prison riot in the United States occurred in McAlester, Oklahoma, in 1973. The general background of this novel comes from that occurrence. However, all of the events and characters depicted herein are purely fictional and have no connection with that event.

ISBN: 0-8061-2917-4

Text design by Cathy Carney Imboden. Text typeface is Trump Mediaeval; display typefaces are Eras Contour and Eras Ultra.

The paper in this book meets the guidelines for permanence and durability of the Committee on Production Guidelines for Book Longevity of the Council on Library Resources, Inc. ♾

1 2 3 4 5 6 7 8 9 10

CONTENTS

RIDE THE LIGHTNING

PROLOGUE

June 28, 1966—The chains were wrapped around Larry Baker's waist and fastened to the manacles around his wrists. They felt heavy and cold. He shuffled awkwardly down the dim corridor. The bindings around his bare ankles made him feel helpless and humiliated. It was 102 degrees outside, probably at least that inside. Ribbons of perspiration rolled down his belly. Still, fear did not overwhelm Larry until the moment he sat down on the straight-backed wooden chair and faced the five members of the pardon and parole board. He allowed his old friend, anger, to rise up within him just enough to control his bowels.

"Do you swear to tell the truth, the whole truth, and nothing but the truth, so help you God?" asked the young, heavyset man, glancing up only briefly at the inmate.

"Yes, sir," Larry answered in a deep voice. He fortified himself with memories of when he'd been on top of it all. The stud. The man who could do anything, the one everyone admired—or feared, which was just as good. But that was before her. *How in God's name,* he asked himself, *did I let Bitch put me in here?* He searched his mind for details. His birthday. That was the day she'd had him served with divorce papers. *Bitch didn't know much, but she sure did know how to hurt.*

"Mr. Baker," the fat young inquisitor almost shouted, startling Larry and all the observers. Chester Wyndott was serving his first term as chairman of the pardon and parole board. All eyes fixed on the chairman. The small parole hearing room was filled to overflowing with reporters from all over the country. It was the first parole board in state history to be asked to stay an execution. Along with the reporters, only a handful of corrections officials were allowed in the room. Advocates both for and against capital punishment had been excluded as potentially disruptive.

Wyndott's voice lowered two octaves, and he assumed an almost melancholy tone, his gaze back on the papers in front of him. "The transcript shows that on June 1, 1959, your wife, Betty, instituted divorce proceedings. You contested the divorce over the custody of your two-year-old son. According to your wife's attorney, you were cited for contempt, for beating your wife, hiding in her home, going to her place of employment with a loaded shotgun, failing to pay child support, and hitting your wife with your car. Visitation rights were terminated based on allegations of neglect and abuse."

Larry fought to control his features, to hide his feelings behind calm eyes. *Should have killed Bitch then,* he thought, *before all the rest happened. I shouldn't be in here, damn it. He was MY son.* Larry Baker sat up straighter in his chair as Wyndott continued reading.

"On August 23, 1959, you were removed by the police from your hiding place in the crawl space beneath your wife's home. At the time of your arrest, you told police officers you were going to kill your wife, her parents, her attorney, and the judge. Later that day, you told another officer you would kill any police officer who tried to stop you. Further, in October 1959 you told a mechanic at Dwayne's Auto Repair in Okmulgee that you might just go down and blow your wife's brains out."

Larry felt his face muscles twitch. *I don't remember that,* he thought, *but I should have done it.* Wyndott's voice continued, sounding more and more like Larry's father—commanding, controlled. *The self-righteous son of a bitch drank, fucked around, and beat Mama. Beat the shit out of me every day, too. Till I left home at fifteen and joined the army. Best thing I ever done, though. Army was better than home. Even fuckin' Korea was an improvement. At least there the enemy didn't look like my old man.*

"Testimony also shows," Wyndott continued, "that when the divorce action was pending, your mood progressively worsened. You became depressed and, while incarcerated for contempt, attempted to commit suicide. Later, after your release, the police found you in a tree across the street from your wife's residence. You were armed and wearing camouflage clothing and face paint. You told the officers that you were, and I quote, 'watching out' for your son."

Larry felt himself begin to tremble, not with fear but with rage. *It was my house! My kid, to do with as I pleased. Bitch left like I knew she would. Goddamn worthless whore. But he was my kid! I'd never have hurt him, never have done what my Dad did to me.* Tears threatened to fall for the first time in many years. But when he shut his eyes to try and stop them, something worse happened. He saw that night, just as it had happened so many years ago, as though it were projected on a screen in front of him.

He'd been about nine at the time, a scrawny little kid. Mom had taken him fishing. Dad was gone somewhere. It was summer. Hot. After a big meal of fried catfish and cold watermelon, Mom said he could sleep naked in the bed set up in one corner of the screened-in back porch. She tucked him in, something she didn't do when his father was home, and as she kissed him and held him close she whispered, "Don't you never forget this day, will you?" He promised he wouldn't, she went back inside, and he fell asleep quickly and deeply.

He had no idea how much time had passed before he

 awoke to the sound of his own voice screaming for his mother as he struggled beneath a rain of blows. The odors of sweat and whiskey filled his nostrils. He scrunched up against the wall, as far from his attacker as he could get. Then he heard something metal hit the floor. After a moment he breathed a sigh of relief. *It's over,* he thought. *All over.*

But it wasn't.

He remembered Dad's drunken voice, swearing. As Dad picked up his belt with the heavy silver buckle off the floor. Dad's huge, rough hands grabbed his legs, pulling him over to the edge of the bed. "Please, no, Dad! No, Daddy!" he'd cried. But Daddy held him face down, and continued the beating, this time with the belt.

"Hold still," Daddy hissed between gritted teeth, "hold still, ya little bastard, or I'll kill ya quick as shit."

Where's Mama? he thought. *Why won't she come?* Then the terror struck him. *If she could come, she would. So . . . she must be dead!*

Shock and grief hit him like a truck. He gave up, gave in, and lay still and limp as his father swore and sweated. His father continued to beat him, hurt him as he'd never been hurt before, made him ache and bleed and wish he was dead. *Like Mama,* he thought. *Just like Mama.*

Afterward, he lay moaning on the sheets, slick with sweat and blood.

"Shut up, ya little pussy," Daddy growled. "You and your whore of a mother are just alike." He left then, slamming the screen door behind him.

Larry remembered his surprise the next morning when he scoured the house, searching for Mama's body while Daddy lay snoring on the couch. But she was gone, and so was everything that once belonged to her, including the old truck she drove when they had a few pennies for gas. There was no blood, no broken furniture, no note.

Later, Daddy told him she'd left them. "Just took off, Sonny," he'd said. Then the old bastard went on a binge, drinking and crying and tearing the place up for weeks. When that was over, the old man settled down and stayed drunk on a regular basis. He never touched Larry again, in either love or anger. And he never apologized for what he'd done to him. Larry doubted he even remembered. They never spoke of his mother or of the night she left. Larry never saw or heard from her again.

Thinking back, he figured that night had taught him two hard lessons. Important ones. Don't trust anyone, and don't cry, because it doesn't do any good. He swallowed hard, wanting to wipe his wet cheeks but afraid to lift his arm, afraid to make the chains rattle. Then he thought, *Maybe these tears are a good thing. Maybe I can use them. They can't read my mind. Maybe the old lady, the one who kept trying to look away . . .* He opened his eyes.

Wyndott glanced up, leered at Larry, obviously enjoying his discomfort, then reluctantly turned to the other board members and asked, "Any questions so far?" When the vice chairman turned his head to look at Larry, something like embarrassment crossed his features for an instant and he murmured, "Would you like to take a break, young man?"

"No, thanks, sir," Larry answered, his voice far too ragged for his own liking. He cleared his throat. "I think we need to go on."

Individual board members either looked down at the papers in front of them, shifted in their seats, or shuffled their feet. Larry fought to focus his attention on the chairman, to keep the image of the big oaken electric chair two floors below the meeting room out of his mind. Wyndott cleared his throat and continued.

"The transcript shows that on October 16, 1959, you followed your wife as she traveled to her parents' home in the country. During a stop for gasoline you forced her into your car. The two of you picked up your son at the babysitter's house, telling the woman that you and your family planned to spend the day together. Your wife called and spoke to her employer three times that day. He reported that she seemed upset and was crying until her final call, during which she sounded resigned.

"With permission of the board," the chairman continued, "I think I'll read directly from the transcripts of the police officers' reports and the testimony at Mr. Baker's trial."

Larry closed his eyes and allowed the monotonous voice to carry him back in time once more.

"At three-fifteen P.M.," Wyndott said, "Baker, his wife, Betty, and their son stopped at a gasoline station in north Okmulgee. Baker put gasoline in the car and bought a soft drink. As he returned to the car, Betty, who was holding a handgun, exited the car and began shooting at Baker, who ran around the outside of the station as she fired. She entered the station and went into a storage room. Baker, who was also armed, followed her into the station and pointed a gun at the station attendant. Baker fired twice, over the attendant's head. Then, after the attendant crawled under the counter, Baker went into the storage room.

"The attendant heard several more gunshots. Betty screamed. Baker returned to the front of the station, pushing her in front of him. Neither was armed. Two weapons—a .25 caliber and a .38 caliber—were found in the storage room at the station.

"The attendant left his hiding place and watched Baker drag Betty to the car, open the trunk, and attempt to put her inside. She resisted. He removed a double-barreled shotgun from the trunk, closed it, and pushed her ahead of him into the driver's side of the car. He got in the car and drove south.

"The attendant watched as Baker and Betty drove about an eighth of a mile down the highway. They seemed to be wrestling over something. The attendant heard a shotgun blast, saw the windshield shatter, and watched as Baker pulled off the road. He got out of the car, dragging Betty behind him. They fought and quarreled loudly, the attendant said. Betty ran to the rear of the car. Baker opened the rear passenger door on the driver's side. Then, holding the boy with one arm and the shotgun in the other, Baker advanced toward his wife. Betty turned and began to run across the highway. Baker, still holding the child, fired at her. Betty fell to the ground. Baker then walked over, stood above his wife, lowered his son to the ground, reloaded, placed the barrel of the shotgun against her face, and destroyed her head with one blast."

Wyndott stopped reading. Larry opened his eyes and stared across the table. The old man who was the vice chairman of the board from the western part of the state was swallowing hard. He ran a big, wrinkled hand over his face. A fly buzzed somewhere and the ceiling fans turned slowly overhead. No one moved. A few board members sat staring, their mouths slightly open. One younger board member shook his head slowly and wiped his sweating brow with a clean, white handkerchief. The chairman looked back down at the papers in his hands, coughed, and resumed reading.

"Baker turned and kneeled before his son. Two truck drivers arriving on the scene testified that they saw Larry Baker kiss his crying son on the cheek, then turn the boy around, place the shotgun to the back of his small head, and pull the trigger.

"Both witnesses were treated for shock but were able to testify."

The ticking of the pendulum clock seemed to grow louder. The sole woman member of the board, with tears streaming down her pale face, quietly asked for a recess. The chairman granted her request, and the board members filed out of the room like sleepwalkers, except for Wyndott, who remained seated, staring at Baker. Wyndott leaned forward and whispered in a voice audible only to Baker, "You think you are going to cry your way out of this, little love-butt boy?" Startled, Baker rose to his feet as the guards approached. Over his shoulder he glanced back at the demonic grin on Wyndott's face. The guards grabbed his elbows and led him out of the room, up the narrow hall, and into a holding cell.

Alone, Larry leaned against the wall. *They don't understand,* he thought. *I did what I had to do. Poor little Larry Jr. didn't have a chance anyway. His whore of a mama dead, his daddy a murderer. The only other family he had was his fuckin' grandpa, and I sure as hell wasn't about to see him end up there. I did the kid a favor. Hell, I loved him, he knew that. Fuckheads won't never understand.*

Fifteen minutes later the guards came back. Once again Larry shuffled back down the hall and into the crowded room. As he sat down, the chairman called the meeting to order.

Dr. Pallin, the psychiatrist who had interviewed him, was called to testify. Larry almost smiled as the short, dumpy man with fringes of gray hair sprouting above his ears on his otherwise bald head entered the room and sat down in a chair next to him. Half glasses perched perilously on the thin ridge of his nose, Pallin rummaged in his battered briefcase for the file that contained his opinion of Larry Baker. Heaving a deep sigh that stressed the buttons on the checkered vest stretching across his paunch, Pallin began his testimony.

"Although Mr. Baker possesses some of the features of a paranoid personality, he is also the kind of person who gets things done. He is industrious, a meticulous, precise, hard-driving perfectionist. If there isn't a job, he will make one and become obsessed with it. He is impulsive, yet strongly impressed with his responsibility in every area of endeavor. A bit overly prudent and controlling, he likes to be in charge of things and feels threatened by anyone whom he perceives as wanting to run his show. He can also be stubborn and secretive, particularly in regard to discussing his childhood. This is a fairly sure sign that his problems stem from extreme childhood trauma. Also, the fact that he sometimes, if pushed too far, becomes negativistic, drags his feet, and does the opposite of what he feels he really ought to do—"

"Doctor," Wyndott interrupted tersely, "what are we dealing with here? A spoiled child or a convicted murderer? We only have a limited amount of time in which to make our decision. So for Mr. Baker's sake if for no one else's, please get to the point."

Pallin raised one bushy eyebrow before closing the file and continuing without benefit of his notes. "Very well, sir. Mr. Baker reveals, through his compulsive manner of speech and his attention to details, that he is a man who leaves nothing to chance. Again, he easily feels threatened. I believe that the circumstances of the divorce and the subsequent custody battle over the child led to a breakdown. Mr. Baker could not, during this time, distinguish right from wrong." The board members stared stiffly at the psychiatrist. He cleared his throat and added, "I further do not believe that Mr. Baker, at the time, fully understood what the consequences of his actions would be."

It was all Baker could do to keep from laughing. *What a crock of shit,* he thought. In the murmur-filled pause that followed, one of the reporters attending the hearing spoke up.

"Mr. Chairman," he said, "may I have your permission to ask Mr. Baker a question?"

Wyndott looked up sharply. A silence fell over the room as Wyndott paused, narrowing his eyes. "Well, we don't normally allow questions from the press during these hearings", Wyndott answered. "However, since you have conducted yourself with dignity and decorum uncommon among members of the press, I will allow you one question and one question only."

"Thank you, sir," the young man said. He turned toward Larry. "Mr. Baker, I can understand your problems with your wife and sympathize with you if, as Dr. Pallin implies, yours was an unhappy childhood. But shouldn't this have made you even more sensitive to your own child? Why the boy, Mr. Baker?"

Larry shook his head. He'd known, in his gut, that they'd never understand. The hope he'd felt had been a lie he told himself, a way to keep on going all this time. Nobody really gave a shit. Nothing mattered anymore. Still, he supposed the question deserved as honest an answer as he could give.

"Well, sir," Larry drawled, "I guess it was just my turn to play God. 'Cause, see, if there really was a God, he wouldn't have let things go on like they had. And . . . well, I reckon if God had been there that day . . . I don't know. I guess I might have killed him too."

At 8 P.M. on June 29, 1966, twenty-four hours after the board turned down his final bid for clemency, Larry Baker took his last steps across a fifty-foot walkway and down two flights of concrete steps in McHenry Penitentiary. In the center of a cool, damp basement room with peeling gray walls was a raised platform. On that platform stood a massive, dark wooden chair.

Because his legs were weak, Larry let himself be guided forward until his knees touched the front edge of the chair. He turned and nearly fell into the well-worn seat. The manacles were removed and his feet and hands were immediately strapped to the arms of the chair with broad leather thongs. Quick hands attached an aluminum skullcap to his shaven head. Four multicolored wires hung down from the top of the cap, trailed along the floor, and passed through a small opening cut in a white-painted plywood wall.

The wall concealed from the prisoner and other watchers the identity of the man who, with a flip of a switch on a metal panel, would send twenty-five hundred volts of electricity pulsing through Larry Baker's body.

Four law enforcement officials, one reporter chosen by lottery, and a priest muttering in Latin watched Larry as the executioner—who would receive fifty dollars for this, his three-hundredth job for the state—sat on the opposite side of the plywood wall with his hand poised above the bright red switch.

Dwight Talbot shifted in his chair, ran trembling hands through his greasy, black hair, and licked his lips as he watched the nameless inmate brought in. Talbot never bothered to learn their names. Passing by the door they all looked the same. Especially their eyes. But this one was too quiet. He liked it better when they cried or prayed or shouted.

Talbot listened as the inmate's chains dropped to the floor. He couldn't actually see the preparations, but he could imagine the guards' hands strapping the cap on the inmate's clean-shaven head, fastening both arms and legs to the chair. Talbot could almost taste the bile in the inmate's mouth, feel in his own body the tension mounting in his bowels.

Talbot awaited the warden's nod. When it came, he slammed the switch forward.

As the first surge hit Baker's body and he began his

 dance with death, Talbot moaned softly. He sent Larry Baker on his way not with a hymn but with a deep, satisfied sigh.

"Ride the lightning, boy!" he murmured, his head cocked, listening to the dying man's frantic, involuntary movements in the room beyond the white wall. A broad, mossy grin spread across the executioner's face. "Ride the lightning!"

1

DREAMS AND DISAPPOINTMENTS

May 28, 1990—Eric Williams shivered as he pulled his lean, naked body out of the backyard pool and dried himself. The dew was leaving the grass, even though the sun hadn't quite cleared the privacy fence at the far end of the garden. The warmth brought on by exertion—twenty laps today and every day for the past twelve years—eased but never replaced the numbness spreading across all facets of his life but one: his first political appointment. Hands above his head, back arched, Eric stretched before jogging back into the house. Dark hazel eyes stared back at him as he wiped fog from the mirror above his sink. They were lifeless. Dead. He shaved slowly, staring at his reflection and wondering why his clients, friends, and colleagues hadn't noticed. He'd heard it said that all good trial attorneys were consummate actors. Perhaps he was one of the best. But when, he asked himself, had his private life evolved into a staged performance? Why was he—the highest-paid divorce attorney in the state—refusing to agree to a divorce that everyone else seemed to believe was inevitable?

His father's military straight razor clattered into the marble sink, breaking Eric's reverie. The corners of his lips curled involuntarily into a wry grin. Blood oozed from a cut on his cleft chin. *What the hell,* he thought, dabbing at the scratch with a scrap of toilet tissue. He still had a full head of hair and the stubborn hope that, someday, he and Mary Jane could work things out.

Hope. That's what this appointment offer meant. He wasn't naive enough to think an appointment to the state's pardon and parole board would solve everything. But it would give him time to think. Time to feel good about himself again. And feeling anything, right now, sounded good. It was a tragedy that two parole board members had been killed in a car accident on their way to a meeting. Sometimes fate intervenes in a tragic way.

Eric dressed and hurried downstairs. On his way through the living room his eye was caught once again by the letters on the dining room table. The first one carried the ornate seal of the state in the center of the blue stationery. Underneath were the words CHIEF JUSTICE OF THE SUPREME COURT, flanked on either side by duplicate pictures of a blindfolded lady holding the scales of justice aloft. Eric recognized the signature on the letter as that of the chief justice of the state supreme court. The letter read,

Dear Eric:

On behalf of the Supreme Court, I am pleased to inform you that we have asked you to become our appointee on the state pardon and parole board in accordance with Article VI, Section X of the state's constitution. Your term will be served coterminous with the current governor. I might add that you would be subject to reappointment or replacement by the Supreme Court at the end of the current governor's term.

Our knowledge of your capabilities as a lawyer, the ethical standards that you have displayed during your time of practice, your volunteer work within the political system, and your reputation in the community were all factors that led the court to unanimously select your name as our nominee.

We would appreciate your informing the marshal of the court as soon as possible after receipt of this letter of your acceptance or rejection of this appointment.

I personally hope that you will take this appointment, for it truly is one of the most important appointed positions in our state government and one that is important to all citizens.

Sincerely,
Jonathan R. Rutherford,

copy to: Governor David Horton
Chester Wyndott, Chairman,
Pardon and Parole Board
Stephen Erman Brown, Executive Director,
Pardon and Parole Board

That letter gave Eric a great sense of pride and satisfaction. He already had decided where that framed letter would hang in his office.

Eric's attention was then focused on the second letter he had received by special delivery, just hours after receiving the chief justice's letter. That letter also had the seal of the state centered at the top of the stationery. The only indication of where the letter came from within state government was in the upper left-hand corner, where the block words STATE PARDON AND PAROLE BOARD were imprinted. That letter read,

Dear Mr. Williams:

Allow me to introduce myself. My name is Stephen Erman Brown, and I am the executive director of the state pardon and parole board. I was pleased to be informed of your appointment to the board by the Supreme Court, effective immediately.

In the interest of time, I wanted to invite you to meet in my office this Thursday, May 31, for an orientation prior to the first parole board meeting. My office is located within the McHenry Penitentiary, which, as you know, is the main and maximum security prison for our state. Once you have arrived at the main gate, just give the gatekeeper your name, and you will be directed from there.

As you probably know, the Governor is also appointing a new member to the parole board at this time. Hopefully, that appointee will soon be known and I will be able to meet with both of you.

I look forward to working with you. See you Thursday. In the meantime, if you have any questions whatsoever, do not hesitate to call me.

Stephen Erman Brown
(Please call me Earl)

copy to: Chester Wyndott, Chairman,
Pardon and Parole Board

 They were presumptuous and fast, if nothing else, Eric mused.

After his initial rush of adrenaline at rereading the letters, a dark cloud overcame him as he thought of Mary Jane. "How she hated sharing my attention," he said out loud. Shaking his head, reflecting on his inability to cope with her insecurities, he dismissed it from his mind and quickly walked out the door. Normally, Eric's swim made him ravenous. Now, after his initial excitement, his appetite had died abruptly. He left the house, stopped at a 7-Eleven on his way to work, and grabbed a cup of coffee and a Danish. As he walked in the front door of his office, having barely sipped at his coffee and not having touched the Danish, his secretary, Jolene, was waiting with a broad smile, which always made him feel better. He thought he detected something more in her smile as she quickly rose. "Well, I'm certainly glad you wore your tie this morning," she said, her smile ever broadening. Before Eric could ask, Jolene gushed, "I've rearranged your schedule, since you seem to have an important luncheon engagement today. Your old pal the governor wants to have lunch with you, out in public! Before you ask, I don't know—except that he called personally and insisted on it. I delayed all of your appointments for two hours after lunch so you can have plenty of time."

Eric smiled. "Everything seems to happen at once. That's probably best."

Three hours later, Eric passed through the heavy oaken doors of the Falcon's Nest, an elite restaurant on the revolving top floor of the Tower that catered to the capital city's wealthy movers, shakers, and wannabes. It was 1:30 P.M., a little late for lunch. Most patrons had downed their requisite two drinks and had either returned to their offices or were answering the beckoning call of golf or tennis. Eric was standing near the entrance when Tony, the owner and manager, materialized out of nowhere, smiling and offering his hand.

"Mr. Williams! Good afternoon. Governor Horton has been expecting you." The small, dark man led Eric to a table on the far side. Two burly men sitting nearby glanced up from their salads, nodded their recognition, and returned to their meals.

"Eric!" David Horton, the man known as the evangelist governor, rose to his full six-foot-three-inch height behind an elegant table set for two. In a state of fundamentalist churchgoers, the politician who could sound like the local minister had a leg up on his opponents. A soothing, ministerial voice and uncanny ability to remember names and faces had endeared Horton to the public since the beginning of his political career. In spite of himself, Eric, too, felt warmed by the man's friendly demeanor. Horton had shed fifty pounds, and his formerly unruly shock of white hair was now professionally coiffed and swept back at the sides.

The governor flashed a dazzling, boyish smile filled with perfectly even, perfectly white teeth, and extended his hand. "Good to see you, son!" he said.

"Governor," Eric responded, shaking his ex-boss's hand, "nice to see you again."

Eric gazed briefly into the eyes of the man who, alone among all the former candidates and governors of the state, seemed invincible. Yet to a certain degree, he was still a mystery, even to his closest supporters. Eric had always wondered, while working on Horton's gubernatorial campaign, why Cornelius Hermann had only parried and had never actually attacked Horton on the basis of either his politics or his personal finances. Hermann, an enthusiastic member of the opposing party, not only monopolized the state's media—print, radio, and television—but also administered an oil and gas empire. His wealth made him virtually immune to the usual financial temptations offered by politicos, so Eric felt sure no financial deal had been made. The only reason he could find for Hermann's laissez-faire attitude was that Horton might well be privy to more secrets about more people in the state than any one man had a right to know. Billy Reardon, the governor's campaign groomer and handler and now a valued aide, was one of the best information gatherers Eric had ever met and no doubt had suggested this meeting.

Horton extended his well-manicured hand, enveloped Eric's, and chuckled. "Son, we've worked together too closely and too long for formality. Call me David." The governor seated himself, and watched as Eric did the same. "So how's my favorite ex-assistant D.A.?"

"Fine, just fine. Makin' big money off the misery of others, as they say on the south side. But you know me . . ." Eric sipped his water, carefully unfolded his napkin, and spread it over his lap.

"You never really liked the criminal stuff, did you?" the governor asked, snapping his own napkin open with a flourish.

Eric peered at the governor over the rim of his crystal water glass. "No . . . not really, David," he answered, vaguely worried that his old friend and mentor might think him soft. Or worse, lazy.

"I know you're doing well financially," the governor said, deftly skewering a radish on his fork.

Eric smiled. He knew full well Reardon would have run a thorough check—credit rating, surveillance—in advance of this meeting. The governor was cautious and smart, attributes that serve the career politician well.

"Eric, I've always thought you had the best intuition of any man on my staff. You can burrow down inside people, get to truth—and motive—better than anyone I

know." The governor grinned. "No one pulls the wool over
your eyes, do they? Eh? By the way, how's Mary Jane?"

Eric shrugged, grinned back at Horton, buttered a roll, and said, "Fine." He knew stories about his floundering marriage must have reached Horton. But Mary Jane always managed to put on a good face for the society pages. She hadn't sought treatment, had never actually filed for divorce. There were no domestic violence reports on record. Nothing. Plenty of cash and her own innate sense of discretion made witnesses and loose motel receipts unlikely. Their twelve-year, childless marriage was a classic case of a disaster in disguise, a model of caring, compassionate love reduced by waning passion to sophisticated indifference. Mary Jane didn't drink. Her method of self-destruction was different, and she wasn't totally out of control. Yet. She respected him enough not to choose her lovers from among his close friends or bitter enemies. Her trysts were conducted far from home. *Bless her heart,* Eric mused. *May her sweet soul rot in hell for the mess she's making of our marriage.* Still, as close as they were, Eric wasn't about to share any secrets with this man. He'd learned too much from and about him.

Tony graciously served the veal entrée. The governor picked at his food a bit before laying down his fork and leaning forward, hands clasped in front of him in the gesture that always translated well as sincerity on Bible Belt news cuts. "I'll be straight with you, Eric," he said. "I've got a problem with my appointment to the pardon and parole board now that this tragic car wreck has occurred. It's important now, with the federal government after us for prison reform and with the overcrowding problem, that we maintain reason."

Here it comes, Eric thought. The rumor mill had been running full speed ever since the car accident had left the two vacancies. The governor, Eric knew, would believe that with Eric's appointment by the supreme court he would have an extra vote to rely upon. It was obvious that Horton wanted to have no problems with the parole board and wanted to confirm Eric's help. The governor needed to have control over a potentially volatile board that could have devastating political backlash. Guilt by association and all that.

"I know that you're a reasonable man and you'll be good at your job." Horton smiled benevolently. "I don't think the supreme court could have made a better choice, and I just want to take this opportunity to encourage you to take that appointment and let you know that we're in the same corner."

Eric covered his momentary lapse of attention with a slow grin.

"We share a strong sense of justice, Eric, an unwavering respect for the rights of the innocent and for those who have paid their dues. And I know you feel as strongly as I do, Eric, about serving the people of this state."

Eric tried to sound surprised. "Yes. Well, David, I don't quite know what to say . . ."

The governor smiled. "Attorneys always think they have to make speeches. All I want is for you to be loyal to your governor and be available for input from my office. After all, the people did elect me, Eric."

Eric answered with a smile. "You know I'll do what I can to help you, Governor." It was not lost on Eric that Horton clearly wanted another ally on the parole board. By the looks of it, the governor felt compelled to appoint, as a political favor, someone he considered less reliable than Eric. Eric was flattered but knew his friend the governor all too well. The governor might not like some of his decisions. *Ah, well,* Eric thought, *we'll let the cards fall as they will.* He was not going to lose this moment. Now the governor could use his appointment to either satisfy a political debt or create a new debt for his reelection campaign.

As Eric left his meeting with the governor, his mind was firmly made up. When he returned to his office, he called Justice Rutherford's office and accepted the appointment. The appointment would combine the best of both worlds for Eric. It would be a diversion and, more important, satisfy his need to have a meaningful effect on people's lives through government service.

Thursday morning, one week after his official appointment, Eric jumped into his silver Jaguar. He switched on the radio and scanned the dial. When the pounding bass notes of Johnny Cash's "Folsom Prison Blues" rolled out of the speakers, he chuckled, turned off the air conditioner, and rolled down his window. Moist heat flooded the car, but the breeze in his face felt refreshing and seemed to shorten the two-hour trip.

Beneath the dark bases of the towering white clouds ahead of him, a black whirlwind of turkey vultures—spring's tribunals in this part of the state—spiraled skyward until all were airborne beyond his visual range. Eric's gaze drifted back to the horizon. His destination, McHenry Penitentiary, site of his first meeting with the state pardon and parole board, seemed to rise up out of the pale green prairie before him and float on the surface like the gross, bloated carcass of a beached whale.

From a distance the place looked like any monolithic institution—anonymous and unyielding. The closer he drove, the more ominous the scene became. Maybe it was the weather, he told himself. The time of year. Or the landscape.

He exited the turnpike just before reaching the town of McHenry and drove down the narrow blacktop toward the prison. Red-tailed hawks swooped from their fencepost perches, snatching field mice as they scurried toward scattered, ragged clumps of red buffalo grass.

Eric drove up to the iron outer gates and stopped at the gatekeeper's house. A large man with crooked teeth stepped out in front of his car holding his hand out, his belt buckle obscured by his huge belly. He sauntered around to the driver's side. Eric lowered his window. The gatekeeper leaned down, hand casually on the butt of his pistol at his side. "Morning, sir, can I help you?" he drawled.

"Yes, sir," Eric answered, holding up his new identification badge. "I'm with the pardon and parole board. This is my first trip."

The guard grinned, took the badge out of his hand, and looked at it closely before handing it back. "Sir, you'll need to pin that to your shirt while you're inside the penitentiary. Welcome to McHenry. There'll be a parking place for you right in front of the entrance to the main penitentiary. It should have your name on it." He stepped back and gave a smart salute as the outer gates whispered open in electronic welcome. Once inside, Eric parked the Jag, switched off the radio, and sat listening.

Shouts and cries mingled with rock music, and the incessant clanging of metal against metal merged into a weird cacophony of human desperation and violence. Eric got out of the car, locked the door, and stepped around to the trunk to retrieve his files. After shouldering the forty-pound box, he shut the trunk and walked up the worn, stone steps of McHenry Penitentiary.

2

THE GETAWAY ROOM

Eric stopped for a moment to shift the box of files. In the shadow of the building, another, darker shadow moved toward him, eclipsing his already dim view of a heavily barred door. As Eric waited impatiently for his eyes to adjust, the shade spoke.

"Billy L. Washington, number 54682, suh." A gold star imbedded in an enormous white front tooth flashed in the face of a tall, powerfully built black man dressed in a neatly starched uniform and polished shoes. "I'm here to hep you in any way I can."

Eric managed a smile as his new aide relieved him of his burden and with a smart, military about-face preceded him toward the door.

"Kindly folla me, suh," the deep voice said. "I'll show ya to Mr. Earl's office, and if you needs me later, I'll take you to the getaway room."

At the press of a button, the barred door slid open, and Eric followed Washington toward the entrance to the prison. At the doorway, Eric glanced up and saw the foot-high letters of a sign that read "CRIME DOES NOT PAY" hanging directly over another series of steps leading to yet another barred door.

His guide stood smartly aside as the door slid open. Eric passed by him into a small cubicle. A tall, grim-faced guard in a blue uniform recited, "Sir, would you kindly remove your shoes, empty your pockets, and allow yourself to be electronically and physically examined."

The cement floor felt like ice under Eric's feet, and the

jangle of keys and change in his pockets echoed off the walls of the cramped space. The search didn't take long, but he felt uncomfortable. Violated. Washington held the box as the guard slipped his hand between and around the files. Having found no weapons or contraband, the guard signaled Washington, who shouldered his load and clicked his heels together smartly.

A gateway on the other end of the cubicle slid back into the wall, and Eric again followed his guide forward, ducked through the low gateway, stood upright, and then took an involuntary step backward. Surrounding him, the cells within the bowels of the prison formed a circle three stories high, with guard runs facing the center on each level. Men in blue uniform shirts, pressed jeans, black cowboy hats, and boots prowled the catwalks. Strapped on their hand-tooled belts were .44 Magnums. Each guard cradled what Eric assumed was a loaded shotgun across his chest. An eerie feeling of having been transported back to the wild, lawless frontier days came over him.

Eric returned his attention to the ground floor, where a line of inmates started across the black-and-white-tiled rotunda floor. A disjointed group of individuals walked spiritlessly in a long, slow, wavering line. As they passed by him, Eric noticed—with a mild sense of shock and curiosity—the haunting fear in the eyes of one inmate. But it was the indescribable blankness—neither fear nor resignation—in the eyes of another man that sent a chill up from the base of Eric's spine, over his scalp, and out to his fingertips. Something lay dormant at the core of that gaze, a silent, ready violence that was at the same time unfathomable and yet horrifying and real.

Everywhere Eric looked there were inmates. They were jammed in the cells he could see from where he was standing. A large group of inmates was forming at the head of one of the runs to begin a march across the rotunda, and still others were seated in lines along the walls. He turned to Washington. "You've got an awful lot of inmates here, Mr. Washington. Do you happen to know how many are housed in the penitentiary?"

Billy's face darkened and his perpetual smile disappeared. "Yes, sir, Mr. Williams. There are over three thousand inmates in this penitentiary."

Eric looked startled. "But the information that I read said that it was only built to house six hundred inmates."

Washington smiled sardonically. "That's correct, sir. There are four to six men in two-man cells. The inmates' time on the yard outside for recreation and exercise is only an hour a day. Because there are so many of us, they only let the inmates out in shifts. Actually, there's even fights over jobs, 'cause there's not enough to go around. There's not enough books, not enough movies, not enough facilities for recreation. Hell, there's not even enough water to go around in these hot summer months. Most inmates, unless they're lucky like me and get on trustee status, have to just sit in their cells, day after day. You see lots of fights here, Mr. Williams, lots of fights."

A new apprehension seized Eric as the line of inmates disappeared into one of the passageways to a cell block off the rotunda. Washington's voice reclaimed his attention.

"This way, Mr. Williams. Right up here, suh."

Together the two men climbed a set of narrow stairs that, Washington told him, led to the ring of offices that lay between the cells and the outer walls and fences of the building. Later, Eric would discover the elevator and realize that Washington had brought him the long way and, in the process, had provided him with a valuable, if terrifying, prisoner's introduction to the facility.

Eric continued to follow his guide down a staircase and through a doorway, the door of which was hinged so as to snap shut and offer an appearance of security. At the time Eric didn't question why the prison would use a cheap, hollow-core door that could so easily be removed by anyone with access to a screwdriver or a broad, powerful shoulder.

Beyond the door was a narrow corridor leading to the hearing room. Eric hesitated. He stood gazing at the men and women lining the walls on both sides of the corridor. The line stretched all the way to the hearing room. "This way, suh," Billy Washington said. "Mr. Earl's office is at the other end of the hall. That's the getaway room down there, but you won't need to go there yet." Eric, suddenly confused and apprehensive after seeing the number of people in the hall, was thankful for his guide's direction.

Eric walked from the silent crowd and from the smoke that hung like a dense fog beneath the low ceiling. In that brief moment that he had stood in confusion, he had felt prisoners sizing him up slowly and carefully. Some stole brief glances. Most averted their eyes, avoiding direct contact. Here again were those blank stares, the smoldering coals that burned into Eric and left behind an odd, empty coldness in the pit of his stomach.

Washington stepped aside, still shouldering Eric's box so Eric could go through the glass doors that read "Administrative Offices—State Pardon and Parole Board." Eric stepped through the door onto the worn, gray carpet. A gray, stainless-steel war surplus desk between the two interoffice doorways, unmistakably intended as a receptionist's desk, now stood empty. He didn't see the man's arm or anticipate the blow that hit his shoulder, but he couldn't miss his assailant's bellow.

"Hey! You must be the new kid on the block."

Eric wheeled around and found himself face to face with a snaggle-toothed grin as genuine as the owner's cowhide belt and boots.

"It's shore good to have ya here, Mr. Williams. I heard

a lot about you from the governor's folks. They seem to think you might be a stayer for us. Name's Earl Brown. I'm the executive director of this here tea party you were foolish enough to join. Hope you got my letter."

Eric forced himself not to rub his smarting shoulder as the huge man, who might have stepped out of a Louis L'Amour novel, grasped his hand and pumped it up and down enthusiastically.

"I did get your letter, and I appreciate it. I've also heard about you, Earl," Eric said. "Hope you can help me find my way to the toilet."

The big man's belly laugh matched his six-foot-four, 250-pound frame. "Why, Mr. Williams," he said, "this whole place is nothin' but a big ole cesspool anyway, so I imagine that'll be the easiest thing I could do for ya."

Earl, too, had a friend in the governor's mansion. Eric had asked the governor about Earl after his appointment. Horton had spoken favorably to Eric about him, the oldest of four children all born and raised on a ten-acre hog farm not far from where Horton had grown up. According to the governor, Earl was a hard drinker and a hard fighter, like his daddy. Both of them, the governor had said, were "tough old fellas. Kind of ornery, but the most honest gentlemen you'd ever care to meet."

Eric had listened for well over thirty minutes as the governor reminisced about how, when Earl's daddy was crushed and killed in an accident involving a snapped tie rod on an old tractor, Earl had become the man of the house at the tender age of fourteen. "His mama had a breakdown after that," Horton had said. "She was institutionalized. Earl tried to keep his brothers and sisters together, but the welfare department eventually split them all up. Earl managed to keep up with them, though. Even after he ran away to Fort Worth and talked his way into jobs by lying about his age."

Then, at eighteen, Horton had said, Earl applied to the police department. He lied about his education, which only extended partway through the ninth grade. Because his test scores were so high, however, no one bothered to check the facts. So, unbeknownst to the authorities, Earl became the youngest rookie in the city's history.

As a patrolman assigned to the stockyards and adjacent bars, Earl had apparently learned the hard way that there was more to police work than simply arresting criminals and prostitutes.

Horton had laughed when he remembered Earl's memories concerning his loss of innocence. "Old Earl said, 'I just thought you was s'pose to arrest everybody that broke the law. Thought I'd just stop all the crime and then everybody would just naturally be decent folks and things would be all right.' "

Eric had been surprised when Horton, whom he'd always considered to be the leading liberal in the state, had said, "Eric, Earl discovered years ago that there will always be greed and there will always be users and cheaters. You'll learn, too, son. You just can't reform them all. As Earl says, 'That's why we got prisons.' He's learned that the hard way."

Earl ushered Eric into his office, where a man was standing with his hands clasped behind him gazing out the window. Eric recognized the owner of the long, white hair that tumbled over his shoulders as that belonging to the head of William Cullen Bryan Jacks. Jacks turned as Earl said, "Senator, I want you to meet a fellow rookie of this here crowd."

The white mane and trademark western-cut suit made Willie Jacks a dead ringer for the country singer Charlie Rich. Rich's most popular song, "Behind Closed Doors," also described the way Jacks operated. He smiled in Eric's general direction, looking around to see if any reporters were there, or perhaps young ladies, who would be of more interest to the former senator.

"Just call me Willie, son," he said, grasping Eric's warm, damp hand in his own cool, dry one.

Eric remembered that Willie Jacks had been a flamboyant state senator until his defeat by the most notorious of political enemies—wine, women, and the belief that, once elected, a candidate becomes bullet proof and invisible. He never suspected that anyone would find out about his drinking and womanizing, and he certainly had not believed that, after twenty years, he could be defeated. Eric had learned from his friends in the governor's office that Jacks was desperate to get back into the public eye. He had called in a marker with the new governor for an appointment to the parole board so that, while there, he could attempt to establish a new base of support while doing the governor's bidding. The governor, Eric surmised, had quickly understood the old axiom that some appointments are "just politics." With Willie Jacks, the governor had solved both problems.

Willie Jacks's greeting was purely political and delivered with all the sincerity of a Bible Belt evangelist on the green, scented trail of donations. Eric suspected that Willie Jacks could not care less about what the parole board did or did not do as long as he came out ahead.

"Now that y'all have met," Earl continued, "I want to tell you that I appreciate you coming and thought I'd give you a little background on the parole board. I know, Senator Jacks, that you're familiar with all the state government workings. I thought it might help both of you to know a bit about the personality of the board."

"With all due respect, Mr. Brown, personality of the board doesn't matter to me as much as the personality of the press and maybe a few of these female inmates," Jacks said, winking at Eric. Eric felt a sinking feeling in his stomach. *I am going to have to deal with this guy on the parole board,* he thought. *He's still most interested in what got him in trouble.* A frown crossed Eric's face, but he recovered quickly before Jacks turned his attention back to Earl.

"I would like to know, Earl, how long we have to sit in these meetings. I'm certain with my busy schedule, I won't be able to make all the meetings. You just tell me what needs to get done, and we'll make sure it gets done," Jacks said.

Eric felt a momentary blast of heat from Earl. With an obviously forced grin, Earl said, "We'll just work it out, Senator. You know we meet the third weekend of every month for two days and sometimes three days, depending on the number of inmates. With the overcrowding situation here, we may even be meeting for a fourth day, but we can make sure that your schedule is accommodated. Now, if you don't mind, I know it may be an imposition for you, but I'd like to tell Mr. Williams here a little bit about how we work."

"Well, that'll be fine, Earl. I probably could use a little information myself, since I've never attended a parole board meeting. Don't get me wrong," Jacks intoned. "I'm here to serve." With that he sat down, crossed his legs, and started paying close attention to his manicured fingernails.

Earl hoisted one cheek onto his desk, swung a cowhide cowboy boot back and forth, and turned his full attention to Eric. "Mr. Williams, as you may or may not know, the parole board is composed of five members. That doesn't count me—I'm the administrator, but I don't vote. Three members are appointed by the governor, one by the state supreme court, which is you, and one by the court of criminal appeals. Your counterpart on the court of criminal appeals is Mr. Hoyt Hurst. Mr. Hurst is an old newspaper reporter who votes his conscience. I think you'll find him to be very conscientious. This is his second term now on the board, having been reappointed by the court of criminal appeals. And I'm sure you've heard of our chairman, Chester Wyndott."

Eric interrupted him. "Yes, I'm familiar with 'Mr. Parole.' " Eric was not particularly anxious to meet him. Chester Wyndotte was well known to anyone who had read the state newspaper over the last twenty-five years about parole board concerns. He was always available to the press, who liked his seeming candor. It was also well known in political circles that Chester Wyndotte had a cruel streak that frequently was directed at inmates, particularly the helpless and abused ones.

"The remaining member of the board is Ethel Wilson."

"Yes, Dr. Wilson," Eric noted. He was familiar with her work as a respected leader of the capital city's black community.

"Well, then, Mr. Williams, you appear to have done your homework on the board members. Are you just as familiar with our procedures?"

"No, I'm not, Earl, and I wish you could help me out some."

"Well, as you can see from all of the documents you received from us, there is an extensive amount of material on each of these fellas and gals. We form our own records from those of the Department of Corrections and our individual investigator's review of the files at the district attorney's office and the various district courts where they have convictions. We also do a background study through personal interviews with the case manager at the penitentiary, as well as the inmate himself. All of our investigator's reports are confidential and are only to be seen by the staff members cleared, as well as you members of the parole board. Of course, since the governor has to make the final determination, his office is also privy to the records. But ordinarily they leave it up to us. We then elicit an opinion from the case manager who works with the inmate on a daily basis. From that we assign an assessment level, taking into consideration all of those factors that you received in our manual, such as family background, drug and alcohol history, education, employment, and so forth. After all that, our investigator gives you his opinion as to whether the inmate is a good or bad risk to go on parole."

"Earl, I've read those with quite a bit of interest, and I find it enlightening. It really gives you a full picture of the inmate. But how do you know when someone is a good risk to be returned to society?" asked Eric.

Earl chuckled. "Well, you really don't. That's when it comes down to human nature and instinct. There will be those who will show immaculate records but who are nothing more than sociopaths and always will be all their lives. There will be others who will have worse crimes that they've committed, mostly when they were young and mostly under the influence of alcohol or drugs, and they can come out okay. If you want my opinion, you could turn out the prison population today, and sixty percent of them wouldn't come back. Those are the ones who are mostly self-motivated, mostly made a mistake that they recognize and they decided to change themselves.

"We don't change nobody in this prison system, Mr. Williams. Some just can't be changed. Others don't want to change. Some do, and those are the ones you're trying to find. It's not an easy job, and for the most part it's a thankless job. "I know this doesn't sound like much fun to start with, but I reckon you need to know all the facts."

"Earl," Eric said, "I appreciate it, and I want you to know I'll still be calling on you for help as time goes by."

In the meantime Willie Jacks, having decided to catch

up on his sleep during Earl's dissertation, was snoring ever so slightly.

Earl winked, said in a loud voice, "Well, it's time to go to the meeting," and clamped a big hand on Jacks's shoulder. Jacks started, immediately rose to his feet, and said, "Well, I'm ready to go anytime," straightening his coat lapel and walking swiftly out the door.

Earl chuckled and ushered Eric out behind him. Immediately the smoke-enshrouded passageway brought Eric forcefully back to the reality of how his vote would determine the future of not only the inmates but many other people who might be affected by an inmate's release. The closeness of the narrow corridor leading to the hearing room was oppressive. Eric hesitated again, his gaze on the men and women lining the walls on both sides. Corrections officials, family members, and friends of inmates searched his face, each trying nonverbally to transmit pleas, hopes, and warnings. The walk to the getaway room lasted less than a minute but seemed to take forever.

3

THE MEETING

He had expected a courtroom setting, complete with board members sitting judicially above some of the inmates and other inmates attending to the needs of the board members. Instead, Eric found himself in a room that barely accommodated a dozen people, including the inmate who, he expected, would soon sit in the straight-backed wooden chair at a small table six feet in front of the semicircular board members' table. Behind the inmate's chair was a half-paneled, half-glass room from where, Eric supposed, families and other spectators would observe the meeting. A bored highway patrol trooper sitting by the door was the security for the board. Eric briefly wondered how one trooper would fare with three thousand inmates. Three reporters, whom he recognized as representatives of the state's major news services, nodded at him from their front row seats. Eric had never enjoyed seeing his name in print. Now, more than ever, the shyness that had always been at odds with his lawyerly bravado overwhelmed him and his dread of personal publicity returned.

After reaching the parole hearing room, Earl ushered Eric around the small room, introducing him to the three other members of the board. First came the chairman, Chester Wyndott. Though shorter than Earl by some three inches, Wyndott weighed over three hundred pounds and cultivated a jolly fat man image that Eric suspected masked shrewd perceptions and political staying power. Thus Wyndott, a small-town doctor whose need for attention and prominence led him to a career as a parole board member, had moved up to chairman of the board and had then held on to his position for twenty-five years in spite of the shifting sands of administrations. His huge head, topped by a thin, closely cropped mantle of gray hair, constantly dripped beads of perspiration that became rivulets and flowed down the wrinkled, red gullies of his jowls. Only his eyes were small, set astride a wide, flat nose that seemed as though it had sunk into his face over the years. His wide mouth revealed small, crooked teeth set like half-sunken tombstones in an old cemetery. His meaty hand swallowed Eric's, and every other inane sentence was punctuated with a chuckle.

A large, dark-haired man in a shiny black suit came striding purposefully into the hearing room. Wyndott immediately turned his attention to the dark stranger.

"Why, Senator Tobias, what a pleasant surprise," Wyndott gushed.

Eric recognized the name. Anyone in the state who could read or watch television had heard of Glen Tobias, the dean of the state senate and unquestionably the most powerful senator in the state. With his wealth and influence in the majority political party, he was one of the most influential politician in the southwestern United States. He also had powerful enemies, including the state's leading newspaper, which kept his character and motivations under constant scrutiny. Eric had been warned by his friends in the governor's office that Tobias considered McHenry prison and all that went with it as his personal territory.

"Senator, I want you to meet Eric Williams, our newest parole board member."

Tobias turned his full attention to Eric. He grabbed Eric's proffered hand.

"Mr. Williams, welcome to my district. You have all my sympathy." Tobias flashed an even row of gleaming white teeth. "I'm not sure why anyone except Chester here would take on this thankless undertaking," he said with a wink. "But I can assure you that you're doing a service to your state, and if there is anything I can do for you while you're here, don't hesitate to call my office."

"Thank you, Senator, I'll keep that in mind."

Tobias turned to Wyndott. "I don't want to take any more of your time Mr. Chairman. Just wanted to say hello to the board and meet Mr. Williams. Call me later."

With that, Senator Tobias quickly shook hands with the rest of the board and left.

He sure as hell is charming, Eric thought. The moment passed as Earl carefully extracted Eric from the clutches of the chairman, who had returned to sucking up, hoping Eric would join his personal bandwagon. Wyndott liked his job.

Turning Eric away from the man, Earl whispered, "Watch out for that fella. He's one mean son of a bitch. God forbid any of the inmates ever catch him out."

"Really? That bad?" Eric asked around a knowing smile.

"What about Tobias?"

"Same thing, except for the inmates. They love him. He's the attorney for half the prison population. You'll see. Just wait." Earl whispered, then reached out and gently touched the suited arm of an attractive, well-dressed black woman. "Ethel? I'd like you to meet our newest member, Mr. Eric Williams."

Eric stared into the warm brown eyes of a woman whose life work he had followed since the 1960s. Ethel Wilson, at sixty-five years of age, was not only a respected leader of the capital city's black community, she was also nationally famous for her dignity and courage during the civil rights activities of the 1950's.

"Dr. Wilson," Eric said, addressing her with the honorary title she'd received from his own alma mater, "it's a pleasure to meet you."

"Please, call me Ethel. The pleasure is mine, young man," the handsome older woman answered. "I hope you will find your work with this board as rewarding as I have."

Eric remembered having read that Wilson tended to pose the same question to all the inmates who came before the board, namely, "What have you done to improve your skills?" Her sincere desire to relieve the suffering of the disadvantaged was legendary and went far beyond racial barriers. Her willingness to tackle one of the toughest jobs in state government as the only female member of an all-male pardon and parole board seemed neither unusual nor unfitting.

"Mr. Williams," she said, "I'd like to introduce you to another member of our little group, Mr. Hoyt Hurst." As Ms. Wilson introduced him, Hurst's eyes narrowed behind his wire-framed spectacles. Eric could almost hear the man's mental wheels whir and click beneath his bald dome.

"Let me see now," he said. "Your daddy was Richard Williams, wasn't he? A war hero. I remember hearing about him. And you were a hot contender for the Olympic diving team during law school, weren't you? Pleasure to meet you, young man."

When Earl laughed, Eric realized he'd been staring open-mouthed at Hurst.

"Don't mind old Hoyt, here, Eric," Earl said, "He's got a mind like flypaper. Owns a bunch of small-town newspapers in which he publishes his version of the facts."

"Earl's just jealous, Eric," the rangy, middle-aged man said, punching Earl's arm playfully. "Oughta know better than to rile someone who buys ink by the barrel, eh? Actually," Hoyt nodded in the direction of their esteemed but dripping board chairman, "my job is to balance the old teeter-totter. Sometimes our late-night free-for-alls are a whole lot of fun. Welcome aboard, son."

As Chairman Wyndott called the meeting to order, Earl whispered in Eric's ear.

"Just remember, Chester will vote whatever's politically expedient, which usually means whatever is least likely to raise a stink in the media and make him look bad. Ethel and Hoyt, on the other hand, will ordinarily vote how they feel, and the media and all the second-guessers be damned. Ethel will listen to the governor if he calls her and makes a strong argument for or against somebody. But Hoyt won't listen to nobody. I'll bet a bucket of hog slop that Willie Jacks is going to vote with Chester every time."

Eric nodded and sat down between Chester and Hoyt. Earl retired to the executive director's chair, directly behind Eric, near the door through which the inmates entered the room, and close enough to the table that he could respond immediately to the board members' needs.

The board secretary, Sue White, whose deep gravelly voice was the result of smoking at least four packs a day since childhood, called the first inmate in and announced the particulars.

"Inmate Jeremy Slade, number 54621, number forty-one in your packet," she intoned. "There has been one recent sexual misconduct within the last thirty days."

Earl leaned forward and whispered over Eric's shoulder. "She always gives the misconducts first. Any assigned within the last thirty days won't be mentioned in your packet. Reports are prepared a month in advance of the meetings." Earl handed Eric a single sheet of paper.

Eric nodded his thanks and smiled, until he looked over at the chairman.

A smile like that of a maniacal jack-o'-lantern was spreading like oil across Wyndott's face, as the prisoner, a pale, thin young man with an ugly red streak on the left side of his neck, was being escorted to his chair.

Eric scanned the addendum Earl had handed him. The information had been provided by an obviously conscientious case worker, who stated that the young man's recent misconduct involved a rape at knifepoint. The case manager had carefully included all the information needed to prove beyond question that the young man had been the victim of a crime. The system, however, decreed that he, too, must be punished for his participation in the infraction of the prison's rules. Eric suddenly knew for certain that the Constitution and Bill of Rights did not exist here. Once an individual left society, became an inmate, and received a number, he or she entered an alien world devoid of individual rights and ruled by one simple concept—survival.

The young man raised his left hand by mistake when being sworn in. The hand trembled. Wyndott laughed and mocked the boy by raising his own left hand before asking, "Do you swear to tell the truth, the whole truth, and nothing but the truth, so help you God?"

"Y-yes," answered the young man. Then, as though his knees had given out, he stumbled backward into the chair behind him.

After repeating his name and his crimes, Wyndott chuckled and, with a lascivious leer, asked, "Been havin' a little fun with the boys in here, have you?"

Tears stood in the boy's eyes. Eric figured they were as much from frustration over how to answer in a way that would please the board as they were a result of his memories of the attack. Eric interrupted the chairman's next question before it could leave his lips. Surprise and anger at being deprived of his little game with the inmate was evident on Wyndotte's bloated red face. Before he could speak, Eric hurried on.

"Jeremy, have you done anything about the drug problem you had when you came in here?"

Visibly grateful to be asked a question he could answer, the young man responded that he was currently undergoing treatment, but that it was difficult to continue since he had been placed on protection.

"I'm new here, Jeremy. Explain what 'protection' is, if you don't mind," Eric said.

"Well, sir, when a guy has troubles with other prisoners who, uh, you know, think the guy is a snitch, or who owes everybody money, or if they think the guy is someone they c-can, you know . . ."

"Yes, Jeremy, go on," Eric encouraged him.

"Well, then they put you on protection. It's about the same as being on death row, sir. They keep you away from the other prisoners and you exercise in a little walled-in area. You're alone all the time, sir, even during meals. Not that I'm complaining, sir," Jeremy swallowed, "I'd rather be in there than . . ."

"Yes, I imagine so," Eric said. "Can you tell us what sort of progress you were making in your treatment program before you were placed on protection?" Jeremy Slade told the board about his treatment, hesitantly at first, then more fluently. He told the board how he got involved in drugs and how he intended to avoid them when he got out. But when he had finished, he glanced at Wyndott and began fidgeting his hands.

Wyndott, his eyes narrowed, sat staring at Eric and chewing on the inside of his cheeks.

"Thank you, Mr. Slade," Eric said quietly. "Mr. Chairman, I return the questioning to you."

Wyndott, without removing his eyes from Eric, said, "You may be excused, inmate!"

No one said a word as Jeremy Slade was led out of the room, but Earl and Hoyt were grinning. Ethel nodded.

Willie Jacks shuffled papers and said nothing. The great, sweating bulk of Chairman Wyndott leaned slowly forward on his elbows and continued to stare at Eric as Jeremy Slade was led out of the room.

Eric cleared his throat and inhaled, enjoying the old, familiar feeling of victory as it washed over him.

"Well," Hoyt murmured gleefully as he leaned toward Eric, "you sure as hell like to start things off with a bang, don't you, Mr. Williams?"

4

JOHN AND AL

As the meeting continued upstairs, out in the exercise yard a silent sign passed between two men, both inmates, whose status within the walls made them immune to interference.

Tall, gaunt Albert McDougal strode about the yard unmolested. When he stopped to whisper a few words to one of the older guards on duty, Al's Adam's apple bobbed up and down like a bouncing ball. His nose, hooked down at the end, was bracketed by slate gray eyes, as dead as the color of a tombstone. His hair was black and greased straight back from his forehead.

Meanwhile, his conversation partner, John Jeffries, stood in the shade sucking his thick lips thoughtfully in and out of his cavernous mouth. At either side of his remarkable sky blue eyes and bushy eyebrows and stretching around the back of his short neck grew bright, curly red hair. Thick as it was around the sides, the top strands were stringy and barely stretched across his gleaming bald head. His most notable feature, however, was a protruding belly that hung out over a hand-tooled belt fastened by a peculiar buckle—a large scorpion he had trapped in the exercise yard and encased in clear plastic.

What the two men had in common was life and death. Both were convicted murders whose death sentences had been commuted to life by the U.S. Supreme Court's decision to outlaw the death penalty in 1972.

The specific talents of each man, which drew them to one another, also set them apart from the run-of-the-mill inmates. While Al had a coyote's knowledge of all things sinister and outside the law, the ideas belonged to John.

Once a kingpin in gambling, drugs, prostitution, and theft in the western half of the state, John, along with his small but efficient crew, had specialized in the theft of oil field equipment and residential burglaries. His straight sources of income had been a mildly successful plumbing business and a very successful bar and roadhouse near the turnpike and just outside the county where a future governor named David Horton was the state's most vigorous county prosecutor. Horton had never been able to touch him. The roadhouse had also featured illegal late-night gambling and had been a safe haven for the planning of nefarious adventures.

John's only little mistake, as he referred to it, had occurred when he attempted to eliminate a witness who was to testify against him before a statewide grand jury. The state's key witness had agreed to pinpoint John at the scene of several burglaries and transactions, thus making an indictment possible and a trial inevitable. First, he got the state's fastest-rising politician and leading criminal lawyer to represent him—Senator Glen Tobias, who quickly got him bailed out of jail. John was amazed at how much Tobias had learned about the case between the time Tobias had received the phone call and the time he had appeared in the court on the bail hearing. John was also pleased and surprised to find his bail was something he could afford and not what the district attorney had requested. There was a big difference between fifty thousand and one million dollars.

In their first conversation, Tobias indicated that John just needed to lie low, and he would take care of everything. Lying low was not John's style. He got impatient sitting around and waiting for the justice system to move along. So John, who took great pride in his demolition talents, personally wired dynamite to the underside of the witness's shiny new Chevy pickup truck. Ironically, this occurred on a morning when the battery had died in the wife's old Oldsmobile. The witness hitched a ride to work with a friend, giving his wife—a waitress in a local cafe—permission to drive his pride and joy. When she turned the key in the ignition, she was blown through the roof of the truck and over a nearby barn. Police discovered her head a hundred yards away from her legs and torso.

The district attorney's office now had two cases against John Jeffries. The racketeering case for which he had been indicted and had hired Senator Tobias now took a back seat to the capital case for murder. Jeffries had made the mistake of crossing the county line in order to eliminate the witness against him, and in his mistake of killing the wife had committed the act within the jurisdiction of county attorney David Horton. Horton saw this as a springboard to a brilliant political career. He threw the entire district attorney's office into months of intensive investigation in order to piece together enough forensic evidence to get an indictment and bring John Jeffries to trial for capital murder.

Once again, Jeffries turned to Senator Glen Tobias for representation.

Painstakingly, the district attorney's office, under the guidance of Horton, assembled an ironclad case against Jeffries. The forensic evidence revealed that some of the explosive materials had come directly out of the plumbing shop of John Jeffries. He had been careless in his belief that all of the evidence would be obliterated by the explosion. Horton had enlisted the help of the FBI technical laboratory in Washington, D.C., to help find the source of the wiring leading to the explosives. It was a brilliant piece of strategy, and Horton carried the FBI laboratory personnel hrough a series of questions that pieced together the jigsaw into a perfect picture of guilt.

Senator Tobias had only one strategy left that had not been presented to the jury. He gave Jeffries, who had no alibi, the choice of whether or not to testify, knowing full well the risk of cross-examination in the face of the thorough investigation and background check that had been made by Horton's office. Though his lawyer had cautioned him of the pitfalls of testifying and even counseled against it, Jeffries figured that he could convince the jury himself that he had nothing to do with the crime and would walk out the door a free man. That was John Jeffries's second mistake. Though Jeffries appeared relaxed and displayed an absolute glibness for lying, Horton had done his homework. Under skillful cross-examination, Jeffries not only was left without an alibi for the time period involved, but tacitly had to admit that the materials in making up the explosives were the same as those that he kept in his shop. Combined with the horror of the death itself, it didn't take the jury long to reach its verdict. Jeffries was convicted of first-degree murder and received the death penalty. David Horton had taken the first giant step to his eventual election as governor of the state.

After the verdicts were read, John broke out in a wide grin, and as he left the courtroom, he turned to an emotionless Glen Tobias and said, "I'll never see that old oaken chair. But there'll be some folks who'll see me again." The grin belied the turmoil behind his ice blue eyes.

John had later confided to his friend Al that maybe he might even get him a lawyer or two. "Sumbitches cost me an arm and a leg and a part of my ass, and all that just to get me the death penalty." John was not grinning this time.

Al McDougal, on the other hand, was less overzealous

than he was careless. His favorite line of endeavor was killings for hire. He too had been involved in prostitution and gambling, but his home was in the eastern half of the state, an area that held no interest for John.

Prior to their convictions, the two men had maintained a friendly, arm's length rivalry. Al liked to say that he and John just lived and let live. In fact, Al's last mistake started in John's roadhouse bar, when an acquaintance of Al's by the name of Pete sidled up beside him and asked if he would like to help him "say farewell to a fella."

Al asked how much was in it for him. Pete replied, "I've got five thousand dollars, twenty-five hundred down and twenty-five hundred when we finish the job. I'll split it with ya." He produced an envelope filled with twenty-five one-hundred-dollar bills.

With his new partner Al drove out into the countryside to view the grave site Pete had already dug in preparation for the body. It wasn't until they were gazing into the grave that Al finally asked, offhandedly, "Who are we killing?" Then, when Pete named one of Al's close friends, Al took offense, coolly took out his .357, shot Pete, recovered the money from Pete's body, and buried his would-be client in the grave painstakingly dug for another man.

Unfortunately, Al had not scouted the area and was unfamiliar with his surroundings. Shooting Pete was a spur-of-the-moment thing, something no self-respecting businessman ever did if he hoped to cover his tracks.

A lone deer hunter had observed Al from a tree stand in a nearby thicket and was able to give local law enforcement a good enough description. Yet the description and physical evidence found at the scene were still not enough to convict Al. He might have gone free had it not been for his second little mistake.

It seems Pete had been the pimp and lover of one of the capital city's leading prostitutes, Cleo Abrams. Following a relatively short period of mourning, Cleo's grief turned to anger, and she marched into the police station shouting that she wanted to see someone about her boyfriend's murder. Once again, David Horton had an opportunity to put behind bars one of the most notorious criminals in state history. The jewel he discovered in Cleo's testimony was the information that Al's current girlfriend worked for Cleo. As he had done many times before, Al had used his girlfriend as an alibi. Cleo blew Al's cover.

Unfortunately, she didn't live long enough to celebrate her victory. Al later confided to a friend that he had "dumped Cleo's fat ass north of town where nobody would ever find her." Although the remains of Pete's loyal, vengeful lover were never recovered, her testimony damned him from beyond a hidden shallow grave. The combination of testimony and crime scene evidence once again aided David Horton. The ambitious district attorney was able to obtain his second conviction of a major crime figure, yet another man whom he had pursued over a period of several years.

Al's only regret was that he had been convicted over such a paltry amount of money. "It should have been for at least twenty-five thousand," he'd moaned.

Jeffries, however, wasn't concerned about money. For years he had been brooding about the past, wanting revenge, and planning a future that would allow him to get it.

Later that day, while the five members of the pardon and parole board were still hard at work just two floors up, Al McDougal and John Jeffries met in the shadows of the east cell block.

"Twenty minutes is all I can give you, boys," whispered a voice from above them on the catwalk, "then it's chow time."

"Why, thanks, Johnson," John hollered back, "mighty nice of you to remind us of the day's schedule."

Al chuckled, amazed at his friend's audacity. He lit two cigarettes, handed one to John, and waited for his friend to settle down and outline his plan.

John took a drag and leaned against the cold concrete wall.

"Al, ole buddy, I believe now is the time to line out our plan for escape. We're going to need some help from some of your boys. We also need to get that new Aryan white-supremacy group lined out. I don't believe we'll have much problem, because of the overcrowding and the summer heat. You've got to be my trigger man. I need the hard-core boys out on the E cell block to start a riot. I'll make sure we'll have some dope available. They already have a moonshine whiskey operation. I'll leave it to you and your boys to make sure that things are stirred up. As for the Aryan gang, they've organized themselves into what they call the Church of the New Sun. Our devout warden, with the help of my lawyer, Tobias, allows them to hold services in the cannery building. That many crazies in the cannery can easily overpower what guards are around. Once the cannery is taken, that'll allow them to take over the whole south end of the grounds. I'll handle that end. The Muslims will take care of themselves. I'm counting on them to block off the end of the west cell block. If they decide to come out for more territory, then there'll just be more riot. It should all fall together. Think you can handle your end, Al?"

"Sure, whatever you say, John." The anticipation of that much bloodshed brought a smile to Al's face.

"I want you to get that punk of yours, Roger Dale, to recruit the new guys coming in. I want armed robbers, rapists, and kidnappers. No burglars or dopers. They either don't know what they're doing or would sell out their own mothers for a hit of crack. I figure the best time will be on a Friday. All of the administration is ready to go home to spend the weekend. No one's mind will be on business. Let's aim for the September pardon and parole board meeting. There'll be a group of inmates outside the getaway room. We need to get those guys free from their chains and get them to take over the administration wing. I don't see how that could be a problem, since most of them know they're not going to be paroled anyway. Once they've taken over the administration offices, that'll give us access to the guard catwalks. And once we have the catwalks, it'll be nothing to take over the central control panel in the rotunda and open up all the cell houses. That's your job."

"You got it! What's the plan of escape?" Al asked.

"A little project is going to be done to remodel some of the prison utilities. I'm going to be the head of the crew to do those repairs. You'll be on my crew, and that'll give us total access to move freely, getting tools, and having access to places where the screws can't get to us, except one or two at a time. That we can handle. It also fits in with the timing. It probably won't get started till late August or September. The boys will be ripe for a riot by then. Also, it gives me time to get a few people outside to help us when we stage the break. I'll take care of it and tell you in plenty of time when to act and how we blow this joint."

"Sounds good, John. I've got to hand it to you. Crowds mean you can hide. Crowds create diversion. Diversion means nobody is looking for you. That'll be good. But how do we communicate? How do we let everybody know when the time has come?"

"That's the final part of the picture, Al. We seek a little help from George Davis. He's being transferred here."

"You mean the guy that started the con newspaper upstate?"

"Same one. The warden thinks a con newspaper will make him look good. The paper will be our message service. They're calling it *Concepts.* Ain't that cute."

Al dropped his cigarette. The ashes flared brightly in the gathering gloom. He said slowly, "George Davis is one smart son of a bitch, John. You sure you want to get him involved in this? He comes up for parole next month because of all his goody-goody shit. Hell, he wasn't supposed to be up till the year 2000."

John snaked his arm around Al's shoulder and jerked his head closer. He whispered sagely, "I happen to know that ole George is going to be turned down for parole. The warden wants him here. Yeah, George is gonna be ripe for the pickin' when he finds out. Without us, he ain't gettin' out of here til he's too old to take a piss by himself."

Al shook his head slowly. "But I still don't understand how George Davis—"

A voice from above them on the guard run whispered, "All right, you two. Break it up."

John patted his old friend's shoulder as they walked toward their cells, and in a voice as cold as ice, replied, "Trust me Al, the best is yet to come."

III When Eric's first board meeting ended, his head felt heavy with stories. Earl escorted him out of the prison, this time by way of the elevator and the front steps. A storm had passed unnoticed by those inside. Stars shone wetly high above the well-lit parking lot. The two men stopped walking near the rear of Eric's Jaguar.

"Don't need to ask how you liked your first day, Mr. Williams," Earl said, grinning and scratching one edge of his grizzled jaw line. "I can see it on your face."

Eric nodded, opened the trunk, and nearly dropped the heavy file box inside.

"Hard to believe people really live like that, ain't it?"

The older man gazed sympathetically down into Eric's upturned face.

"Earl," Eric replied, turning to shut the trunk, "I assumed I'd run into a lot of drug-related stuff. But, Jesus, I had no idea of the amount of abuse and neglect going on in these people's families, or that alcohol plays such a major role."

Earl chuckled. "Makes ya wanna turn temperance, huh? Resurrect that woman from Kansas—Carrie Nation?—and go swing an ax or two?"

Eric nodded and gazed into the prairie night out beyond the wall and the rings of barbed and electric fences.

"But, then again," Earl said, rubbing the back of his neck and flashing his best Will Rogers grin, "it shore makes a strong man wish he had a drink, too. Don't it?"

Eric got in his car and smiled up at his new friend. "Lead on, Earl."

Earl ambled over to a well-used red Dodge pickup truck, hefted himself in, and slammed the door. Then he leaned out the open window and yelled, "I know where there's good service, edible food, and plenty of cold beer. Let's see if we can't put the color back in them young cheeks of yours, Mr. Williams!"

Eric climbed into the Jag, started it up, and followed Earl's pickup out through the gates and onto the turnpike. After five or six miles, they took an exit and made a left at a stop sign. As Eric followed Earl's taillights through the night, windows down, on a narrow, paved road headed toward a few twinkling lights on the horizon, he began to relax. Fireflies danced and crickets chirped in the tall grass alongside the road. The full, rising moon hammered a small farm pond into a medallion of pure silver.

As he drove, Eric reflected back on a day that had felt more like a nightmare. First, his thoughts of Mary Jane and his lonely drive. Then, the curious journey into the heart of the prison. Finally, he thought back over all the inmates he'd seen and the stories he'd heard. Exhausted as he was, Eric still felt challenged, exhilarated, and certain that he hadn't made a mistake by accepting the job. Maybe, just maybe, he thought, I can discover a rule of reason that can help these people and their families.

Ahead of him, Earl's truck slowed down and pulled off the farm-to-market road and into a crowded, muddy parking lot. The place didn't look like much on the outside, just an old 1920s house that had been converted into a bar and restaurant. The ornate front porch, still intact, gave the place a little character. Still, he'd seen many houses like this, built with no plumbing or electricity. Many of them still had no plumbing or electricity and provided only minimal shelter for sad, lonely children who, very likely, would become dark, hopeless adults like those he'd seen all day. The pink neon sign blinking "Jo's Place" seemed garish and out of place.

He followed Earl into the dimly lit bar. Inside, a huge, round-topped jukebox blared country western music at the far end of a surprisingly large dance floor. A couple dozen dancers were dressed up, paired off, and happily scooting their boots in a counterclockwise circle at the outer edges of the highly polished wood floor. Thirty or forty men and women—all arrayed in denim, cotton, and leather—drank longnecks, smoked cigarettes or chewed tobacco, and generally washed down and talked out their daily troubles. The busy bar ran the length of the wall from the entryway to the back. Earl led Eric through the crowd to a table in the far corner, away from the jukebox.

"Earl, you old fool! Hang on and I'll be right there!" a shrill voice shouted from somewhere in the room.

Eric saw a hand wave briefly above a couple of cowboy hats near the bar and then disappear. The hand soon reappeared, however, attached to a short, stout blonde woman in blue jeans that seemed ready to burst away from her 250-pound body at any moment.

"This the new one, Earl?" the woman crooned as she bounced into Earl's lap.

"Umfph!" Earl groaned, "Bomber, you little bitch, still trying to kill me? And I thought you loved me all this time." The big man grinned. "Mr. Williams, meet Bomber. She runs this here joint and don't need no bouncers to take care of trouble."

After planting a big kiss on Earl's beefy face, Bomber stood up and shook Eric's hand. "Nice to meet ya, Mr. Williams. Ah can tell Earl here likes ya, and if he likes ya, ah'll like ya too. Drinks on the house. What can ah git for y'all?"

"The usual, Bomber. Same for Eric, but make it light, right, Eric?"

Eric grinned and nodded.

"Damn young pups," Earl groused. "Worry too much about their weight."

"Comin' right up, boys," Bomber promised and bounced off like a badly released bowling ball on a warped lane. Eric had no doubt that if ten people were standing at the end of that lane Bomber would make an easy strike.

Earl grinned as his gaze followed her across the room. Then he laughed. "Ain't that a lot of woman, now? Wait'll you see her dance, son!"

Eric spent the next hour watching the crowd, drinking beer, listening to Earl talk, and wolfing down one of the biggest, juiciest steaks he'd ever eaten. For dessert, he watched in amazement as Earl whirled Bomber around the dance floor to the "Tennessee Waltz." After four beers, Eric was beginning to feel as though the building had landed on his head.

"Earl," he said as his new friend stumbled back toward his chair, "I think I better go to bed."

Earl squinted at him and popped a toothpick in the corner of his mouth. Then he sat down, reached like a slightly clumsy bear through the mess of empties on the table, and put a massive paw on Eric's shoulder. "Mr. Williams," he shouted above the crowd noise, "I'm gonna warn ya, 'bout one thing, jest 'cause I like ya. Don't take on the cause of every inmate. Stay above it and stay away from it. If you don't, you won't last a month. Most of these folks you just can't help, bad as you want to. That's the reason we got prisons. Remember that and you'll do just fine." Earl laughed and pounded Eric's shoulder. "Shore was proud of the way you came out of the gate today. Yessiree."

Eric stood and turned to go, then faced his friend again and shouted, "Thanks, Earl. That may be the nicest compliment I've ever received."

5

MARY JANE

Twenty minutes later, Eric closed the door of his room at Motel 6, checked his watch, and sat down on the edge of the bed to call Mary Jane. He had told her he would call to discuss the divorce settlement. It was 11:45. He dialed and got her answering machine, but no Mary Jane. Sick dread made him perspire. But he was also full and exhausted. He lay back on the bed and seconds later fell into a troubled sleep.

The Dream, as always, seemed to go on forever. Eric shivered as he drifted into the Dream. Everything about it was familiar. The odors of chlorine and mildew, the hum of voices, even the turquoise-tinted air. Standing on the edge of the high dive, he looked out across the pool and watched his mother's delicate, proud face float out of his memory and into focus among those of the judges. Except for the fact that his mother had been dead for five years before he graduated, everything else in the beginning of the Dream was just as it had happened that day. He'd spent more time working out than he ever spent studying; getting up at seven A.M. every morning, every day of each semester, to work for two hours before running to his law classes.

Sunlight flooded through the windows of the gym, fractured the surface of the silvery water and reflected back up, waltzing across the walls, over the ceiling, and into the hot, moist air that entered his lungs. Sure as gravity, confident of winning a place on the Olympic team, Eric waited for the high-pitched whistle that always echoed through the rest of the Dream. When it came, the weight of his dream body balanced itself on the balls of his feet. The sandy grit of the board's surface tickled his toes. Every muscle strained for height as he launched himself, first up, then out, then over and over and down and down through bottomless, hollow space and endless time. Seconds became minutes and minutes turned into days as he moved and twisted, free-falling toward the shining surface of the water that stretched itself upward to meet him. He tensed, ready for the ultimate ecstasy of contact, ready to cut the surface cleanly, leaving no ripples behind. But he couldn't do it, couldn't reach the water. Instead, as he fell closer and closer, the water seemed to move farther and farther away.

Eric awoke in a cold sweat to the sound of his own heartbeat fading beneath the persistent ring of the telephone. The dream images rearranged themselves into digital numbers on the bedside clock radio—6:00 A.M. It was his wake-up call. Friday morning.

Eric tried again to phone Mary Jane. Again he got her machine, so he dressed, grabbed a quick breakfast in the motel restaurant, and spent until seven that evening at the prison reviewing inmates. After trying her apartment one more time from a pay phone, he made the long drive home.

When he arrived around ten that evening, the house was pitch dark. He could tell Mary Jane had been there. He unlocked the front door, expecting to find a note, even knowing where he'd find it. He stopped to mix a drink before picking the small lavender notecard off the dining room table and heading down the hall toward the den. Just inside the doorway, he flipped on the light and read.

Eric,

I'm sorry I missed your call. I will be leaving town for a while.

I will call you about the terms of the settlement. Believe me when I say I'll always love you, but I can't be with you.

M.J.

When he looked up from the note, Eric realized he was staring at the photograph Mary Jane had framed and given to him on his birthday a year after their honeymoon. There she stood, beside him, facing the camera held by a cooperative Virgin Islander. Slender, tan arms clasped above her head, smiling, her long, silky dark hair contrasting perfectly against the sun-kissed sand. The ocean, the sky, and her eyes—all an incredible bright blue.

Eric remembered the last morning they'd been together. He remembered it like it was yesterday rather than a month ago. He had awakened and turned to gaze across the king-size gulf of blue satin where the still-sleeping form of his wife, Mary Jane, with the sheet and comforter wrapped around her legs and her slender bare back, turned toward him. A warm flow spread from Eric's gut toward his groin. Daylight crept through the space between the bottom of the blinds and the window sill.

Eric lay transfixed, watching as a fine line of morning fire spread across Mary Jane's thick, dark hair, haloed the soft curve of her shoulder, and illuminated the graceful valley between her waist and the full curve of her hip. He longed to pull her close, nestle her warm, smooth curves against his cool arms, chest, and thighs. He reached out and, this time, actually managed to touch her shoulder before the tidal wave hit. Desire receded like a massive undertow, and he jerked his hand back just as Mary Jane rolled over on her stomach and turned her face toward him.

Repulsed by the beauty that had once attracted him, furious that it still could, Eric waited until her breathing steadied once more. He did not awaken her, nor did he lose himself in her cold blue eyes and moist interiors, did not—as he had before—demand she tell him where she'd been all night. Who she'd been with. He'd made her promise not to lie, but the last thing he wanted to hear that morning was the truth.

Eric remembered finally rolling to the edge of the bed, standing up, and shaking his dark, curly head of hair. Snatching his dark green terry robe off the bedside chair, he padded across the off-white Berber carpet and out into the silent hall. While drying himself off after his usual twenty-minute swim, he reentered the house, and on his way through the living room a slight movement in the corner of the curtained room caught his attention. Mary Jane, wrapped in her white satin robe and sitting with her long, tanned legs beneath her, had been waiting for him. He expected her to rise, offer him breakfast, and head toward the kitchen as usual. Instead, she sat staring at the floor in mute silence. Finally, he moved toward the stairway.

"Eric . . ." she began. He remembered turning to face her as she continued speaking.

"It's just not working. Something must be done. If nothing changes, I'll leave you."

It crossed his mind to fight and say, "Sugar, you already did, years ago." The words hung heavy in the roof of his mouth. He gagged them down and replied gently. "Honey," he had said, "I think we ought to try. I'll try to stay home more often. Honest."

Tears glimmered on her cheeks, Eric remembered, as she said, "Eric, I remember a time when I had to push you out of bed to get you to leave me and go to work every morning."

He had stopped himself, afraid of what his real, gut-level feelings, his honesty, might have done to her. Waves of anger and guilt had washed over him. He knew she couldn't help herself, knew she didn't want to push him away. But she always had.

"You should know better than anyone else," Mary Jane had said. "I'm lonely, Eric. Horribly, terribly lonely."

He had known Mary Jane was referring to the affair—really, a one-night stand—he'd had with a colleague's secretary. It had happened during the weeks that Mary Jane was spending every night at her dying father's bedside. She might never have known about his transgression, his single fall from grace, if guilt hadn't gotten the better of him.

His advice to clients in similar positions had always been to confess to a minister, a priest, a therapist—anyone but their spouses—because, he believed, such a confession only widened the gulf between husband and wife.

But he hadn't been able to follow his own advice, and he still wondered why. Had his confession truly been motivated by a desire to receive absolution? Or had he consciously sought to punish Mary Jane? He didn't know, but it had backfired.

She had held one hand filled with kindness and forgiveness outstretched toward him, and with the other hand she shoved her own numerous, ongoing affairs under his nose.

The note still in his hand, Eric sat down heavily in his chair. Somehow, at times like this, all the anger and pain left him and he was able to remember her as she had been, as they had been together, in the beginning.

During the early years, Mary Jane's insecurity had seemed like a manifestation of her girlish charm, her feminine vulnerability. He felt flattered, wanted, and necessary when she fell so hard, so fast. At the time, she insisted that her anxiety about his comings and goings, her questions about his old girlfriends, and her tendency to want to make love anytime they had even a minor disagreement were all expressions of her deep love for him. But it didn't seem to matter how many times he reassured her, she couldn't seem to trust him. It took Eric a few years to realize what was happening. When he did, he began to pity her. As the neglected daughter of an oil-rich, strict fundamentalist father and a social climbing, holier-than-thou mother, it was no wonder Mary Jane so desperately sought attention and affection. In high school she'd discovered that sex was a satisfactory, if only temporary, substitute for true intimacy.

That discovery resulted in pregnancy, disinheritance at the age of sixteen, and a shotgun wedding with a boy who assumed he was marrying into money.

Later, the boy resented his new wife and her pregnant, penniless condition. Arguments escalated into fights, fights led to beatings, and Mary Jane miscarried during the seventh month of her pregnancy. A neighbor helped her find the courage to file for divorce a few months later.

But Mary Jane's hopes for a reconciliation with her family ended abruptly when her father, in response to her pleas for acceptance back into the family fold, decreed that the miscarriage—and her subsequent sterility—were God's retribution for her sin of fornication. He would have nothing more to do with his daughter. Mary Jane's mother didn't go to the hospital when her daughter miscarried, and later she made sure that Mary Jane became persona non grata among her sisters.

Intellectually, Mary Jane knew her exile was unjust. But emotionally, she so desperately needed her father's love, support, and approval that she became depressed and shut everyone else out, including Eric. She awoke crying every night for weeks and began to fantasize that suicide would end her misery. Then, after her father's death, and that of her mother, which came only a few months later, the nightmares and suicidal thoughts ceased and her promiscuous behavior began. *Funny,* Eric thought, *how in the beginning everything had seemed so filled with promise.*

He came to accept the fact that Mary Jane had no confidence in herself as a woman, as a wife, or as a daughter. Still, he felt, she might have outgrown some of her insecurities had her father not managed to lay upon her one final curse.

Eric could still picture her, standing eagerly at her father's bedside, a beautiful, shy, guilt-ridden child hoping for the loving forgiveness that would free her from the pain of familial isolation. Instead, from his hospital bed, her father had raised his voice like a crazed prophet and pronounced judgment, called her a whore, blamed his financial fall from grace on her moral turpitude, and damned her to the hell she'd been taught all her life to fear.

Mary Jane had come close, then, to a complete emotional collapse. Her promiscuous behavior started. *Fueled, no doubt, by my infidelity,* Eric thought. Still, she refused to seek counseling. Finally, about six months into his own recurring dream, Eric had sought help himself. After only a few sessions, Carolyn, his counselor, had presented the dilemma concisely.

"Eric," the petite redhead said, "you'll just have to decide whether you can live with Mary Jane's demons. Right now, she seems determined to let them destroy her and your marriage. Maybe over time, with your constant love and encouragement, she'll come around. Maybe not. All you can do is hope . . . or find a good divorce attorney."

Eric drained his drink and slipped the note into the corner of the frame so that it just covered her image. Now, in the photo and in life, he stood alone. Finally, he could do what had once seemed impossible—let go of the pain, turn away, leave her in the darkness, and close the door behind him.

6

THE SMELL OF DANGER

It was Saturday morning, Eric's first weekend alone in the house. He cut his usual morning swim short by five laps and, still dripping beneath his terry robe, filled a cup with decaffeinated coffee and headed down the hall to the den. The first file he pulled from the box belonged to George Davis. Eric had asked Jolene to gather all the *Daily Herald* microfiche articles on Davis and add them in with the rest. He spent an hour at his desk going over the contents of the six-inch-thick file before moving to the battered old recliner Mary Jane had always called "The Womb." He rubbed his eyes and sighed.

Of all the men whose files he'd read over the past few days, Eric considered George the least likely to belong in the prison system. Although he'd been repeatedly decorated for heroism in Vietnam, George had become a drug addict and, ultimately, a murderer. Eric had heard and read enough over the past week to begin to doubt some of the stories inmates told. But he felt as though he was beginning to understand the complexity of problems that brought them to prison. At least he felt he understood about as much as any law-abiding citizen could.

Although the tragic details made each case unique, many inmates shared similar backgrounds, and their stories were generally about the same. Most offenders came from the lower socioeconomic levels. Almost all, male and female, had been abused as children by one or more family members. Nearly all had been involved with some form of substance abuse, usually alcohol. They had been taught that education was of no importance and that the only attention they could hope to attract would be negative and self-created. Among the men, there seemed to be a scarcity of positive male role models, which set them up for adoption by older, seasoned criminals. Their initial crimes were committed while drinking or using other drugs that helped them suppress their fears and self-doubts.

Eric smiled bitterly when he thought of all the federal and state money pouring into efforts to eliminate street drugs—cocaine, heroin, and marijuana—when beer and whiskey seemed by far the biggest problem. His research had shown that three times as many crimes involved alcohol as involved the other drugs. Methamphetamines ran second to alcohol by a wide margin. And according to Earl, guards allowed the more seasoned, discreet inmates to smoke marijuana because it kept them mellow. And thanks to the so-called war on drugs, mandatory drug sentences had only worsened prison overcrowding throughout the United States.

Eric had to agree with Earl's assessment of the war on drugs. Just two nights before, around a mouthful of Jo's famous steak, Earl had said, "The way to get elected is to scare the shit out of the voters about somethin' they know nothin' about. Don't mess with the general population's greed and self-indulgence. It's called politics as usual, Mr. Williams, and it's been goin' on since caveman days."

Eric held George Davis's file closed in his lap. *Here,* he thought, *is a life worth saving.* It wouldn't be easy. George was serving a five-hundred-year sentence for first-degree murder and armed robbery. However, although he was only thirty-eight, George had already used his prison time to become an accomplished artist and writer and had cultivated the leadership potential that had cropped up while he was in the military. Unfortunately, his drug problem had begun in Vietnam as well. Eric felt he needed more direct, personal information. The state attorney general, Barry Morris, had a brother, Clint, who had served in Vietnam with Davis. Eric didn't have to look long for Clint Morris's number.

The phone rang only twice.

"Hello?" The line was clear, but the voice sounded fuzzy.

"Clint? Eric Williams here. I doubt you'll remember me, but—"

"Why, sure, Eric," the gradually reviving voice responded. "We met at the inaugural reception, and then, let's see . . . you were also at Barry's Christmas open house, right? Heard you're on the parole board now. Congratulations! How's it going?" The man's voice sounded slightly strained, as though he might be shifting from a horizontal position to a vertical one.

"Thanks, everything's fine, Clint, just fine. Except . . ." Eric paused and then continued, "Look, I hate to bother you on a Saturday, but—"

"No, hey. What can I do for you?"

"Well, I need a favor. Some information on a guy I think you know. George Davis."

"George? Yeah! He up for parole already?"

"Uh-huh. File shows he's been a model prisoner, but I really don't know much about his life prior to conviction."

Clint sighed. "That was a long time ago, Eric. But George and I used to be pretty tight, so maybe I can help you. I'm not sure, but I think he was born in a little bitty town down in the southwest corner of the state. Bessie? I think that's it, but I wouldn't swear on it. He had a bunch of brothers and a couple of sisters. Oh, yeah, his dad worked a hundred-and-sixty-acre farm, most of which he leased. Seems like he had forty acres or so of his own around the home place. Guess you'd say they were typical, hard-working, God-fearing, early-to-be-worn-out farmers. His family always seemed too large for the amount of ground they worked and the prices they could get at the market."

Eric smiled to himself. Clint wasn't head of a large public relations firm for nothing. "Was he the only son who went to Nam?" Eric asked, feeling his usual twinge of embarrassment over the fact that, as the only son of a widow, he had not been invited to join in the conflict.

"Yep. In fact, it was sort of a big deal, if I remember right. Two of the other boys might have gone if one hadn't married at sixteen and had two kids and the other hadn't sliced off half his foot when his ax slipped off the log he was chopping. But George was young, healthy, and athletic—the perfect candidate for a less than perfect war, right?"

Clint paused, so Eric probed a bit deeper. "His file says he was a rifleman in your Ranger platoon, an expert marksman."

"Sure. Shooting jackrabbits on the prairie was good practice, I guess. But George had other talents, too."

"Like what?"

"Well, he could move like a ghost. And, better yet, that boy could pinpoint the source of even the slightest sound. He usually got assigned point man on recon and ambush squads. Let's see . . . well, hell, he could take a man out at a thousand yards and—"

"Jesus!" Eric interjected, picturing the distance.

"Yea! But hey, listen, man." Clint's voice sounded both awed and excited. "You ain't gonna believe this part. Davis could literally smell the enemy." "Ah, come on, Clint, get serious! I need your help, man."

"Listen, Eric," Clint whispered, "the first time he stopped in the middle of a driving rain and whispered that he could smell the enemy twenty-five yards to our right,

I thought he was a nut case for sure. I mean, there's no way, right? So, well, I probably made a big mistake then—at least where George was concerned."

"Why? What'd you do, fart?"

"Very funny, counselor! No, I told our commanding officer, who promptly shoved ole George into the damp undergrowth and told him to go on in and bring back the enemy he thought he smelled. Well, the joke was on both of us."

"What do you mean?"

"Well, George reappeared less than thirty minutes later dragging behind him a Vietcong sniper with an army knife sticking out of his chest."

"Christ!"

"Hey, we all sat up and took notice. This was the old man's third war, see, and I'm sure he really didn't care whether George saw, heard, or smelled what was out there. But the fact that George could sense danger saved our butts plenty of times. Definitely hit Colonel Coltrane where he lived, so to speak."

"I bet," Eric murmured. A current of shock rushed through him. He hadn't heard that name spoken since his mother's death. A Colonel Coltrane had been his father's best friend during the war. In fact, it was Coltrane who had written the bad news to his mother and, later, stopped by often, for a while, to see them. He hadn't realized, when he read Davis's file, that this Coltrane might be the same man.

"Listen, Eric." Clint's voice was suddenly submerging beneath what sounded like a television running cartoons full blast. "The kids are up. Can you call back later? Meanwhile, see if you can get in touch with our old C.O., Theodore H. Coltrane. Ted's retired, but he's still alive and kickin' here in the city. Number's in the book."

"Right, Clint. Thanks." Eric hung up the phone, opened

the file again, and reread the letter of commendation signed by Colonel Theodore H. Coltrane. It was worth a shot.

The gravelly voice on the other end of the line sounded glad to hear from him. Coltrane said he'd read about his appointment to the pardon and parole board in the paper. When Eric told him he was working on George Davis's parole, the colonel immediately offered him a breakfast he couldn't refuse. Homemade chicken fried steak, cream gravy, biscuits, grits, and "coffee hot as hell and sweet as heaven." With Mary Jane gone, and the rest of the weekend to himself, Eric figured he had nothing to lose. He didn't bother to shave, just pulled on a pair of jeans, a polo shirt, and his sneakers and started out in the Jag for the south side.

Thirty minutes later, Eric stood in a neat and orderly Airstream trailer staring at a faded black-and-white photo of his father and Coltrane, their arms draped over one another's shoulders. Frozen in time, two smiling young men in their green years stood, side by side, somewhere in Italy. For a moment, Eric felt the same sharp stab of anger he'd felt for the first few years after his father's death, when the most important man in his life was suddenly reduced to dozens of photos and certificates on his mother's bedroom wall that had hung there until after her death. Now he was standing in the trailer of an old man whose life was summed up in a wall covered with photos. Italy. Korea. Vietnam.

"You know, I'm sorry I didn't make it to your mother's funeral," Coltrane murmured. "She was a wonderful, beautiful woman. Always felt bad that she wouldn't go out with me."

"Is that right?" Eric was surprised. "I didn't even know you'd asked her."

"Several times, as a matter of fact," Coltrane said as he headed into the kitchen. "But she wouldn't have me. And I never wanted anyone else."

Eric felt both proud and sad. His mother had depended on him, and he on her, right up until her death. He wondered how he would have accepted Coltrane, or any man, as a replacement for his father back then. Although he was an easy eighty years old, the tall, handsome colonel had probably shrunk only a couple of inches in height since the photo on the wall had been taken.

In a few minutes the two men were sitting at the tiny dining room table indulging in a cholesterol junkie's fantasy and loving every minute of it. Eric noticed that, for all his battles, Coltrane seemed fit and at least physically unscathed. Eric commented on the fact around a succulent mouthful of biscuit and honey.

"Well," Coltrane beamed, "I still work out." He patted his nonexistent gut. "And I don't drink nearly as much beer as I used to. In Nam, we drank more beer than water. Safer, ya know?"

Eric nodded, trying to find a way to steer the conversation to the topic he had originally come to explore. Finally, he just asked. "Colonel, what can you tell me about George Davis?"

The old man rubbed his grizzled chin. His gray eyes narrowed a bit. "What exactly do you want to know?" he asked, his voice cooling like a breeze over a glacier.

Eric coughed. "Well, for starters, how much do you think his military service had to do with his drug problem? What was he like when he served under you?"

Coltrane laid both hands on the edge of the table as though he might, in a feat of strength, dislodge it from the wall and push it over on Eric without blinking an eye. But he didn't. After what seemed like a long time, the colonel relaxed, refilled his coffee mug from the old, blue enamel pot, and simply began to talk.

"You know, Eric, I look back on it now, considering what happened to George, and I wonder if I was right to put so much pressure on that boy. Making him platoon sniper and permanent point man, I mean. After Nixon ordered us into Cambodia for the Parrot's Beak excursion, George got real shaky. He said there was just too much death in the air. Then his best friend got shot in the neck and bled to death."

"I noticed that he received the Silver and Bronze Stars for his valor in that excursion, thanks to your recommendations."

"Well, son, he had those medals coming. But . . ."

Eric wiped his mouth on his napkin and waited.

"Son, I saw this happen maybe once or twice while I was serving in Europe and in Korea. Usually, it began with a young man who'd been hospitalized for an injury. But I saw it far too often among the eighteen-, nineteen-year-old kids fighting in Vietnam." Coltrane reached for the coffee pot and filled Eric's cup. "You were lucky you didn't have to go."

Eric was startled. He'd always felt guilty for his exempt status, as if he hadn't deserved it. He'd often wondered if his father might have thought him a coward. Now here was his father's best friend telling him he was lucky, in a sense, to have lost his father and not himself.

"I think," Coltrane continued, "that, as time went by, George began to see himself as capable of nothing but killing."

"Why? Did he enjoy it that much?"

Coltrane scowled, then sighed. "No, son. He wasn't that kind of crazy. Mostly, like many young men, he felt he should have been able to save his buddy's life. He blamed himself. But I guess I didn't help much either."

"You had him discharged before he'd served his full hitch. Do you wish, now, that you'd sent him home even sooner?"

"Hell, no! He was too damn valuable. Listen, Eric."

 The old man stared intently into Eric's gaze. "He saved our asses so many times I quit counting. So I used the kid. But to be honest, I've often wondered if he might have been better off if he'd died a hero's death out there in that damn jungle."

The colonel stopped talking and stared down at the table. When he showed no signs of continuing, Eric filled the old man in on George's efforts at improving his life while in prison. Coltrane seemed pleased and more relaxed, so Eric posed another question.

"When did his drug problem start, sir?" Eric asked quietly.

Anger flashed in the old man's eyes. "I don't care what anybody says, Eric! Those who served in Europe and Korea and then applauded when their sons went off to the jungles of Southeast Asia didn't have a clue what they were sending them into. They just couldn't fathom that Vietnam wasn't World War Two or Korea. Those boys came home with wounds nobody wanted to see, let alone help to heal." The old man shook his head and cleared his throat. "In Nam, those who felt like George did—and there were plenty—got to where they drank more than usual, even for soldiers. Pot was easy to get. So were opium, heroin, morphine."

"Was George a big drinker?" Eric asked.

"Hell, no!" the old man said, shaking his head. "George was a clean-cut farm kid. His mama hadn't raised him to be a drinker. He'd never even smoked cigarettes, let alone pot."

"But he came home with a drug problem, sir. When did it start?"

Coltrane stared past Eric to the wall behind him covered with framed medals, certificates of honor, and awards. Eric didn't want to push, was even a little afraid the old

man would order him to leave. But he needed to know—
if not for Davis, then for himself.

"Well, one day," Coltrane began softly, "George came in from the jungle waving the epaulets from five Chinese soldiers, sobbing and covered with blood. I thought I was going to have to send him home. He wasn't doing drugs, wasn't even drinking. Then. But he was going right out of his mind, screaming and carrying on that we were fighting the whole goddamn oriental empire. 'Course, nobody paid much attention because, even though folks at home didn't realize it at the time, we had always been fighting the Chinese. Guess the president didn't want anyone worrying about the possible use of nuclear weapons."

Eric poured himself half a cup of coffee and waited.

The old man rubbed his face hard with both hands. His pale gray, red-rimmed eyes fastened on Eric. "If you're wondering whether I noticed a change in him, the answer is yes. After he came in that day, I sent him to Saigon for a little R & R. Hoped some time with the ladies would gentle him down. Women can do that, you know, especially during wartime."

"Did it work?" Eric asked.

"Seemed to. When he got back, he was still suffering, but at least he was useful. In a strange way he was even more deadly, more focused. Hell, he was crazy with the pain of living to see so damn much death. The drugs helped ease that, I imagine. The Saigon whores probably turned him on to the stuff the first time. After that, he got his own."

"So is that when you sent him home, sir?" Eric asked.

"No. At first I just ignored it. Hoped he'd snap out of it when he got home." Coltrane shook his head and stared at the floor. "Hell, that man was amazing. Stoked to the gills, he still functioned better than most of my men did when they were straight. And we'd come to depend on his talents to such an extent . . ."

Eric tried to conceal his disappointment.

"Shit, Eric, of course I kept him in the field!" The old man sat still with his palms over his eyes and his head bowed. "What else could I do?"

Eric cleared the plates from the table while Coltrane composed himself. When he sat back down, the colonel went on.

"I let it go on and told myself it was for the greater good of my troops. I played a major role in the ruination of that boy's life, probably contributed to his being in prison today."

The old man stood up and walked a few steps over to the living room window, his hands shoved deep into his khaki slacks. Suddenly, the old warrior looked every bit his age.

"He was facing court martial over his drug use when I managed to get him sent home. Yes, Eric, I used him. But so did the army, the jungle, and the United States government. We were all used! And we used him and thousands of other poor boys right up and then let them throw what was left of themselves away. For nothing." The colonel straightened his back, turned, and looked levelly at Eric. "If there is ever anything I can do for George Davis, Eric, you can be damn sure I'll do it."

Eric nodded. After a short silence, he offered to help with the dishes. Coltrane shook his head. They both said good-bye and made vague promises to see each other again. Eric thanked him for the meal before walking back out into the shimmering midday heat.

About nine-fifteen that evening, as Eric sat alone, thinking, out by the pool, the doorbell rang. It rang on, insistently, as he passed through the house on his way to the front door.

Clint Morris stood on the front porch. His blond hair was disheveled and his nose was red. At first, Eric thought he was suffering from either an allergy or a sinus problem. Then it occurred to him that Clint might be indulging in cocaine, the current yuppie drug of choice. Clint blew his nose twice as he followed Eric back out to the pool. Eric wondered if the attorney general knew that his brother had a drug problem.

"Man, it was all the lies, the cover-ups." Clint, having sprawled into a lounge chair, rattled away as Eric mixed a drink at the bar just inside the sliding doors to the patio. He handed him a gin and tonic and sat down with his Budweiser in the deck chair near by.

"That's what finally done ole George in," Clint went on. "He got home and his daddy had lost all but the family's original forty acres. By then, George had it so bad he couldn't begin to help anyone. Not even himself. Fucker used to call me and cry 'cause he just couldn't talk to his dad anymore."

"Was he using?" Eric asked.

Clint laughed bitterly. "Shit, yes! 'Ludes, speed, coke, horse, anything he could get in and keep down. Then he'd strap on a sidearm and go nuts, actin' like a damn gunslinger. I was lucky. My family was supportive and my wife was glad to have me home. I went to school on the GI Bill and stayed there till I finished. Don't know if I could have made it without Sue and the kids to live for. Even then, it wasn't easy. Used to wake up havin' nightmares like I was right back in the jungle, man. All wet with perspiration and shakin' like hell." Clint paused for a minute and took a long pull on his drink.

"Ever get any counseling?" Eric asked.

"Yeah, well . . . I joined a vet support group. That helped some. Used to stop by George's place fairly often back then. Tried to get him to go, but he wouldn't. We smoked a little dope together once in a while. I told him about a few jobs, even gave him references a time or two. But he couldn't keep a job long."

"Clint, did you know he was robbing pharmacies?"

Clint exploded out of his chair and paced along the edge of the pool, waving his arms. "Hell, no, man! He was so full of shit, half the time you couldn't understand what he was talkin' about." Clint stopped and stood staring out into the pool. "Look, Eric, I knew he always had good, clean stuff, okay? But in those days, it wasn't always smart to ask where it came from."

"Did you talk to him that night?"

Clint sat back down and finished off his drink. He nodded slowly. "Well, yeah, he talked about how he might do it, how he thought he could get away with it. But I just thought it was more crazy talk, y know? George was a sweet guy, really! I still can't imagine him doing anything like that, not even when he was high."

Clint's voice dropped almost to a whisper. "The night he flipped, he must have been having major problems. It was a lot like tonight, real hot and humid. He'd never been to my place before. And there he was, big as life and wearing his fucking fatigues. Christ, some criminal! The asshole still had his name printed on his pocket!" Clint laughed bitterly. "He was strung out, man. Smelled like whiskey and looked like shit. He wanted to talk, but I was embarrassed. You know, the wife and kids and all. But I asked him to stay for dinner. One of those polite offers you extend hoping someone will refuse? George understood. Shook his head and said he had things to do. Jesus."

Eric twirled the ice in his glass. "Papers said the pharmacist shot first and missed by a mile."

"Tryin' to be a hero, I guess. Don't reckon he knew who he was dealing with, did he?" Sweat poured off of

Clint's forehead as he formed an imaginary .45 with the fingers of his right hand as it lay in his lap. "Hell, George was way up by the front entrance of the grocery store. The pharmacist must have been a football field away! George was good, though, man." Clint smiled, shook his head, raised his imaginary .45 to eye level, and pointed it into the darkness. "Bang-bang, motherfucker! Right . . . between . . . the eyes."

The crickets suddenly sounded unusually loud. The lights glowing below the surface of the pool reminded Eric of the Dream. He shook himself mentally and tried to imagine what must have been going on inside George that night, strung out and hyped up as he was. The police report stated that they'd found him standing in the parking lot stuffing aspirin in his mouth and mumbling incoherently.

George's trial had not gone well. He had been prosecuted by David Horton, at that time the state's best-known county prosecutor and newest political star. Horton argued that even though Davis had been a war hero, he had betrayed his country by committing criminal acts and taking innocent people's lives. A news clipping Jolene had slipped into George's file quoted the foreman as saying that most of the jury members agreed with Horton. They had convicted George of murder in the second degree. Eric thought perhaps the only reason George hadn't received murder one, and with it the death penalty, was that a witness had described his shot as "unlucky."

"Funny thing is," Clint said, his quiet voice interrupting Eric's thoughts, "George must have smelled danger that night, too. Otherwise, he'd have bought it. I asked him once, what it smelled like, you know?"

Eric nodded.

"He said that the danger of imminent death smelled a lot like pussy—rich and sweet and overpowering." Clint's words were becoming more and more slurred. "Said he learned to smell danger when he was a kid. He and his family were floatin' down the Barren Fork River on inner tubes toward one of them Army Corps of Engineers' lakes they have down there."

Eric smiled to himself. "Cheap entertainment, huh?"

"Yeah. Anyway, George's tube was hooked to his mom's. They came to a place where the current began to spin them around toward the bank and under some overhanging trees."

"Sounds exciting," Eric said.

"Yeah. Well, after they hit the bank and were heading back into the current, George said his mama commenced to scream, 'It's in the trees! It's in the trees!' George said he and his mama paddled and kicked for all they were worth!" Clint laughed until tears rolled down his cheeks. Then he wiped his eyes, blew his nose, and sat still and silent.

"So they ended up okay?" Eric asked, unsure about the point of the story.

"Yeah, yeah, but listen, now! When they got back into the current, George looked toward shore, and a six-foot water moccasin was heading across the top of the water back toward land. George said there were tooth marks in the tube near where his mother's hand had been draped over the edge. Ain't that the goddamndest thing you ever heard?"

Eric shook his head.

"Hey," Clint said, "George said it happened. I don't doubt it for a minute."

Eric took the glass from Clint's shaking hand as the sobbing took hold of him. Eric put his arms around Clint's shoulders and held him. The crying escalated until he released a high-pitched wail, the sound of an animal in pain. When the wail died away into ragged breathing, Eric loosened his grip, and Clint slumped sideways onto the

lounge chair. Eric looked at his watch and stood up quietly.
He was about to step inside and phone Clint's wife, Sue, when Clint opened his eyes.

"Eric?" he said, his voice like that of a frightened little boy, "George said his mama told him all evil things have a certain smell. Guess that's why we listened to him, why we made it out of that hell hole. 'Cept some of us haven't quite made it far enough out. We still get sucked back in . . . now and again."

Eric shivered. "You gonna be all right, man?"

Clint shut his eyes and nodded.

A few minutes later, Eric called Sue. She sounded calm, said she'd seen it coming on earlier that day, after his call. She had also known there was little she could do until Clint broke down.

"Thanks, Eric," she said quietly, once he'd reassured her Clint was sleeping. "Sometimes he just needs someone to listen."

Clint spent the night by the pool, but was gone when Eric awoke the next day.

7

GEORGE DAVIS

While Eric was sleeping fitfully in his king-size bed and Clint lay snoring in the lounge chair by the pool, George Davis lay awake and perspiring on a narrow bunk. He stared at the dark ceiling and knew, without glancing at the luminous dial of his clock, that it was after midnight. Most nights he was tired and dropped off into sleep immediately. Tonight was different—hot and humid. George lay worrying about all the things he didn't understand, the things over which he had no control. And he found himself reliving other times in life when he'd had similar, unpleasant feelings.

As a rule, he seldom thought about Nam anymore. Those horrors had been replaced by new ones. Like the day he read the trial transcripts he'd ordered through the prison library. It wasn't his crime that had bothered George so much. What was done was done. He couldn't go back and change the facts, so he'd resigned himself to paying his dues. The bad thing was that he didn't remember his trial at all. Not one minute of it.

Often, on nights like this, when despair threatened to overwhelm him, George forced himself to run scenes from his childhood through his head as though the ceiling of the cell was a movie screen and his eyes were projectors. He could remember a lot from when he was a kid. But when he tried to work his way up through time to his days in Nam, or to the few years between his discharge and his imprisonment, that's when things got either fuzzy or scary.

The childhood scenes he ran through his head were

realistic, vivid, colorful, and three dimensional. He could also remember smells, good smells—like cornbread and beans and fried pies—but lots of bad smells, too. And sounds. In fact, it was from smells and sounds that he reconstructed the few, very vivid scenes from those hard-to-remember years. Still, the movie had no plot. Nothing held the scenes together or gave them a reason for being, especially for the later scenes. He couldn't remember, for instance, where in Nam he'd been when Donnie, his childhood friend, had died in his arms. All he could remember was the way Donnie's eyelashes had fluttered as the blood just kept pumping, pumping, pumping out of what was left of his neck and how someone—he didn't know who—kept screaming, "Medic!" over and over again.

After reading the transcript of his trial, George developed a sudden interest in reading what history books had to say about Vietnam. He tried to trace where he'd gone, what he'd done, partly because he'd finally dried out and was bored, but mostly because he felt as though a huge, black hole had sucked in a big part of his life and had sent it plummeting to the other side of the universe. From the psychology classes he'd started taking on the advice of his case manager, he'd learned that, because of the trauma of those years, his subconscious might be preventing him from remembering much of what had happened because his conscious mind wasn't ready to deal with the memories yet. It was as though he'd gone too far, asked too many questions for which he had no answers.

For months he felt bursts of frustration and anger. Through it all, George had managed to keep a calm, quiet exterior. Then one night, something inside him snapped.

He was taking a shower when they came at him like a pack of dogs, sniffing out his fear, ready to do whatever it took to ensure their dominance. But they didn't just want to fight. They wanted his body and soul.

An older inmate and two younger men jumped him in the showers on E run, a place reserved for inmates serving long sentences for violent crimes. George had been standing with his back to the doorway, his eyes closed, when that old, familiar smell entered his nostrils. It was a few seconds before he actually heard their footsteps coming toward him. It took less time for him to sense why they were there, what they wanted. As he stood facing the blue-tiled wall, George's incubating anger and frustration blossomed into a full-blown rage.

All he'd been taught about hand-to-hand combat, all the tricks that had kept him alive in the jungle, came back in a rush. He couldn't remember the fight itself because, by the time he turned around to face them, he'd snapped. It was as though his instincts took hold and sent his conscious self on vacation. He couldn't remember the face of the young man he'd nearly killed before the older inmate came running in with the same guards he'd paid off earlier to avoid the E run that night. But he did remember the shock on the faces of the guards, the five of them who pulled him off the second young man, and who later said that everyone involved had "slipped" on the wet floor.

George was written up, as were the two younger inmates. But the older convict spread the word, "Lay off George." Word got out that he was "psycho," not to be messed with.

George had never been a threat to the leaders among the convicts. After all, he was just an out-of-control drug addict, not a career criminal. Now, however, he'd shown special talents and a willingness to use them—both of which were attributes that made him a potential leader. Nobody wanted competition.

Two days after the incident, George awoke to find a pad of writing paper, some art supplies, and pens—things he'd wanted for months—under the gate to his cell. Suddenly, keeping him happy and out of the way had become a priority for one or more of the boss inmates.

While taking the college classes offered inside, George discovered his writing talent. He conceived the idea of starting a convict paper while he was in the maximum security facility and was allowed to write, print, and have distributed one sheet, more a newsletter than a newspaper. The rules were stringent. He had to pass every issue through the warden before it went to press. But George quickly learned what would be cut and what would not. The paper wasn't quite what he had in mind. There were no poems, articles, or stories by inmates other than himself, and those he wrote didn't reflect the vicious realities of prison life—but it was a start.

So when word came down from the administration that George was to be transferred from his current maximum security facility to start a real prison newspaper, George wondered why. Would he now be able to have a newspaper with more freedom to put what he wanted in the paper without prison officials' vetoes? George's confusion was compounded when he heard that John Jeffries, "a powerful con," was supporting his paper strongly. George didn't know why Jeffries, a man he didn't even know, was encouraging the administration of McHenry Penitentiary to let him start the publication. And he didn't care. All he knew was that, using his own talent and intelligence, he might be able to influence the parole board to consider his parole. He had also been promised that the paper would be more than just an organ of the administration, that prisoners would have an opportunity to submit poetry, articles, and letters that aired grievances without fear of retribution.

The theory was that this would divert convicts from expressing themselves in other, less productive ways. It was true that, since George had begun his newspaper, the number of prison deaths had fallen. Even given the limitations placed on him, George had been able to influence the convicts in a positive way. It was a source of pride for George. The administration was grateful. It was, therefore, with great reluctance that his current warden agreed to allow George Davis to be transferred to McHenry and start a paper there.

At three A.M. George's heart beat wildly as he tried to imagine himself walking down the streets of Bessie as a free man. His appointment with the pardon and parole board was coming up in a few weeks, and although George was prepared to be turned down for parole, there still was that one trace of hope that something different would happen and he would be paroled early. Under normal rules and regulations that applied to a violent criminal with a long sentence, George knew his case shouldn't be reviewed for several years. That had all changed when his good buddy Clint, brother of the current attorney general, Barry Morris, had come to see him a week ago. It was good fortune that had brought Clint back into the picture. The one thing for sure was that if it all fell together, it was his ticket to freedom.

Meanwhile, across the state in McHenry Penitentiary, John Jeffries slept soundly, certain that his plans were moving along according to schedule.

8

POLITICS AS USUAL

"Fuck 'em!" Horton growled, his jutting lower jaw completing the picture Billy Reardon had projected so well to the public during the exciting days of Horton's campaign for governor. As he sat in the dark green leather wing chair facing the governor's huge, native cedar desk, Reardon knew no actor could have filled the role of the evangelist governor as convincing as this man, the former prosecutor who had brought John Jeffries and Albert McDougal to justice.

David Horton possessed all the determination and ambition of a Caesar and every bit of the vanity and arrogance. But these were facets of his personality only a trusted few knew existed. Nothing about the governor was a mystery to Reardon, his former campaign manager and closest adviser.

Reardon, a small, pockmarked, and seemingly insignificant figure, viewed his role as the behind-the-scenes director of a political drama for which new twists in the plot were constantly being written. Today his job was to be the bearer of bad tidings.

"Now, Governor—"

"Don't 'Now, Governor' me, Billy!" Horton held out his hand like a traffic cop and walked over to the window of his second-floor office overlooking the capitol grounds. He stood gazing down on the derricks and pumps that had become world-famous symbols of the state's fragile boom-to-bust economy. When he continued, Horton's voice had softened only slightly.

He proceeded to tell Reardon that he would not approve "one damn penny more" for corrections. He lambasted "that flop-footed attorney general" and his lost cause. Horton wondered aloud why his supposed friend, the attorney general, was giving speeches all over the state about prison reform. "You think maybe he covets my job, Billy? Well, if he does, he's barking up the wrong tree. The public already perceives prisoners as pampered darlings. Doesn't matter what you or I think, how much we spend on advertising, or what the best damn P.R. man in the business says. Voters hear the words 'prison reform' and immediately visualize new cells, televisions, ruffled curtains, carpeting, even maid service, for Chrissakes!"

"But corrections reform is what got you elected, David," Reardon lied. He knew Horton had won the election for one reason and one reason only. He, Billy Reardon, had handed it to him on a silver platter.

As Horton's campaign manager, Reardon had realized early in the game that securing the endorsement of the state's media magnate, eighty-year-old Cornelius Hermann, was vital. At first it seemed his only hope was damage control. He racked his brain for ways to prevent a serious bloodletting once Hermann's reporters unearthed the damning details of candidate David Horton's past. After investigating Hermann's past, however, Reardon had come up with a plan, the success of which depended on appealing to old man Hermann's one weak spot—his sorrow over the tragic accidental death of his only son while he had been serving overseas during World War II.

First, Reardon set up a "chance" meeting in old man Hermann's favorite breakfast haunt, the Toddle House, a small diner established in the 1920s by Hermann's father. After hours of drill and coaching, Reardon dropped Horton off at the Toddle House.

According to his own report, Horton's performance had been brilliant. Reardon, who knew the governor's ability to charm the pants off even the toughest jury, hadn't doubted for a moment that his boss could do the job if he would just follow the script. But Reardon worried that Horton might decide to improvise. Since Reardon liked to sleep peacefully at night, he hedged his bets. Which is why—in his home safe, among his other important insurance policies—Reardon had assembled a veritable library of videotapes and transcripts not only of the conversation between Horton and Hermann but of other, equally sensitive meetings. If all went well, Horton need never know any of it existed. If not, well . . .

Not that old man Hermann had said much during the meeting. His politics being just to the right of Genghis Khan, the media emperor had simply made it clear to Horton that he would never endorse his bid for governor and would do all in his power—which was considerable—to prevent his election.

Horton, following Reardon's script, had assured Hermann that he would never expect a man of Hermann's ironclad moral character and impeccable journalistic ethics to do anything less than serve as a vigilant public watchdog. Then, like a magician, the candidate had deftly diverted the old man's attention.

He thanked Hermann for having hired him as a paperboy back when he was struggling to support his widowed mother. Then he praised the kindness of Hermann's now-deceased wife, whom he had known because of his close friendship with their son. In fact, he told the old man, it was Mrs. Hermann who had suggested he apply for the job.

Reardon's script was a masterful blend of fact and fancy. Horton had indeed lived in the same neighborhood as the Hermanns and had actually worked as a paperboy during his early years. Delivered by Horton, with just the right amount of gratitude and respect, the entire story seemed plausible.

Reardon had spent hours in the archives of the paper gleaning every bit of information he could find on Hermann's son. Hermann had received compassionate leave to return from the European war to attend his son's funeral. While home, Hermann laid out in loving detail his son's short life in his newspaper. It was the first and only emotion expressed in his otherwise dogmatic ultraconservative newspaper. It was like discovering a gold mine for Reardon. As luck would have it, while he was researching in the newspaper, he ran into an old man who had been a young printer during those early days. He had recalled under Reardon's questioning that Cornelius Hermann had a pet name for his son that he had heard him use over and over in those early days. It was a name that he never used again after his son's death. His son's name was Mike, and Cornelius Hermann called him Mookie. While Horton was telling a suspicious Hermann about his relationship with his son, he casually dropped in a fictitious event where he and Mookie were playing a game. A startled Hermann instantly questioned Horton about how he had learned that name. Horton had told him his son liked the name because his father had used it, but he only wanted his best friend to know about it, for fear the other kids would laugh at him. With Hermann's wife dead and no other family members to confirm or deny Horton's story, and given Cornelius Hermann's advancing senility, it was the perfect hit on the old man.

After that fateful meeting, the employees at the newspaper were amazed at the close relationship that came to develop between Cornelius Hermann and David Horton. Horton was one of the few who could drop in on the old man at any time and be ushered immediately into his office. No one at the paper or in Hermann's small circle of acquaintances would dare ask him about it because of the imposing presence of the old man and his intense desire for privacy. So the relationship between Horton and Hermann remained a mystery, even to the most inquisitive of reporters.

Consequently, during Horton's campaign for governor, the most astute political analysts noticed a surprising lack of investigative reporting on candidate Horton. Reardon recognized that Horton had more talent for bullshit than anyone he had ever seen. But he, and others close to the governor, knew that without Reardon as his chief aide, Horton's talents had no focus.

"Billy," the governor said, turning from the window to face Reardon, "I got elected by being an active district attorney and by prosecuting bastards who are rotting in prison right now. Hell, it's roads that make money. That and pork barrel projects like rattlesnake hunts and peanut festivals. Makes local representatives look good, and they in turn make me look good."

Reardon nodded. To some extent, he knew, the governor was right. But he also knew that the governor was avoiding the main issue. Money. He, after all, was the governor's bagman, the money man, and had been since he'd produced the first ten thousand in cash contributions to the campaign. Engineers, architects, contractors, nursing home operators, car dealers, and some of the biggest ranchers and oil men in the state had all supported Horton's bid for office.

Reardon's divorce, following Horton's election, and his subsequent remarriage to an equally ruthless woman lawyer who physically towered over him, had ensured that the cost of doing business in the state would continue to rise. Reardon made sure Horton's campaign promise to "Keep business going and money flowing" was also a personal reality. Reardon's wife now served on the bank and savings and loan licensing board. Together the Reardons were building a sizable retirement fund. Every fourth license granted or renewed filled another bank box.

Most of those who visited Billy Reardon's office seeking favors from the governor didn't care where the money went as long as they got their licenses, contracts, and permits. Horton knew about the election funds, but no one had guts enough to ask him about the stiff remuneration being doled out to his aide. The whole process was very discreet. Reardon and his moneyed guests were both shy of electronic surveillance. Unless, of course, it was their own.

"Governor," Reardon said, propping his chin on the steepled fingers of both hands, "I know everybody wants to lock these people up and throw away the key. But the fact is, we're facing a real crisis. McHenry was built in 1917 to house six hundred prisoners. We've got nearly three thousand men and women in there today, not counting the ones overcrowding all the other penitentiaries.

"On top of that, the hot season has already started. It was ninety-three degrees here yesterday, which makes it about a hundred and twenty inside those cells. Think how hot it'll be in July, August, and September. With four to six men to a cell, it means incredible control problems for the guards. My latest report from the Department of Corrections shows that over the past six months we've had at least one killing every month, all of them directly attributable to these guys having nothing to do and being crammed into those cells like cattle in a railroad car. We've got to do something, or we're going to get a lawsuit from the feds and God knows how many civil rights lawsuits from inmates and their families. I hate to say it, Governor, but we could have a full-scale riot on our hands."

Horton crossed both beefy arms over his massive chest and resolutely shook his head. The sun was setting, and its slanting, golden rays reflected off his snow-white mane as though off a snowfield.

"Listen, David," Reardon said, trying mightily to rein in his rising impatience. "The feds have managed to push a case through the Supreme Court that opens the door for federally mandated prison reform."

"Goddamn busybodies," Horton growled.

"Hell, David, the guidelines have already been established!" Reardon lowered his voice. "They aren't mandatory yet, but it's only a matter of time before all three branches of the federal government will be standing behind a wholesale list of reforms."

"Fuck the feds," Horton murmured, and stalked over to sit back down at his desk.

Reardon shrugged and cleared his throat before administering his well-timed coup de grâce. "I also have it on good authority that Senator Tobias is prepared to introduce legislation to remodel the prisons—"

"And fuck Tobias, Billy!" Horton shouted, leaning forward in his chair, both hands clutching the armrests.

"And you know he'll seize the advantage," Reardon said mildly. Then he paused, waiting for the bombshell to inflict maximum damage.

Horton leaned both elbows on his blotter and rubbed his temples with his fingertips. "Ah, yes," he sighed. "The Dark Prince." He inhaled deeply, held his breath for a moment, and then exhaled before continuing. "Billy," he said, his voice deceptively calm, "I'm well aware that Tobias wants jobs for his district so more money can flow into his pockets. He also wants to be governor so he can speed up the process. So now I've got not only Senator Tobias and our busybody little attorney general but the whole federal government working against me!"

Reardon rose restlessly from the wing chair and sauntered toward the window. Behind him, Horton opened and closed his top desk drawer. It was his most notable nervous habit. The sound of the drawer sliding back and forth made Reardon think of a pendulum clock. Slide. Click. Slide. Click. Slide. Click. *Bang!* The drawer slammed shut. At the window, Reardon wheeled around and looked at Horton.

"What I want, Mr. Reardon," the governor said steadily, "is that son of a bitch's balls."

Reardon swallowed hard.

"What I want," Horton said, "is for our crippled pit bull of an attorney general, Mr. Barry Morris, to call a grand jury investigation." Reardon started to speak but was interrupted by a wave of the governor's hand. "I know that the feds are going to indict Tobias, and he's going to come up for trial soon. I just want to give the IRS a little help. If for some reason our friends at the IRS can't make their charges stick, then I want to be ready for him with our own grand jury. Indict the bastard and put him right back up for trial again. He won't have time to worry about bills for corrections, much less running for governor. Incidentally, I don't care what he's indicted for. Just find something. That, Mr. Reardon, will be part of your responsibility."

Reardon nodded, grinned, and glanced at his watch. "Well, sir," he said, "you can tell Mr. Morris that yourself. He should be here any minute now."

III As he limped past one of the many small offices just off the long corridor leading to the governor's office, Attorney General Barry Morris heard a familiar giggle. While he would have liked to believe the sound was a sign of some comely young woman's barely suppressed sexual excitement, he knew better. His stooped figure and odd gait made him ridiculous in most women's eyes, no matter how much money he made or how much he was willing to spend on his wardrobe or on entertainment. Women saw his deformity as clownish. Morris couldn't really blame them. The haunting, hated sound of his splay feet slapping the marble flooring had echoed in his own ears for over thirty years.

Barry Morris would never forget the hot, windy June day when, in celebration of his sixth birthday, his father had allowed him to ride on the outside of the combine during wheat harvest. The terrifying fall, down between the reels and threshers of the huge, lumbering machine, resulted in a frantic pickup ride to a hospital in the state capital. An orthopedic surgeon, after fusing the bones of Barry's ankles, warned his parents that their small, bright son might never walk again.

Lying in his hospital bed, Barry overheard the whispered prognosis. His immediate reaction was anger—at the doctor, at God, at his parent's easy acceptance, at life. Gradually, however, the anger evolved into an iron determination to prove them all wrong.

Later, as captain of the state's champion high school debate team, Barry proudly received the compliments of the guest speaker. The governor shook his hand and said, "Mr. Morris, I'm glad you're not old enough to run for office. Otherwise my position would be in serious jeopardy." The remark became Barry Morris's inspiration.

Still, after he had become the youngest state representative in state history, after he had served four terms (one as House majority leader), even after he'd won election to the office of state attorney general, each step Morris took reminded him that he would always have to be tougher and smarter than those who freely, recklessly strode the halls of power.

Nevertheless, Barry Morris couldn't help chuckling at

 the irony of his present situation. He had won election primarily because he had attacked a popular incumbent's ineffective prosecution of criminals and his reluctance to pursue death sentences. Now, however, there seemed to be no way to settle the prison controversy without disappointing allies and turning them into enemies. Federal courts were threatening to either shut down the state's prison system or take it over. His constituents wouldn't stand for that. And now the governor and the most influential senator in the state had made the issue the major bone of contention over which their next electoral dogfight would be waged. The fact that all the players belonged to the same party complicated a problem that Morris knew would take more than politics as usual to solve.

His knock on the door of the governor's inner sanctum was answered by Reardon, a man Morris and so many others who worked with Horton had learned to hate with unmitigated passion. When Reardon smiled, Morris envisioned the big collared lizards he used to blow to pieces with a .22 on the ranch where he had grown up.

"Hello, Billy," Morris said genially, shaking Reardon's hand. "Good to see you."

The governor bestowed upon Morris one of his own beatific smiles and said, "I hope you're not riding in here on Billy's hobbyhorse to warn me that the feds are coming."

The last thing Morris wanted was to join hands with the governor's bagman. He knew that the secret to any political dash to the top was cash in exchange for favors. Lines had formed very quickly in front of Reardon's campaign office. While Morris suspected that huge amounts of money were flowing into Reardon's worn leather briefcase on a daily basis, he also knew there was no way in hell he could ever prove it.

After the campaign, Reardon had continued to wield

power, this time in the form of an only slightly more discreet funneling of cash. Two thousand appointments to boards and commissions and control of every conceivable license in the state lay at his fingertips. Morris figured that, although Horton probably worried a bit about Reardon's tactics, he was more concerned about what might happen to his political career if his bagman's plundering were brought to light.

No sooner were all the men seated than the phone on Horton's desk rang. Reardon reached forward to answer it. Horton eyed his aide ominously and picked up the receiver. Morris suppressed a grin when Reardon snatched his hand back as though it had been burned.

"Hello," the governor said. He paused a moment before continuing. "Why, yes, Chester, what can I do for you?"

Morris figured the caller had to be Chester Wyndott, head of the pardon and parole board. His own inside source had informed him not thirty minutes earlier that Chester was not a happy man.

As he listened, Horton's face flushed bright red. "I don't give a goddamn what the senator said about paroling people, Chester!" Horton shouted. "I want you to stick with the hard line. That's why I kept you on as chairman." Horton bounced the end of his gold Parker pen solidly against his desk blotter. "Now, if you need some butts kicked, Chester, you just call me and we'll take care of that. I know I can rely on you." During the thirty-second pause that followed, Horton regained his normal color and a smile spread across his broad face. Finally he nodded and said, "Excellent, Mr. Chairman. You do that. And congratulations on another fine job you're doing for our state."

As the receiver hit its cradle, Horton swiveled in his chair, a broad grin on his face. "Checkmate this time, Senator!"

"Sir, I think the time is right," Morris said, plunging to

 the attack. "Take the lead on prison reform before you're forced to do it."

"Why, sure, Barry," the governor said, his voice dripping with sarcasm. "I'll just do that. And then you and I and Billy here can go stand in the unemployment line together. No, dammit! I'm not ready to make history yet. My career isn't over yet." He sat back down in his chair, then quickly bounded to his feet again and pointed his finger at Morris. What had been unspoken and carefully danced around over the past two weeks was now bellowed forth by the governor towering over the attorney general. "What I want you to do first, Mr. Attorney General, is to quit giving speeches all over the state talking about prison reform. Corrections was mentioned in my campaign. But as you and I both know, that's the quickest way to the back door of politics. Your talking about it all the time doesn't help me one little bit. Plus, you're giving Glen Tobias a platform from which to attack me. What in the world has gotten into you, Barry? Whatever it is, I'm not sure I even want to know. What I do want you to do next, Mr. Attorney General, is fight this federal action with every ounce of your intelligence and every assistant in your office. Then I want a grand jury investigation of that black hearted son of a bitch Tobias, since I'm not at all sure that the Justice Department is going to convict him on home ground. Let's keep the man's feet so hot he'll be too busy to cause any trouble."

Morris shook his head and sighed. He'd known this would be neither easy nor pretty. "Governor, folks in Tobias's part of the state are pretty closed-mouthed about what goes on," he murmured.

"Hell, Barry," the governor said, "Tobias has mines, farms, mills—you name it! Surely we can find out where his money is coming from. We damn sure can see where it ends up."

"Governor," Morris replied patiently, "the FBI and the IRS have poured countless hours and millions of dollars into trying to catch Tobias and bring him to trial. They have the manpower to pursue him even if he is hard to pin down. This last mess is a perfect example of—"

"Sniff around the prison system, then!" Horton shouted. "Anybody with as much power as Tobias has in that county—and in the whole damn prison system, for that matter—is bound to have his hand in somebody's cookie jar. Do what you can. In the meantime, I'm going to talk with the Speaker of the House and the president pro tem of the Senate. I'll quash any appropriation bill for new prisons if it's the last thing I do."

Morris shivered at the possibility that the governor's comments might well become prophetic. Quietly, he reminded Horton of Governor George Wallace and the disaster that had occurred when the FBI forced desegregation in Alabama. During his speech, Reardon sat quietly, chewing the frayed end of a toothpick, his eyes giving nothing away. When Morris finished, the three men sat silently for a moment or two before the attorney general spoke again, his voice smooth and soothing.

"Well, David, why not do a little remodeling project?"

Horton scowled at his aide, and Morris felt a rush of adrenalin. He forced his voice to remain under control.

"If nothing else," Morris continued, his voice mild, "take care of the sewer systems. That way, you could strike a compromise with the Speaker and the president pro tem of the Senate and at least make it look to the feds as though you're trying to solve the prison problem on your own."

Horton stared at the wall behind Morris and Reardon as though trying to visualize the consequences of such a move. Finally, he cleared his throat to speak and stared directly at Morris.

"Mr. Attorney General," he said, "that may be the most politically astute thing you've said all morning." After that Reardon turned and favored Barry Morris with a bright smile.

Morris immediately thought of Reardon's worn leather briefcase. He knew the aide's smile was most likely in anticipation of construction kickbacks and not a reflection of his compliments to the attorney general of the state.

"Well, sir," Morris said, glancing at his watch, "I have a meeting with the press in a few minutes to protest parole consideration for John Jeffries." He reached out to shake Horton's hand as he rose from his seat. "If this is settled, and it sounds as though it is, I'd better be going."

The two men accompanied him to the door of the office. Horton put his arm over Morris's shoulder. "We seldom agree, Billy and I," the governor confided, "but I don't know what I'd do without him to help me think things through, and I know we both agree with your fine idea. Thanks again, Barry."

As Morris turned to leave, the governor stopped him with an arm around his shoulder. "But do me one favor, Barry, no more speeches," wagging his finger in front of his face. The attorney general smiled and walked through the door.

Morris continued to smile as he made his slow way down the hall toward the circular staircase that descended from the rotunda. Actors, he had heard someone say, are like children. David Horton and Billy Reardon were both proof of the maxim. Without Reardon at his side, Horton would be nothing. Without Horton, Reardon would only have been a petty thief and a con man. But this time, Morris mused as he pressed the elevator button, he had been in control. He had directed the scene. And neither Reardon nor Horton was smart enough to realize it.

9

THE PRINCE

On the same afternoon, three blocks from McHenry Penitentiary, in an office kept deliberately shabby by its owner, another strategy meeting was about to convene. The last of a long line of favor seekers, an elderly coal miner, backed smiling and bowing out of the front door and onto the sidewalk. State Senator Glen Tobias leaned his bulk easily against the door frame and waved good-bye, his impatience masked by the paternal, reassuring smile he'd been doling out to the inhabitants of this smallest and poorest county in the state for nigh on twenty-five years. In all that time, Tobias had fought only one close election battle: his first. And now he was preparing for the most important battle of his career: the governorship. From there, he knew, there was no telling how far he could go. The feds were trying to interrupt his plans, but all he needed was to get to trial. *Wait till they see what I've got waiting for them*, he thought to himself with obvious pleasure.

As the elderly man climbed into the driver's side of a battered red Ford pickup, Tobias closed to the door to his office and locked it. Not since he'd first run for office, at the tender age of twenty-one, had he felt so exhilarated. More than anything else, Tobias wanted to end this day knowing he was not only on top of the impending prison crisis, but that he would stay on top when the situation inevitably unraveled.

Although he was six feet, two inches tall and weighed two hundred pounds, Tobias's large hands and feet made him appear even larger. His blue-black, wavy hair was full and thick, swept back in pompadour not unlike that of the rockabilly singing star idolized by many of his female constituents. His features were full and, according to his many lady friends, sensuous. Most impressive of all, however, were his coal-black eyes, flecked with gold, and set beneath heavy, dark eyebrows. This combination of features, combined with his piercing stare, lent even more credence to the name his numerous enemies had assigned him—the Dark Prince.

Tobias stepped down the dim, narrow hall and into the back room where his staff sat waiting around what served as a conference table, the old, oak family dining table from his boyhood home. The men and women who surrounded the senator were, without exception, loyal friends who had hugged his coattails for a quarter of a century. He understood and accepted the fact that their loyalty and respect were based on three things: empathy, admiration, and money. Tobias's father, like their own, had emerged from the coal mines with a permanent cough and no pension. Like their own fathers, the elder Tobias had died shortly after retirement. He left behind a son whose memories of poverty, pain, loss, and injustice eventually inspired him to seek political office in an effort to improve the quality of life for those in his district, many of whom were unemployed.

Encouraged by his mother and teachers, Glen Tobias had studied hard, earned a full-ride scholarship to law school, become a member of the state legislature during the later months of his senior year, passed the bar exam on his first try, and finished law school in record time. As a crack trial attorney and the youngest legislator in the state, Tobias began accumulating power and prestige. His wealth, and the wealth of those who backed him, came surprisingly easy. By passing selective legislation that either subsidized or removed restrictions placed on oil producers, cattlemen, large lumbering interests, and mine owners, and by shrewdly investing both bribes and honest income, Tobias had solidified his financial power. His rationale was that he was simply creating job opportunities for his constituents by lending his vast influence and money to various projects. Naturally, his constituents were grateful.

However, Tobias's methods had not been lost on the IRS or on the opposing party's U.S. district attorney. Now rumor had it that the governor wanted a grand jury investigation. Still, Tobias wasn't worried. He had known everything he needed to know about Franklin Felix, the federal prosecutor who, he had just learned, had been assigned to his case. He also knew his people were every bit as loyal as those in the Texas hill country who had backed Lyndon Baines Johnson's rise to power. He also had learned he had been indicted and was going to be brought to trial. The trial was to be held in federal court, just one block from his office.

He wasn't worried, and he wasn't going to disturb his staff about it now. He knew he could get a speedy trial—that's all he needed. He had more pressing matters at hand.

Warren Littlefield, Glen Tobias's law partner, sat sipping iced tea from a quart jar and waiting for the meeting to come to order. He'd much rather have been drinking his customary Scotch and soda, a fact to which his swollen nose and ruddy complexion bore testimony. On his right sat Tobias's brother, Clarence, a man not nearly his brother's intellectual equal but, nevertheless, as loyal a man as could be found. To Warren's left sat Kitty, Tobias's faithful secretary of twenty-five years.

Warren rattled the ice in his glass and started the meeting in his usual aggressive manner.

"What we need is a goddamn massive escape at the prison." said Warren. "Better yet, just burn the son of a bitch down. The governor'll look like shit 'cause he hasn't done anything to prevent it by relieving the overcrowding and all that liberal bullshit. Glen, lead the fight for reform! You know damn good and well that after they burn it down, we can get federal money. Voters'll be left with no choice except to rebuild if they want to keep the feds out."

Clarence nodded. "Not to mention that our old T-Mac Construction Company might be able to hire a few folks in this part of the state to rebuild it."

What Clarence didn't have to mention was that the company was carefully set up to funnel profits from the construction company whenever bids were accepted on state jobs.

Senator Tobias allowed his massive head to sink toward his chest, a posture that he knew gave others the impression that he was immersed in thought. Then he placed both his hands on the table, glanced up at the assembly from beneath his dark brows, grinned, and leaned toward his partner.

"Warren," Tobias murmured, "I've always said that if I ever had to pick someone to help me fight my way out of a bar, it would be you."

Warren and Kitty laughed heartily, Clarence blushed, and Tobias addressed his secretary.

"I agree with Warren. We need to take immediate action. Go ahead and draft legislation for improvement of the facilities, including the construction of new cell blocks, outer walls, internal factories, and utilities. They don't have a hope or a prayer of passing, but that doesn't matter. If nothing happens at the prison, we'll still appear to have anticipated and tried to cooperate with federal wishes—in spite of the governor. On the other hand, if those three thousand plus boys at McHenry do decide it's time to tear things up a bit, or leave, then I can say, 'I told you so,' and hand over the only available plan at the crucial moment."

Warren nodded. "Johnny on the spot."

"So let's get it done," Tobias said, rising and stretching. "I'll introduce it as soon as possible."

Warren smiled as those assembled gathered their papers and prepared to leave the office. He waited until Clarence and Kitty had gone and he and Tobias were walking out to the parking lot together. "Glen," he said, patting his old friend on the shoulder, "I've always been impressed by your style. But this time, I got to hand it to you. Your sense of timing is perfect."

Tobias simply smiled and nodded.

The next day it was announced that Senator Glen Tobias had been indicted some three months previously, but that his indictment had remained under seal and had not been publicized except to the parties involved. His trial was set in the Federal Eastern District and would commence the following month, on July 10.

The speed at which the trial was set came as a surprise to most, including the federal prosecutors. It was not a surprise to the Prince, however. He was ready for a showdown with the feds.

10

CHILI

At high noon, guards manacled George Davis, helped him onto the bus, and turned their backs as the bus, headed for McHenry, drove through the gates and onto the freeway.

Meanwhile, on the other side of the state, Eric and the other parole board members, having finished this first full morning of the July board meeting, were climbing onto the small bus that would transport them to McHenry's Women's Maximum Security Prison for lunch. Eric saw the eagerness displayed by Senator Willie Jacks, and he heard Chester Wyndott's crude remarks about looking forward to seeing the ladies one more time. In disgust, Eric hurried past Ethel Wilson and Hoyt Hurst to the back of the van, where he could sit with Earl and not be involved in any conversation with the senator and the chairman.

Although located on the same seventeen hundred acres, the women's facility was eclipsed by the imposing whitewashed vastness of the much larger men's facility that faced the freeway. As he rode in the back seat of the transport van with Earl, Eric glanced out the window and found himself spellbound.

Just outside his window shone the waters of a small lake that seemed to have dropped out of the brilliant blue sky and accidentally landed upon the rocky landscape.

In the very center of the lake's mirrorlike surface, an ancient, peeling rowboat floated like an image lifted from an Andrew Wyeth canvas. In the boat sat a fisherman clad in bib overalls and a western-style straw hat. Water, boat, man, and cane fishing pole were as still as the water surrounding them.

"What's that?" Eric murmured, pointing toward the scene.

"Huh?" Earl leaned across to look out Eric's window. "Oh! That's the waterworks. Supplies both facilities."

"Okay, but who's the guy?"

Earl chuckled and slapped Eric's knee. "Why, he's the sleepout, ole Harvey Gilmore."

"Pardon? What's a sleepout?" Eric asked, wondering if this was the beginning of yet another of Earl's famous put-ons.

"A sleepout's a guy no one expects to make a run for the fences. Harv's been here practically forever. Must be in his eighties. He takes care of the machinery."

Eric smiled.

"Looks gentle enough, don't he?" Earl said, fumbling in his pockets for a cigarette. "But the only reason he's out here is he's too crippled up to run away, and most of the prisoners are scared shitless of the tough old bastard. He'll never make parole."

Eric reached into his own pocket for the new pack he'd bought that morning. He hated that he'd started smoking again, off an on, but kept reassuring himself he'd quit once his divorce was final. He offered one to Earl and, as the bus wound its way around the lake, lit up and gazed at the old man of the lake. "He doesn't seem that dangerous, poor old guy. What'd he do?" Eric asked.

"Well, for starters," Earl said, exhaling, "he's deadly honest. We know just what he'll do if he gets out."

"Which is?"

"Finish what he started thirty years or so ago after he and his old lady split up and got in a big hoorah over the custody of their teenage kids. Harv had always had a runnin' battle goin' with his in-laws, too, over how the kids oughta be raised. Well, to make a long story short, his wife was related to the judge. Harv fought hard but, really, he didn't have a snowball's chance in hell. According to folks who knew him, he seemed to accept the decision pretty well. Then one Sunday night, about a month later, as his wife and in-laws were walking to evening services at the Church of Christ, Harv drove into the parking lot in his old farm truck, just like he'd done for years. But this time, when he got out, he was packin' a shotgun and a .38."

Eric could feel it coming. He was beginning to hate these stories, beginning to anticipate the endings. "So he killed his wife, right?"

"And his father-in-law. Two shots from the double barrel in the chest laid her down real permanent and a .38 slug between the eyes took care of her daddy. Harv's mother-in-law was trying to hightail it out of there. Harv managed to get off five shots, two of which hit home."

Eric shook his head.

"Yeah," Earl agreed. "She lived to testify, though. Which is why ole Harv will never get out of here. I swear that old woman must be a hundred by now. Probably still full of bullets, too, and bound and determined to stay alive just to spite ole Harv. He swears, every time he appears before the board, that he'll get the old bitch yet." Earl laughed. "I reckon if she ever does die, Harv'll be offered parole. But, hell, if I was him, I'd stay right there."

"Why? Think he's too old to readjust to the outside world?"

"Nah. But he'd have a helluva time findin' fishin' this good on the outside!"

The blacktop road ended in a parking lot in front of a red brick building surrounded by a barbed-wire fence. Guard towers rose at all four corners. Without the fence and towers, Eric thought, the building would have looked much like a Victorian dollhouse. The windows and peaked roof were trimmed in fancy, delicate white scallops and concentric circles.

Once past the fences and inside the imposing front door, the iron bars on the inside of the windows didn't seem all that much out of place to Eric, considering how many homeowners in his area of the city had installed them for security.

"Here comes the key man," Earl murmured. "Watch your step."

Eric turned around to see a huge, heavyset woman in a guard uniform that stretched the fabric to its limit. The black roots showing within her blond 1950s beehive hairdo were another clue that she had long ago ceased to worry about her looks.

As Earl introduced her, Eric's extended hand was gripped by one with calluses and viselike strength. Her eyes were cold and gray.

"She's been here thirty years," Earl whispered as they followed the key man toward a barred gate. "Trust me, son. That's a major accomplishment."

The veteran ordered Eric to remove his boots and empty his pockets and then made a cursory patdown of the remainder of this body before passing him through the gate and into the dining hall beyond. Eric jumped as she growled near his ear.

"Watch the whores. Dopers are next. The rest are shit."

He mumbled a bewildered thanks, and she smiled, obviously proud of having imparted her knowledge to someone with authority.

Earl walked straight ahead, but Eric stood for a moment, surveying the scene.

"Hello."

The voice was melodious. Its owner stood at his elbow,

her smooth, light brown features and brilliant sapphire eyes turned up toward him. The resemblance between this woman and Mary Jane was unbelievable. Were it not for the prison uniform and the slightly darker shade of skin, he could have been fooled into believing that it was Mary Jane. As she came closer, he could tell that she was obviously American Indian, with her long, straight black hair glistening a deep blue under the pale light from the barred and curtained windows. Eric felt befuddled.

"Please, read this," the sultry, shy voice pleaded as she slipped an envelope into the palm of his hand. Shocked for a second time, Eric involuntarily thought, *My God, it's even her voice.* Then, as quickly as she'd appeared, she was gone. Eric turned, hoping to follow her, to say something. But she'd faded into the mass of women crowding the room. He slipped the envelope into the breast pocket of his jacket. Suddenly, Earl had him by the elbow and was steering him toward a linen-covered table in the corner of the room.

"Come on, son," he said, "quit your lollygaggin'."

They sat down together at the table amid a flurry of activity. A bevy of well-groomed, uniformed women convicts floated like butterflies about the table, graciously distributing food, coffee, and smiles to all the board members.

Earl cleared his throat and Eric glanced over at him, thankful that this was a new place and knowing that Earl would take his mind off the encounter he had just experienced.

"Watch," Earl murmured. "These ladies fight like cats for the right to rub up against us here. Every one of them has a sad story and wants a chance to whisper it in your ear. Personally, I think we ought to eat in town. But," Earl gestured with a fork full of mashed potatoes and gravy,

"Wyndott likes to eat here every other month. Looks like Willie Jacks likes it too. What a surprise!"

Eric watched the old men surreptitiously running their hands over the carefully proffered backsides of the young women who found reaching across the table to pour coffee easier than walking around. Eric suddenly realized he'd been staring and glanced somewhat shamefaced at Ethel Wilson, who was seated on his right. Ethel's expression was enigmatic, but her eyes twinkled as she wiped the corners of her mouth with her starched napkin.

"One very interesting aspect of this facility as compared to the men's, Mr. Williams," she said quietly, "is the social structure."

"Oh? How's that?" Eric asked, grateful to this dignified woman for drawing his attention away from the behavior of two of their fellow board members.

"Here the women tend to form family units, which supply the same benefits of protection and sex as do the men's gangs. However, these units also provide the women with emotional security."

Eric considered Ethel's words. The women's adjustment to their confinement seemed healthier than that of male convicts. Because he had longed for his father and wished for a brother or sister all his life, Eric thought he could understand the women's need for surrogate family members. After all, hadn't he adopted Mary Jane as a sister, as a cause, rather than as a real wife?

"The strongest women," Ethel said, interrupting his thoughts, "are the father and mother figures. The others are their dependents."

Eric nodded, thinking of his own mother, who had played both roles since he was four. All of a sudden, he felt terribly, horribly alone. He put down his fork and sat thinking. Ethel finished her meal and glanced at her watch. The others were still eating and talking. "We have about fifteen minutes," she said. "Come with me. I'll show you one of the Daddies."

Eric stood and followed Ethel toward a set of swinging metal doors at the back of the room. As they passed the tables filled with women, forks stopped in midair and hundreds of sets of eyes fastened on them. Animated conversation groups fell silent as he and Ethel walked past. Eric felt much as he had when he first walked down the crowded corridor into the getaway room in the men's facility.

Ethel stopped just outside the swinging doors and, with a finger in front of her pursed lips, motioned silence. She nodded toward the small window in the door, and Eric peeked through it into the kitchen.

Women of all ages, shapes, sizes, and colors scurried about preparing food and washing dishes. One woman, however, sat virtually motionless on a high stool in the near corner.

Her fiery red hair curled tightly against her head, and a pair of closely set green eyes flashed above her rather prominent nose. She looked to be about five foot seven, slim but bosomy, and broad shouldered. Her biceps bulged beneath her starched white oxford shirt, the sleeves of which were rolled up to her elbows. A tattoo artist's rendition of a coral and white water moccasin, its head covering most of the back of her right hand, writhed up her right forearm as she flipped cigarette ashes into the cupped palm of her left hand. Eric watched, fascinated by the lifelike motion of the snake's forked tongue sliding down her middle finger and the gold, reptilian eyes blinking at him from either side of the second knuckle. The undulating body of the snake was faintly visible beneath the thin fabric of her shirt sleeve, but its vibrant colors reappeared between her neck and the shirt collar. The snake's tail made an S curve, tapered gracefully over her left breast, and disappeared again, this time into her sweat-slick cleavage. Ethel's voice sounded as though she were a million miles away.

"That's Chili, Eric. Her temper is just as hot as her name. She's been in and out of institutions since she was twelve, but she didn't hit the big time till she was eighteen."

"What happened?" Eric asked, backing away from the window and turning to lean against the nearby wall.

"It's a long story," Ethel said, "and every man's nightmare." She crossed her arms and leaned against the wall beside him. "As a child, Chili was repeatedly raped by her father."

"Where in hell was her mother?" Eric asked, disgust and frustration obvious in his tone. Ethel briefly raised one eyebrow before continuing.

"She died of injuries sustained from a 'bad fall' when Chili was three or four years old. He started abusing Chili shortly after her mother's death."

"How long did it go on?" Eric asked, staring at the black and white floor tiles.

"Until she was twelve," Ethel answered. "One night, after her father had finished with her and fallen asleep, Chili slipped into the kitchen, came back to the bedroom with a butcher knife, and stabbed Daddy five times before he managed to get her under control."

"Good for her," Eric muttered under his breath.

"Yeah, well, someone heard him screaming and called the police. Her father died of his wounds. Neighbors, who had been real closed-mouthed while it was going on, suddenly came to her defense. The police, for once, called it self-defense. But because none of the neighbors would take her in and no relatives came forward, she was placed in the state mental hospital for observation. Physicians and psychiatrists who examined her verified that there had been ongoing sexual abuse. But she didn't receive any treatment."

Eric shook his head grimly. "So what did they finally do with her?"

Ethel paused, then looked up into his eyes. "The state, in its infinite wisdom, placed her with an alcoholic aunt who turned her out a street whore and got her hooked on drugs."

"Great!" Eric murmured.

"Uh-huh. A year after her release, her aunt died in a mysterious house fire."

"Good God—"

"Had nothing to do with this scene, honey," Ethel interjected.

Eric felt embarrassed by his ignorance, but his shock was genuine. "So what happened then, Ethel?"

"Well, Chili did what thousands of girls in her position do, Eric. She shacked up with a pimp and part-time dealer twice her age and gave him and his clients sex in exchange for a steady supply of methamphetamines. When she got pregnant, she talked him into marrying her so their baby would have a real family—"

"Christ!"

"—and after their wedding, he proceeded to beat her regularly. Finally, when she wasn't making enough on the streets, he forced her to sell the baby. That's when she made up her mind to get rid of him."

"Love works in mysterious ways," Eric muttered.

"'Deed it do, Honey, 'cause by this time, Chili had found the first real love of her life. A woman named Marsha. Together they bought a .45 caliber service revolver, hid it, and packed up her things. One night, while her pimp was asleep, Chili and Marsha loaded everything onto his Harley-Davidson."

"Folded her tent and slinked off into the night?" Eric asked. "Doesn't sound very gutsy."

Ethel shook her head and smiled. "You got that right, Sugar. And Chili had become one very gutsy woman. She didn't just leave. She went back into the house and woke that man up with a vengeance! Police report says she crawled into the bedroom, peeked over the foot of the bed to make sure he was lying on his back, and fired the first shot straight through his balls."

Eric's testicles tightened self-protectively. "Jesus!" he whispered.

"That man screamed, moaned, and pleaded for half an hour before Chili finally emptied the rest of the clip into him," Ethel said, shaking her head in wonder.

Eric stepped back over to the window in the kitchen door and searched the face of the woman on the stool. When a young woman came by and whispered something to her, Chili's green eyes brightened and she smiled. But the light in them died quickly, and she went back to watching and directing the work with occasional, short sweeps of her arm.

When he turned away from the window, he noticed Ethel had started back down the gauntlet of staring, smiling women toward the board's table. Eric hurried to catch up. As he came alongside her, Ethel continued her narrative.

"Chili and Marsha went on a robbery spree across three states. When they hit here, they were high on methamphetamines. Instead of doing their usual circle around the store to check things out, they pulled in and parked at the first convenience store with an empty lot. Normally, Chili did the job while Marsha guarded the bike. But this time, Marsha jumped off the bike and ran inside first.

"When she heard the shot, Chili ran into the convenience store and met up with the business end of a shotgun. When she tried to duck, the blast hit her shoulder and knocked her through the glass door and back out into the parking lot.

"Marsha was shot in the face," Ethel continued. "She died instantly. Chili had a bad shoulder wound, but she recovered and faced trial."

"Plea bargain?"

"Uh-huh. Got forty years for manslaughter and five concurrent sentences for armed robbery. She's on the docket for work release now."

"Smart lawyer. If she's paroled—"

"That's right," Ethel agreed, "she'll be paroled for all five robberies." Ethel stopped short three steps from her chair at the table. Then she turned to face Eric, her back to the other board members. Her voice softened and she spoke quietly. "I read in the paper the other day that you've filed for a divorce."

Eric swallowed hard and nodded. He knew the news was bound to get around, but was surprised that Ethel was the one bringing it up. Here. And now.

"Well, honey," she crooned, patting his arm. Her eyes sparkled with mirth. "I know one hot redhead who would probably just love the chance to rock your world. You interested?"

Eric's laughter ricocheted off the dining room walls.

III In the kitchen, Chili grinned to herself as Kim, the young woman who'd intercepted Eric and handed him the envelope, sauntered through the swinging door of the supply room and into the kitchen. Kim smiled broadly at Chili and nodded toward a corner hidden from the guard's view by an industrial-size, stainless-steel freezer.

Chili rose from her perch, nodded at a guard (who promptly turned her back), and let the hypnotic sway of Kim's hips draw her across the crowded, noisy room.

In the corner, Kim turned to face the older woman and leaned against the wall, her arms hanging loose at her sides. Chili's green eyes stared boldly into the younger woman's brown ones as she slid the palms of her hands up Kim's arms, barely touching. She smiled to herself as the tiny, downy hairs beneath her hands rose at the command of her almost imperceptible touch.

Kim gasped as Chili grasped the front of her blouse and jerked it free from her skirt. Slowly, still staring into Kim's eyes, the redhead parted her own dry lips and moistened them with the tip of her wet tongue. Kim remained motionless, mesmerized by Chili's tongue, her eyes, and the sensation of fingertips gliding across smooth skin, up and up over the trembling, taut flesh of her soft belly and her rib cage, moving like live things toward warmth. At last, Chili's warm palms encircled, squeezed, lifted, and weighed the younger woman's firm, heaving breasts.

Chili watched lust clouds move across Kim's eyes and listened with satisfaction to the soft, feathery moans escaping her lips. As Kim's eyes closed, Chili leaned forward, licked the salty beads of moisture outlining Kim's upper lip. First with delicate flicks of her long fingernails, then with firm, insistent pinching of her fingertips, Chili toyed with Kim's erect nipples through her thin lace bra. Kim's head tilted slowly backward as though attached to an invisible string reeled out by her seducer. Months of seconds danced past as Chili rhythmically kneaded Kim's breast with her left hand and whispered to her, over and over.

"You like that, don't you, honey? Yes. Mama can make her baby girl feel so good . . . so, so good."

Kim replied incoherently, and Chili glided her right hand down the younger woman's abdomen, across the waistband of her skirt, and further down, toward the moist heat of her sex radiating through the cotton skirt and sending thick waves of primal incense into Chili's flaring, quivering nostrils. Then, as she firmly pressed her palm against the younger woman's throbbing mound, Chili released Kim's breast and reached inside her own bra for a moist slip of paper. She slid the note slowly and carefully inside the younger woman's satin panties.

"You did real good, honey," Chili crooned, her voice ragged with desire. She stared at the vein pulsing beneath the smooth skin of her lover's proffered throat, consumed by a fantasy in which she leaned forward and drank from that blue river, crushed the smooth muscle of Kim's upper arm in one hand and dug the fingernails of her other hand into the woman's tight, round ass. Instead, Chili abruptly stepped back and watched in triumph as Kim's knees buckled and her head snapped forward. Wisps of long, dark hair lay plastered to the young woman's brow, and sweat glistened in the hollows formed by her collarbones.

"Soon," Chili promised, "Mama's gonna give you your reward. But right now, get your sweet ass back in the supply room and send this note on its way to Mr. Jeffries." Chili's eyes were green fire as she gazed at the young woman. "We play our cards right, Sugar, and you and I will be out of here in no time, with no one to watch or worry about how long we play."

Kim nodded, grinned, and deftly tucked her blouse back into her skirt. She brushed provocatively against Chili on her way back to the supply room.

That night Chili lay on her bunk mentally rehearsing her role in John Jeffries's grand scheme. She consciously fought her fears and reassured herself that, as much as she resented having to trust Jeffries—or any man, for that matter—right now she had no choice. Besides, it just might work. Jeffries wouldn't dare sell her out. He knew that if he did she would kill him. If she wasn't alive when the dust settled, one of her drug suppliers would take care of him. Business was business.

After a short time, Chili sighed with satisfaction. The power balance felt about right. Although John had not revealed the details of the last phase of his plan, she was fairly sure she knew what he'd do. Which was nothing, without her help. If Chili succeeded in getting her work release, then only she would have access to transportation, and the same drug contacts on the outside that solidified her leadership position inside the prison would ensure their safety beyond the walls. Chili relaxed and smiled to herself, let her mind drift back to the kitchen, and to her brief encounter with Kim. Then, for a few precious moments, she went still further back among her memories and savored every detail of the first time, a few months ago, when she'd tasted her newest daughter.

It had been twice as exciting as usual because of the tremendous risk involved in approaching Kim on her own with no lookouts at the entrances to the shower room. But because she felt this one was special, Chili hadn't wanted to frighten her. And, of course, she'd been right. But being right had its price.

Chili had worked slow, approaching Kim as a friend, using her voice and lots of tenderness. No threats. Just like she'd have treated her own, real baby, if she'd been allowed to keep it. She'd known from gossip that Kim had been taken from her mother when she was very young. Chili suspected that the shy, quiet girl craved love and protection from a woman but had never translated her emotional need into a physical act. All this only stimulated Chili's intense desire to take charge, to control others, and best of all, to initiate a new innocent into her world.

Chili prided herself on ruling her family with a an iron fist inside a velvet glove, preferring seduction to rape and grateful, loyal service to terrified compliance. She knew that she was good. Her confidence was what had made it possible, that night, to capture Kim and send her into orbit, helplessly writhing in the clutches of an overwhelming orgasm. However, her confidence sometimes had interfered with her better judgment and her senses. Which was why a guard was able to walk in unannounced and find Chili with her face buried between the young Indian woman's luscious thighs.

Luckily, the guard was the same one who'd been asleep on duty during an escape attempt several months earlier. The escape plan had failed, and though Chili was not part of the attempt, she eagerly took advantage of her opportunity to acquire a chit. As part of the investigation by the warden into the aborted escape, Chili and the guard were questioned. Chili claimed that the woman on duty had been busy helping her deal with an unusually messy and difficult period during the escape attempt. The guard's surprised smile was like money in the bank. Chili hated to use a valuable chit simply to avoid a write-up for sexual misconduct, but she needed a favorable recommendation from the board and knew that she would not get one with a misconduct on her record.

Now, if she and Kim could influence the newest member of the parole board—this liberal asshole, Williams—she'd have her work release and Jeffries's plan would move up to phase four.

Chili drifted off to sleep, dreaming of freedom and someone with whom she could enjoy it once more.

III During the interminable, depressing afternoon meetings, Eric often reached inside his pocket and felt the envelope. The face of the woman who'd handed it to him moved in and out of his mind. His curiosity warred with nagging twinges of guilt. Still, he had to know more about this woman who could have been a twin of Mary Jane's. On the one hand, he knew this kind of contact was expressly forbidden between members of the board and convicts. On the other hand, he had taken this job because of an intense need to help others.

He had better take some time to think about it. He didn't want to make a mistake. The question was, how could he be expected to help if he didn't allow this girl a chance to have her say?

11

THE TRIAL OF THE PRINCE

Crowds of reporters and bystanders were standing on the worn granite steps of the federal courthouse building as Franklin Felix, the pride and joy of the Federal Justice Department's prosecution team, entered the building. The confidence bred by 165 convictions for the Federal Justice Department showed itself in the stride of federal prosecutor Franklin Felix. It was June 10, the day Franklin Felix had called "opening day of hunting season"—the first day of the trial of State Senator Glen Tobias on fraud and tax evasion charges. Felix, looking like a *GQ* ad, paused just before entering the federal courthouse, turned to the crowd of reporters, and assured them that this case was just a matter of laying out the facts. It was an open-and-shut case of multiple violations of federal income tax laws.

As Felix stepped aside to allow his crew of clean-cut young male lawyers to busily push in dolly after dolly loaded with dozens of boxes full of records pertaining to the case, a reporter in a western-cut suit and boots, his pen poised above his yellow legal pad, said, "Mr. Felix, don't you think the party that appointed you to office is going a bit too far by singling out a popular state senator who just happens to be from the opposing party?"

Felix dismissed the question with a pained expression and a wave of his well-manicured hand.

"Check the Constitution and the Rules of Ethics," he said. "The Department of Justice's responsibility is to uphold the Constitution. That applies to a small-town state senator just as it would to any other citizen who violates the law."

Despite Felix's scornful reply, the reporter was grinning as he turned away to return to his office. If there was to be a governor from Felix's party elected in this state, the reporter thought, Tobias, a particularly resourceful, energetic, and popular senator, would have to be dethroned. It reminded the reporter of the time he had asked the president of the state bar association who was the best criminal lawyer in the state. The president had replied, "Glen Tobias when he is sober." When asked who the second-best criminal attorney was, he replied, "Glen Tobias when he is drunk." The reporter laughed out loud as he was retreating down the steps, causing a puzzled frown to cross Felix's face. He immediately dismissed it and started striding purposefully toward the courtroom.

Franklin Felix's wide-set blue eyes and tan features were accented by gray sideburns at his temples and a full head of slicked-back black hair. He was every Hollywood producer's image of the elite prosecutor dedicated to the preservation of the American system of justice. Felix knew he really belonged in New York, Chicago, or Los Angeles and hated to waste time in this rough-and-tumble backwoods courtroom. As he pushed through the courtroom doors, he was taken aback by the chorus of boos that erupted from the overflowing crowd. With a surprised, slightly shocked expression on his face, he hurried to the counsel table.

Senator Tobias sauntered in from the doorway closest to the jury box for a brief visit and was greeted by loud shouts, whistles, and applause. As the senator waved to the crowd, Felix's mouth tightened into a firm, thin line, and the muscles of his jaw worked under the smooth skin of his face. As he turned to open the door for his attorney,

 Tobias's gaze rested for a moment on Felix's face. The Prince smiled. Felix involuntarily shivered. That disgusted him, he thought. *Just another backwoods politician.* But in the deep recesses of his mind, he knew that this asshole played for keeps. "Well, so do I," Felix mumbled under his breath.

As a body, the entire courtroom, with the exception of the FBI men lounging in each corner, rose as if on some silent signal. Senator Tobias and his lawyer had entered the courtroom and were making their way to the counsel table.

The senator's handsome good looks, ramrod straight bearing, and smiling countenance contrasted sharply with the appearance of the little man walking at his side, who might easily have been his grandfather.

The smaller man, Frank Bell, wore a wrinkled gray suit and an outlandish red tie. His shoes were scuffed, and his red hair was too thin to hide the dime-size liver spots on top of his head. All of his features were angular, from his sharp nose to the short, pointed ears standing out perpendicular to his head. His mouth curled downward in a permanent scowl, and the early signs of Parkinson's disease—the stooped back and trembling hands—were apparent.

Frank Bell had changed a great deal since the painting of a portrait of him now hanging in the halls of the law school. He now used his black cane, topped by the silver head of an eagle, more for support than as a stylish accessory.

Tobias, his lawyer on one arm and the elderly man's worn briefcase on the other, looked like a respectful new king wisely seeking the counsel of an elder ruler. Still, the briefcase hardly seemed big enough to hold sufficient material with which to fight a drunk-driving case, let alone a massive political influence and fraud case.

Had he thoroughly researched Bell, Felix would have known that the old man used his appearance to gain an advantage and catch his opponents off guard. They would also have discovered that Bell was a quarter Creek Indian, that he had once been on the tribal council, and that the tribal headquarters of the Creek Nation were located a short three blocks from the courthouse. Fully one fourth of the jury panel was undoubtedly Creek. The Justice Department investigators did inform Felix that Judge Gordon McPherson, the trial judge for this case, had studied under Frank Bell's tutelage in law school. Felix dismissed that tidbit of information as insignificant. It turned out he was wrong.

All the spectators rose again, this time at the bailiff's request. Judge McPherson, the presiding federal judge for the eastern district, a wizened little man with thinning strands of gray hair pulled across his gleaming skull, entered the courtroom through the door behind the judge's dais. Gordon McPherson hailed from the same county as Glen Tobias, and the senator and McPherson were very old, very good friends. McPherson had been appointed by the very senator whom Tobias, as an eager young man, had labored tirelessly to get elected. In fact, it had been young Glen Tobias who had first introduced Gordon McPherson to the very senator who later appointed him to the exalted position from which he would now hear the case of *United States v. Tobias.*

McPherson was eccentric but evenhanded. That he displayed a tendency to be for the underdog in civil cases didn't worry Felix. This was a criminal matter, and McPherson had always shown himself to be a harsh judge in criminal prosecutions. However, the judge seemed to have more than his share of personal problems. His marriage was usually in trouble, probably because he took a somewhat more than passing interest in good Scotch whiskey.

Yet because his was a lifetime appointment, McPherson's difficulties and eccentricities were not as devastating as they might have been to an elected official. In fact, according to a talkative waitress who had served Felix's breakfast, after one particular night of drinking and fighting with his wife, the judge had spent a night in one of the jail cells on the top floor of the federal courthouse building. Despite the rantings and ravings of the drunks in the adjoining cell, he'd apparently declared it the best night's sleep he'd had in ten years.

McPherson sat, requested those present be seated, and immediately removed his thick, rimless glasses and rubbed his eyes, a gesture that both sides would see repeated throughout the trial.

Felix rose, waved his soft, beringed fingers, and began arguing to the court that the courtroom should be cleared.

In response, McPherson honored him for a full minute with an icy glare over the lenses of his glasses, which now rested in deep, reddened ravines alongside his nose. "Mr. Felix," he finally intoned, "it is my understanding that you are a fine government prosecutor. Having you come all the way from Washington to this Eastern District must mean that this case is very important to the government." He then reminded Felix that the same government had appointed him to the bench and that he would like to protect the Constitution also, but reminded him very clearly that the Constitution provided freedoms for fellow citizens who did not work for the government.

At this, a delighted roar went up in the courtroom. A gentle tap of the gavel restored order, and McPherson continued:

"When I start barring people from my courtroom, Mr. Felix, I am telling them that they cannot watch their government in action. Surely secrecy is not the theme of our administration in Washington, Mr. Felix? Regardless, it is not the way I run my courtroom. I would think that you should start concerning yourself with presenting the case for the United States to a jury, rather than worrying about what your fellow citizens are thinking while watching our judicial process. There will be no clearing of this courtroom. Not now, not ever!"

As a reaction erupted in the back of the courtroom, Judge McPherson, obviously anticipating such a demonstration, slammed the gavel down. A sound like an exploding shotgun shell reverberated throughout the room. Once more he spoke into the ensuing silence. "I would also remind everyone here today that this is not a circus. Demonstrations of this sort will not be countenanced. Otherwise, every one of you will discover the fine facilities we have available on the top floor of this building."

Muffled laughter rippled across the crowd. Felix's face grew red, a color change that had nothing to do with the temperature inside the room.

"Now, Mr. Felix," McPherson continued, "do you have any other preliminary matters, or can we get on with the government's business?"

"Nothing further at this time, Your Honor," Felix muttered before retiring to his seat.

Felix considered arguing to the court about the relationship between the jury's composition and his opponent's lawyer. He knew the jury panel was filled with retired and active miners, some if not all of whom undoubtedly knew that Senator Tobias's father had been a miner. He also wasn't sure about the number of people Senator Tobias had represented either as a senator or as a lawyer. He decided to sit motionless and avoid another lecture. He knew he would simply have to take his chances. The trial hadn't even begun, and already beads of perspiration were gathering on Felix's brow.

He proceeded to the voir dire. The questioning of the

 jury to test their qualifications to be fair and impartial provided another nightmare for Franklin Felix. It was obvious that Felix was having a hard time believing the answers, or lack thereof, that he was getting out of the jurors. All the men and women denied knowing or having ever heard of Senator Glen Tobias. Felix's intense cross-examination was abruptly cut short by Judge McPherson, who informed him that he could only have a limited number of questions after the judge himself had voir-dired the jury. By contrast, the judge's voir dire sounded like a father checking on the health and well-being of his children.

Felix drew four retired miners and exercised three challenges to get rid of them. There was little doubt in anyone's mind that the last remaining miner, a big man with gnarled hands and permanently dirty fingernails, would be chosen jury foreman even though, when he denied knowing Senator Tobias's father, the crowded courtroom buzzed like a swarm of mosquitoes.

During opening statements, the judge interrupted Felix several times with admonitions. Opposing counsel, on the other hand, sat with his aged head bowed and only occasionally moved his head to confer quietly with his client. A frustrated, angry Franklin Felix made an impassioned statement about the jury members' duties as patriots and Americans and then abruptly sat down. It then became time for the opening statement of the venerable counsel for Senator Tobias.

Frank Bell rose slowly and with difficulty, supported by the grasp of the senator, who set him on his feet. Bell then shuffled toward the jury, stood for a moment and looked them over, turned slowly toward the court, and finally spoke in a clear, resonant voice with a minimum of accompanying gestures:

"May it please the court, ladies and gentlemen of the jury, I have been astounded by the parade of government employees who have walked through this courtroom carrying load after load of the boxes you see stacked in that corner. I want you to be mindful of those boxes. I want you to listen to the government's lawyer as he takes you through all those boxes. I want you to be mindful, also, of the hundreds and thousands of dollars the government has spent to accumulate those boxes and bring all these government people here to your courtroom to present this case."

The muscles in Felix's jaws were working overtime. Bell continued:

"I know you are all God-fearing, taxpaying, patriotic Americans. You have a right not only to be in this courtroom as jurors but also to know how your tax dollar has been spent.

"I want you to judge the demeanor and the dress of all of these government employees and witnesses. I am certain they are here to do a job. They certainly better be doing a job, since they've got to justify the tax dollars spent to employ them, send them here, clothe them, and feed them."

Felix leaped out of his chair, shouting, "Objection, Your Honor!" and immediately moved to plead his objection. McPherson glared over his glasses and banged his gavel.

"You are out of order, Mr. Felix! Sit down. Your objection is overruled."

With a smile at Frank Bell as if he were apologizing for the unruly misbehavior of a nephew instead of a government representative's intervention, McPherson said, "You may now continue, Mr. Bell."

When Bell turned back to the jury, his face held just the hint of a smile. With his hands in his coat pockets, he continued:

"Thank you, Your Honor. Folks, we've got a young man on trial here by all these government people, and I want you to be mindful of him, too. You've reelected him to be your representative many, many times because of all the good things he's done for this county, for this state, and for you. He's not paid very much to do that by the government, so he has to work as a lawyer. Well, after all, a man's got to do something in order to feed and take care of his family. And I want you to be mindful that, as a lawyer, he represents people and upholds the constitution of this great state and this fine county."

"So, finally, what I want you to do to find the truth in this case is, I want you to compare all those boxes over there and all the work these government people have been doing with what this fine man, Senator Tobias, has done for this county and state and what he will continue to do in the future."

Bell paused, lowered his grizzled head once more, removed his hands from his coat pockets, and placed them in front of him in an almost prayerful pose. Then, slowly, he lifted his head and looked each juror squarely in the face. Finally, Bell whispered into the hushed courtroom:

"When you good men and women finish your comparisons, you send Senator Tobias back home. You send him back home to his wife, his children, and his grandchildren. You send him back to his people and let him continue with his good works for all of his people."

As Bell shuffled back to the counsel table, Felix half rose from his seat to object. He actually opened his mouth, in fact, then closed it and eased back down in his chair. The judge sat ready, his gavel poised. Bell's opening statement had been moving, unethical, and preposterous. Yet half the jurors were dabbing at their eyes with handkerchiefs while the other half sat glaring at Felix.

That afternoon, Raymond Revis, special agent of the IRS and chief of the Enforcement Division, took the stand in his dark, conservative suit. His muted red-checked, burgundy silk tie lay smoothly against his white, button-down oxford shirt. The high polish on his brown wing tips matched the shine of his carefully barbered hair. Revis looked perfect. Too perfect. The man's pale green eyes were cold, calculating, and he had an annoying habit of licking his lips before answering questions.

His delivery was reminiscent of an adding machine totaling a long series of numbers. In an East Coast courtroom, Revis would have been an instant hit, had immediate credibility. But not here. He was not the sort of good old boy any of the jurors would want to spend an evening with, sharing a beer and pickled eggs and maybe playing pool or shuffleboard.

Felix attempted to lead Revis through a long and laborious series of calculations and numbers, comparisons of bank statements, tax returns, and office records that, while necessary for the record, would have put a raging elephant to sleep. Just when it appeared the judge was ready to call it quits, Felix began to wind things up.

"Mr. Revis," he said, "do you have an opinion as to whether or not these records reveal that Glen Tobias reported all his income from the last three years as reflected by his tax returns?"

"Yes, sir," Revis replied, "I do have an opinion."

"And, sir," Felix asked, turning his back to the jury and gazing, for effect, out the window of the courtroom, "what is that opinion?"

"In my opinion, sir," Revis replied, "Mr. Tobias was receiving income from each of those succeeding years, but failed to report it in the appropriate year."

Revis went on to testify about ten instances when Tobias had received an attorney's fee from a client but hadn't reported it on his income tax for that year. The most damning testimony concerned Tobias's complicated cattle transactions. A two-year examination of his cattle operations revealed a failure to report income on the sale of calves. Revis cited specific instances where no income was reported on sales where there was clearly a profit. Deprecation and expenses had also been taken on feed that had not been purchased for cattle that did not exist.

Nevertheless, through all of this testimony, three of the jury members had nodded off, while the others remained impassive. They appeared to be bored with the whole proceeding and ready to move on. Franklin Felix felt his stomach churning. He tried to make his voice louder when asking key questions in hopes that it might stir up the jury. Still they remained impassive.

One hand tucked neatly in his trouser pocket, he sauntered toward the witness. In a loud voice he asked, "In your expert opinion, Mr. Revis, do all of these factors constitute a violation of the statutes governing the Internal Revenue Codes, specifically the United States Code, as to tax filing and reporting?"

"Why, yes, sir," Revis replied as though surprised at the question. "Obviously, not reporting income for the years in which the income was earned constitutes a violation and subjects the individual to all of the criminal and civil penalties, together with interest and costs."

As Felix sat down, Professor Frank Bell rose with the aid of his client and shuffled toward the witness. Halfway to the witness chair, he turned and looked up at the judge, raised a finger, and asked, "Your Honor, may I please have a moment?" The judge nodded, and Bell shuffled back to the counsel table. He leaned precariously over to pick up a yellow pad on which he had been scribbling during Revis's testimony. Then he straightened and looked quizzically up at the witness, dropped the pad on the table, and shuffled straight back toward the witness and began his interrogation.

"Mr. Revis, you are a man quite knowledgeable in your field. I am impressed by your ability to go through all those boxes over there and come up with all those figures. I assume that, while looking through all those figures for the three years in question starting with the year 1986, you also looked at all of the deposits, checks, and tax returns for the years 1987 and 1988, did you not, sir?"

Revis shifted in his chair and said, "Yes, sir."

Bell continued: "And it is your final testimony, Mr. Revis, after all of these hours of going through all those boxes, that Glen Tobias did not report income he received—let me see if I remember correctly—in the amount of four thousand dollars in 1986 and some little checks that amounted to another fifteen hundred dollars or so, on his 1986 return. Is that right?"

"Yes, sir," Revis replied, obviously confused as to what Bell was leading up to.

"Well, Mr. Revis, didn't you find those checks had been deposited into the bank account of Senator Tobias's law firm?"

"Why, yes, that's true, but—"

"And did you not, in looking at the 1987 tax return, see where Mr. Tobias reported that four thousand dollars and that fifteen hundred dollars on his return?"

Revis licked his lips twice. "Well, yes, sir. Of course he did that, but that is a violation—"

"Again, sir, did you not find in 1987, when you found these checks were the same as you had found in 1986, that those were deposited in his account?"

"Yes, sir, but—"

"Well, did you not find that those were reported on his 1988 return?"

The courtroom was silent. Sweat was dripping down Felix's back. A vein had swollen at Revis's right temple and was now visibly pulsating.

"W-w-hy, yes," Revis stuttered, "of course! B-but counsel, that is a violation and against United States Code!"

Felix was obviously stunned. Revis had not told him the same income had been reported in subsequent years. It was, technically, a violation. Nevertheless, it did not constitute massive tax fraud. Felix made himself relax. After all this was a minor part of the prosecution's case. The massive cattle fraud would get this son of a bitch in the end. Felix's confidence returned.

Bell stood like an ancient, twisted live oak in the center of the courtroom. Quietly, he asked, "Are you telling me, Mr. Revis, that our government is now spending hundreds of thousands of dollars to investigate, forcing people to spend money on attorneys, allowing people to be held up for ridicule in the press, and penalizing them simply because the money they earn is not reported in the same year in which it was earned?"

Revis was obviously confused and amazed. "Why, that's exactly what I am saying. We must adhere to the letter of the law! Otherwise, the law has no meaning."

Old man Bell turned his flashing glance on the jury for an instant and then directed it once more at Revis. Revis attempted to go on. "Besides, there are numerous other violations that I have been testifying about, that—"

For the first time Frank Bell's voice rose two octaves, interrupting Revis in his attempt to go on. "I submit to you, Mr. Revis, that to have brought this type of shame and degradation upon this man, to have spent all of these tax dollars based on some bureaucrat's interpretation of the law, is ludicrous!"

Felix leaped to object, but the judge merely waved him

down. "Professor Bell," the judge said kindly, "you may make your point in closing arguments."

The old man looked up at the judge with a flush in his cheeks.

"I'm sorry, Your Honor. I got carried away. Injustice makes me do that. I apologize to the court and to this jury."

Bell turned back to Revis and got him to admit one more time that Tobias did report the income, but not in the year the IRS thought he should have reported it. He then sat down shaking his head. Felix attempted to rehabilitate his witness, but it was obvious the jury was not interested. All during the time Felix asked Revis about the cattle fraud transactions, the jury seemed distracted. They paid more attention to Tobias patting the shoulder of Mr. Bell than to Franklin Felix's loud questions.

Although the trial continued for five more weeks, it mainly consisted of a dry attempt to portray several funds as not reported and diverted for fraudulent purposes. The fine points of accounting were boring and totally confusing to the lay jury. On top of that, Bell managed to back each witness into a corner with cross-examination that never exceeded five minutes. Each witness wound up admitting he or she could not trace certain transactions and that it was difficult to tell whether or not, in gross amounts, everything that should have been reported had in fact been reported. With masterly cross-examination technique, Bell emphasized only the weaknesses in the government's case, never touching on the testimony concerning the cattle fraud. The jury was more than tired of Franklin Felix and the government witnesses and completely enamored with the kindly Frank Bell.

Finally, after five weeks, the government rested its case. It was now time for Franklin Bell to put on his defense of Glen Tobias.

The old man wasted no time. The very next day Glen Tobias took the stand as the only witness for the defense.

Tobias took the oath and, looking like a dark, avenging angel, marched to the witness stand.

Judge McPherson turned to him and said, "Senator Tobias, you are under oath, but you are also an officer of this court and must be mindful of this as you testify."

Tobias nodded and fired the first salvo for the defense in his reply to the judge:

"Your Honor, I could take the oath a hundred times and it would not change my fidelity and faithfulness to our American system. I can assure you that you will hear the truth from me."

As he recited his well-rehearsed statement, Tobias turned slightly in his chair and looked directly at the jury. They all smiled sweetly down upon their native son. Then Bell, as counsel, began his direct examination of Senator Tobias. Mr. Bell deftly carried Glen Tobias through his background and his relationship with the IRS, pinpointing for the jury that he had given access to all of his books and records to them over a period of years. Over the objection of Franklin Felix, he testified that he had provided the "revenuers" with an office at his own expense.

Bell continued with the last series of questions that put the nail in the government's coffin. "Glen, I'm not going to take up any more of these folks' time than we have to. You and I have discussed all of these charges and all of these things that they've said before and during the course of this trial, have we not?"

"Yes, sir."

"It seems to us that there is only one issue that they keep trying to hammer back and forth, and that is whether or not you declared money when you deposited it and if you paid tax on it like every other citizen of these United States. Is that right?"

"Yes, sir."

"Glen, let's talk about 1986, 1987, and 1988. Just tell the court and the jury, in your own words, what that was all about."

Senator Tobias turned his regal head and stared with piercing eyes directly at the jury. In his best oratorical voice, he said, "Ladies and gentlemen of the jury, I don't know how or why these people would lead you to believe that I have not paid my taxes. Each one of these exhibits that I hold in my hand now are canceled checks, deposit slips, and income tax returns. All of them show that I reported every bit of my income and paid taxes on it. I'm shocked and angered that our government would pass such technical laws that seem to serve only to entrap honest citizens. I'm not guilty, and furthermore, if you give me the chance, I'll carry this fight to the halls of Congress so that honesty and fair play can come back into our system as it was intended by our founding fathers when they wrote the Constitution."

With that, once again, all the spectators in the back of the courtroom rose in silent unison and remained standing. Judge McPherson lifted his gavel but slowly laid it back down.

Franklin Felix had now reached the biggest challenge of his life: the cross-examination of Senator Glen Tobias. Every time Felix tried to bore in on the question of the cattle fraud, however, Tobias would turn toward a receptive jury and recite how difficult it was for his good employees to keep up with all the constantly changing regulations from Washington. He would answer, "It's difficult for my good help to be precisely correct, but in the end they've always been honest, just like I was raised by my family to be, and just like all of my friends in this fine county."

Direct examination and presentation of the defense

exhibits had taken Bell less than an hour. The government had put in two years of investigation and five weeks of testimony, ending in a fizzle. The comparison was devastating.

The jury, with hundreds of thousands of documents to go over and reams of instructions to follow, nevertheless returned to the courtroom in twenty-two minutes. Judge McPherson brought his cup of coffee back to the bench with him and set it down carefully to one side. He was still standing, banging his gavel, when the courtroom stopped its anticipatory buzz and settled down to listen with rapt attention.

"Ladies and gentlemen," the judge said, "I want no outburst or demonstration to occur in this courtroom. Now, I have received the verdict, but there is still business to be done by the court. When I leave this bench, I don't give a damn what you do outside this courtroom. While you are here, however, you are to remain absolutely quiet. Bailiff, if you will please return the verdict to me."

The judge glanced at the slip of paper in his hands before handing it back to the bailiff, who returned it to the foreman of the jury. McPherson turned to the defense counsel table.

"Glen Tobias, you will please rise."

As the senator rose, the multitudes in the back of the courtroom silently rose with him. The judge looked up, shrugged, and said, "Mr. Jury Foreman, have you reached a verdict?"

The big miner stood and answered, "Yes, we have, Your Honor."

"Clerk, please read the verdict."

"The jury duly impaneled and upon our oath and all jurors unanimously agreeing, we find the defendant, Glen Tobias, not guilty on all counts."

The judge immediately turned to glare at the crowd,

but aside from a low murmur and a few gasps of joy, there was silence. McPherson then turned to address the prosecution.

"I have never, in all my forty years of practice or on the bench, seen a case so permeated by political implications. I am surprised, Mr. Felix, that the government didn't try to have a star chamber proceeding in order to get at this defendant. This use of the judicial system by my own government is appalling to me. Mr. Felix, you and your co-counsel will appear in my chambers in precisely thirty days for a hearing by this court as to why sanctions should not be imposed against you, the government, and the Department of Justice."

The judge then turned to the defense table and said, "I hope Senator Tobias will carry this experience with him and think often of it as he continues his political career, which has long involved battling against government persecution. This court stands adjourned."

The Dark Prince walked triumphantly from the courtroom, surrounded by reporters and admirers.

That evening, a late-night radio talk show host and amateur political analyst discussed Tobias's trial with callers. He summed up Senator Tobias's stature and the trial with an anecdote. He stated that if the election were held today, Senator Tobias would receive 95 percent of the vote. The deejay went on to joke that if the good senator had been convicted, he probably would have received only 90 percent of the vote in the next election.

12

KIM

Eric was playing catch-up at the office because of the time his parole board duties had taken. As tense as the parole board meetings were, the week that followed was worse, filled with bitter, loveless recitations of grievances by what seemed like an endless parade of divorcing clients. Eric found himself actually looking forward to the next parole board meeting, still a few weeks away. Exhaustion threatened to overwhelm him on Friday, at nine P.M., as he piloted the Jag the short distance up the parkway from his office to his neighborhood on the city's north side. A bright and cheerful array of lights blinked on all around him in determined defiance of his waning energy level.

As he exited the parkway and drove the toward his neighborhood, Eric took solace in the fact that, for the most part, his divorce from Mary Jane was going well. He hadn't seen her for two months now. Not that he really wanted to. Her lawyer, a young guy fresh out of school, said she wanted only a small stipend and the personal items she'd taken with her. Had Eric been one of his own clients, maybe he'd have felt elated, victorious. Maybe.

But he thought he understood better, now, how his clients felt when a mutually agreed-upon settlement fell short of providing emotional closure. Certainly he'd given up on "happily ever after." Still, some kind of friendly resolution would have been nice. He was working longer hours than he had in a very long time, hoping to find peace and contentment in his work. But he realized he'd fallen into a trap of sorts. Now, when he wasn't actually working, Eric felt blurry. His entire life seemed out of focus.

As he steered the Jag into the empty driveway, he wished Mary Jane had accepted his offer of the house. Then he'd have been forced to move out. But that was the problem. He had no idea where he wanted to go. So he stayed.

The two-story brick home was still in good shape. But Mary Jane's flower beds—once lovingly tended and bursting with multicolored zinnias, pink and red roses, Shasta daisies, lavender, and scented geraniums—were drying up and running wild with weeds. Eric gazed at the dusty yellow grass on either side of the walkway. He glanced at the dying blooms of unpicked tea roses turning brown and ugly near the front door as he turned his key in the front door. Watering had always been her job. All he seemed able to manage was regular maintenance of the pool.

He'd considered hiring a kid to do yard work, maybe the son of the housekeeper who now came in twice a week to straighten up and fix meals. Maybe he'd call her. Sometime. But not tonight. Right now all he wanted was a cool drink and a long sleep. The memory of Kim's sudden appearance at his side nagged at him. "She looked so much like Mary Jane," he said aloud to the empty house. He knew he had waited long enough to make his decision. Perhaps too long. It was time to see what he could do to help her.

The television blared its greetings from the brightly lit living room. The entire scenario was an illusion of occupancy Eric had devised to take the edge off the silence. Still, the place felt abandoned, as though its true owners were on vacation and he was merely caretaking until their return.

As he headed upstairs, Eric thought again about selling

and moving into an apartment. Something smaller, closer to his office. Sweet, thoughtful Jolene had started leaving red-circled copies of realtor's apartment listings on his desk.

"Honey," she'd said, "that place isn't really your style at all. Except for the pool, of course. But apartment complexes have those, so you could still swim. That way you'd have a chance to meet . . . people you might want to spend time with."

Bless her heart, Eric thought, smiling to himself. *Jolene the matchmaker*. But he wasn't ready. Not yet.

Eric shrugged off his jacket and tossed it into the cleaning basket in the corner of the bedroom. When he reached into his pockets to empty them out for the cleaners, his hand made contact with the envelope Kim had given him.

Eric started to open the missive from Kim but stopped, kicked off his shoes, and changed to his trunks instead. He grabbed the envelope and, padding barefoot down the carpeted stairs and into the living room, marveled at the way he'd begun to construct elaborate rituals out of the simplest things. Like undressing before opening a beer or pouring a gin and tonic. He realized he was prolonging the experience of opening the letter, caught as he was between mountains of anticipation and rivers of hesitation.

Kicked back in his recliner, his sweating glass making a white circle on the end table beside him, Eric shut his eyes for a moment and pictured the young woman who had handed him the note in the dining room of the women's facility. She was slender, beautiful, just like Mary Jane. The only difference was that Kim was obviously part Indian—not unusual in a state where nearly everyone boasted at least one relative who had married into one of the Five Civilized Tribes or one of the many other tribes in the state.

A part of him didn't want to go any deeper than this, didn't want to find out that, like many inmates, she couldn't write, or that the letter was a cold, emotionless recitation of a soap opera plot. He forced himself to open his eyes, open the envelope, unfold the pages, and begin reading.

To his surprise, the young woman's rambling narration was written in perfect script. Another similarity to his soon-to-be ex-wife. She introduced herself as Kim Whitlock, a half-blood member of the Seminole tribe. Interest was piqued. Like all other children born in this state, he had taken a full course on the Five Civilized Tribes, one of which was the Seminole tribe. Of the Five Civilized Tribes, only the Creeks and the Seminoles were removed to land that later turned out to be the oil patch. They were dispossessed of their minerals by allotment of the tribal estate, and then by court fraud of the individual allottees, not by intermarriage with whites, as many assumed. Just another chapter in the trouble the Native Americans endured in those early years.

Eric read on. Kim wrote that she remembered her full-blood mother but had never known her father, and her mother had never talked about him. When she was eight years old she was taken from her mother and placed with an older white farm couple who lived in the western part of the state. They were strict, religious fundamentalists. They believed in discipline and that a woman's place was in the home, cooking and cleaning for the men. Eric remembered from his studies that in the late 1970s the Indian Child Welfare Act had been passed to protect Indian children from the indiscriminate taking of the children from their Indian parents. Before the passage of that act, 30 percent of the Indian babies had been taken from their mothers by the state and sent to white foster homes. It was a tragedy repeated many times in an obvious design to take children away from their mother and father to get them out of the Indian culture. Often they were sent to boarding schools with a military atmosphere and forbidden to speak their Indian language. By the time they had finished school and went back to the reservation, they were no longer Indians. Their heritage, religion, and culture had been suppressed. Others, like Kim, were sent to white foster homes, many of those homes with a strict fundamentalist background, as Kim experienced. Once more, Eric was faced with a similarity with Mary Jane. It was obvious that Kim was subject to judgmental parents like Mary Jane's.

When she was ten, Kim wrote, her foster father's constant whippings and her foster mother's refusal to interfere or show Kim any type of affection led her to start running away. Kim attempted to transfer her need for love and affection that she was not getting in her foster home to anyone who would show her attention, mistaking that attention many times for love. Eventually her foster father or one of his friends would find her and bring her back to another beating and hours of churchgoing. In her search for love at fourteen, Kim wrote, she became pregnant by her high school counselor, a married man and the first person ever to praise her efforts in art and music. When she told him she was pregnant, "the man packed up his family and moved out of town overnight." Her foster family immediately rejected her (just like Mary Jane's father, Eric mused), and she was institutionalized to have her baby. The baby was taken from her by the Department of Human Services shortly after its birth. From there, Kim was placed in a series of foster homes.

At sixteen, Kim wrote, she ran away and found work as an exotic dancer, taking pride in the fact that she was eventually able to make enough money to move into an apartment and buy furniture. She also fended off the attentions of men who frequented the bars where she worked.

Then one night a bar customer and known drug dealer broke into her car and waited for her after work. When she opened the door, he yelled at her, held her by her jacket sleeves, and slugged her repeatedly in the face. She fought back, eventually dragged out of the car. When he reached into his coat, Kim wrote, she assumed he was going for a gun. She was frightened and, without thinking, fired one shot from a loaded .38 she kept in her purse for protection. The bullet hit his heart. When police discovered bits and pieces of a roll of hundreds and an ounce of pot in the man's blood-soaked shirt, she wrote, "they assumed the incident was the result of a drug deal gone bad."

Kim ended her letter by saying that, while in prison, she was working hard to develop her talents. She had learned to play the piano and was producing paintings that now hung in the warden's office and elsewhere throughout the prison. She had been placed on trustee status two months ago, during which time she had been a model prisoner.

Eric, both impressed and saddened by the letter, sat staring out into the darkening backyard. The pool lights came on, sending eerie, wavy patterns of illumination and shadow dancing across the water and up among the branches of overhanging trees. He knew the letter was meant to elicit his sympathy, that every word had been carefully chosen to convince him that she was worthy of parole. He also knew that Kim quite possibly had not written the letter, at least not by herself, and that it might all be lies. Eric kept going back to the similarities between Mary Jane and Kim. Maybe that is why he wanted to believe her, needed her to be everything she seemed to be—if not exactly pure, then at least honest, talented, bright, and deserving of his special consideration. A special consideration he apparently could not give to Mary Jane. He also knew he needed more information.

Eric absentmindedly reached for the phone, but stopped short of dialing when he noticed the time. Midnight. Earl would be in bed. Eric heaved himself out of his recliner and trudged up the stairs to bed, his mind churning with the ghosts of plans.

Sleep came quickly, but so did the Dream. Only this time it was not his mother Eric saw in the crowd at the edge of the pool. The face was dark and seemed to move with the ripples from the waves on the water. Was it Mary Jane? No. It was Kim. Laughing, swinging her dark hair across her smooth, tan shoulders and firm, naked breasts. As he stood on the board, preparing to dive, the crowd disappeared. Suddenly she was there, in the water, with him. They made love, and her warm, fluid body flowed around, over, and through him, over and over, all night long.

The next morning, immediately after his swim, Eric called Earl and requested Kim's file. Although Earl didn't ask any questions, Eric knew he wasn't imagining the curiosity behind his friend's acquiescence.

Three weeks later, Eric sat in Earl's office at McHenry Prison, waiting for the call to enter the boardroom. He'd thought about Kim a great deal after reading her letter, even more so after reading her file. Although disappointed by the discrepancies between the letter and the contents of the file, he was not particularly surprised. At least Mary Jane had taught him that lesson.

For the most part, though, her letter was backed up by the contents of her file. Police and court reports indicated, however, that in her telling of events leading to her arrest and conviction, Kim had slightly altered the facts of the case. For one thing, her co-workers at the bar had testified that Kim sometimes solicited customers and supplemented her income through prostitution. In fact, on the night in question, she had mentioned to them that she planned to meet that night with the victim, a john with whom she exchanged sex for drugs and money. According to the police report, the john had passed out in her car as he sat waiting for her.

The report also said that Kim appeared to have dragged the victim out of the front seat of the car and onto the street before placing the barrel of her .38 against his chest and firing one shot into his heart. Her face was bruised and one eye had been blackened, but there was no proof that the john had inflicted her wounds. She was stoned and hysterical when arrested.

The court couldn't really determine whether it was a case of self-defense or cold-blooded murder. There were no witnesses, and because the john's blood alcohol was high and there were photos of her injuries, the court accepted a lesser plea of manslaughter.

Eric tapped his fingers on the file, thinking he should drop the inquiry. He knew enough now, surely. She had learned to lie and was probably a murderer and a liar. But she was also a victim of life, a beautiful and talented woman whose past had prepared her for nothing but pain, drugs, and violence. Mary Jane had been lucky to turn one way, while Kim had turned another. It was such a short life as a matter of luck and happenstance. In Kim's case, she had no luck.

Eric had made a point, earlier that morning, of visiting the warden's office to view her artwork. She was good. He felt sure she could land a job as a commercial artist on the outside.

The office door opened and Earl poked his head in. "You still busy in here?" he asked.

"Nah, come on in," Eric said, grinning. "After all, it's your office."

Earl lumbered over to the chair behind his gray metal desk and sat down. Eric knew what was coming, had actually expected a lecture sooner.

"About this Kim girl. . ."

"Yes?" Eric answered brightly.

"Now, don't get me wrong, son," Earl began, running a huge hand over his stubbled jowl. "I know how eager you are to help these folks, and this particular girl would make any man's blood boil—"

"Earl, it's not like that. Really." Eric said, hoping he wasn't blushing. "I'm thinking about writing a research report on rehabilitation. This girl—what's her name?"

"Kim Whitlock," Earl supplied. His voice sounded tired.

"Kim. Yeah," Eric said, glancing at the file. "Well, you know how I feel about the necessity of rehabilitation. This girl just seems to have the talent, brains, and determination she'll need to become a useful member of society. I'd like to interview her and trace her progress. That's all."

Earl raised one eyebrow and gazed for a few moments at Eric. "Well," he drawled, "I suppose that wouldn't be a bad idea, writing a report and all. Would get you some notice and might help change a few attitudes in this backwards old state. But, you know, it's so damn easy to cross the line and—"

"Ah, come on, old buddy," Eric said, laughing. "You don't think I'm dumb enough to get romantically involved with her, do you? Hell, I have plenty of opportunities for that kind of stuff every day in my own office—women just begging for a little attention—and I haven't yielded to temptation yet."

Earl smiled and nodded. "Okay. Fine. I'll set up an

interview for this afternoon as soon as we hear the last review."

As he followed Earl into the boardroom a few minutes later Eric felt excited, relieved, and only a little guilty. He supposed learning to think on his feet in court had made it easier to tell quick, convenient lies. He hated lying to Earl, but he'd learned the wisdom of not always telling the whole truth. Eric's reverie was broken by the announcement of the first inmate to be seen and the appearance of George Davis entering the parole board room to take his place at the media table. Eric had been pleased that the warden would allow George Davis to attend the parole board meeting so that he could write about it in the prison newspaper.

Sue White's gravelly voice announced Jesse Allen Jones, as Eric returned his attention to the file before him.

Jesse Allen Jones, a handsome twenty-five-year-old, had never been in any serious trouble with the law prior to the offense for which he'd been incarcerated. Petty larceny and disturbing the peace were his only juvenile offenses. Though juvenile records are sealed, Eric knew that once a felony had been committed sufficient to incarcerate one in the state penitentiary, then all criminal records, no matter how early, were available to the board. It had proven to be helpful in some cases, but in other cases such as Jesse Allen Jones, the behavior was unexplainable.

One day, while driving down the highway, Jones had been caught speeding. He calmly pulled over on the side of the road, took a pearl-handled .32 caliber revolver out of his pocket, and shot and wounded the patrolman in the arm.

"Son, did you commit this crime?" Wyndott asked.

"Yes, sir," the boy answered, his brown eyes shining. "I did. But I'm a revolutionary and, as such, I believe in order. I believe that all violent criminals should be executed. That should be the law. Second-time offenders who commit nonviolent crimes should be killed, too. Automatic execution."

"Do I hear you right, son?" Wyndott asked, "Are you asking us to order your execution?"

"Yes, sir," the young man replied. He went on to deliver a rambling discourse on violence in American society, explaining how the evil in society could only be purged by fire. Finally, he detailed his own repeated attempts to effect his own death while in prison.

Wyndott interrupted him to read from the report, which stated that high-powered sniper rifles, grenades, and automatic weapons had been found in his apartment.

Eric flashed on news footage of Charles Whitman and Lee Harvey Oswald. The call for a vote took him by surprise. He voted with the board to deny Jones the parole he didn't even want. Eric noticed George Davis had seemingly paid great attention to this case. He was writing furiously.

Still, Eric knew Jones's sentence could only run six more months. *What then*? he thought. *Where will this guy go? And who, when he takes his final bow, will he feel bound to take with him*?

Eric's worry was interrupted by Sue White's call for the next inmate. The next case was not at all humorous. As dark as Eric's thoughts were about Jesse Allen Jones, a darker cloud began to form. A short, heavyset couple were led into the room as Ms. White announced their names. "Larry and Ramona Lindsay."

Eric felt the hairs on the back of his neck stand up. Even though he remembered the names from news reports, when he'd read the details in their case files he'd become sick to his stomach. The pair was serving time for lewd molestation of their five children.

Wyndott read from testimony presented to the board by the district attorney's office. According to the report, the Lindsay family was just planning to pass through the state on their way to California when they ran out of money, food, and gas. The parents set up a tent on the shore of a lake in the western part of the state and went to a local minister asking if he could find someone to take the children in until they could find jobs and housing. The minister found an appropriate foster home, and the children were placed there.

According to the D.A.'s report, the foster parents called the minister the next day saying that the children were behaving like animals. Pressed for details, the shocked foster parents revealed that all five of the Lindsay children were performing sexual acts of every nature among themselves and with the foster family's dog in full view of the foster parents and their other children.

When the children were taken into custody and questioned, the D.A. learned that this activity was a family tradition. The oldest child, an eleven-year-old girl, said her father had asked her, in their previous homes, to perform sexual acts with their landlords in exchange for free rent. According to the D.A.'s report, medical evidence and interviews with the children indicated that the three girls—ages eleven, seven, and six—had been having oral, anal, and vaginal intercourse with their mother, sisters, father, and brothers since babyhood.

Mr. and Mrs. Lindsay regularly taught the children new "games" in which all members of the family participated. The boys, ages two and five, reported having had repeated oral, anal, and vaginal intercourse with both parents, their sisters, and one another. The strongest medical evidence for the astounding amount of abuse reported was the fact that the youngest boy's rectum was a mass of scar tissue and required immediate and extensive surgery.

None of the children seemed aware that what had been happening in their family was not normal or was in any way wrong. The reports stated that none of the children experienced any guilt associated with the acts they had committed, but said that they had only been trying to please their parents.

The D.A.'s office, after consulting various psychiatrists, believed that, because the situation had existed for such a long time, only the two-year-old boy was salvageable. Even if they had been eligible for placement, no foster home would have taken any of the other children. They were summarily institutionalized.

The board voted unanimously to turn down the Lindsays' request for parole. As they stood to leave the room for a break, Earl shook his head. "Damn shame," he whispered to Eric.

"Yeah," Eric responded, numb with despair.

"They only have two more years yet to serve, you know? Then they're back out there, doing it again—either to their own or to someone else's kids."

Eric flushed with sudden anger. He hadn't considered that the parents, having lost their freedom and their family, would not be changed in some way by their prison experience. Yet, on second thought, he realized how wrong his assumption had been. The prison system did not provide any sort of psychological treatment for such offenders.

"It's times like this," Earl growled, "when I truly believe in the death penalty."

Eric sighed and shrugged.

Lunch was a quiet affair—Eric had a sandwich in Earl's office while reviewing Kim's file—followed by the last cases of the day. Eric was half listening to Wyndott's monotonous announcements while thumbing through the contents of the next inmate's file.

Eric was also learning that, just as he and others in his outside world attempted to avoid chaos, destruction, and death by structuring a society to combat evil, so prisoners in their world behind walls attempted to structure a society that would provide and maintain for them a sense of order and hope. Usually, these attempts involved force. Often the use of force was rationalized. Sometimes the excuses were humorous. Such was the case with John Jacob "Howdy Doody" Adams.

It was all Eric could do to keep from laughing out loud as Adams walked loose-jointed to his chair and sat down. He was, in every respect but his prison uniform, the spitting image of the happy-go-lucky television show puppet. His broad grin and freckles spread across a youthful, fifty-two-year-old face. Huge ears protruded on either side of his head. All this was topped by carrot red hair parted down the middle and slicked down with water. As soon as his full, real name was read, he spoke up.

"Now, folks, you just call me Howdy. That's what everybody else calls me, though I never seen this Doody fella. But they tell me I look a lot like him, so that's fine."

The man looked and sounded so young and naive that Eric had a hard time relating his appearance with the facts in his file.

Howdy had been in trouble all his life, beginning with minor infractions of the rules in the children's homes where he'd grown up and extending to a record of over a hundred felonies. He had been incarcerated seventeen times, yet not one of his sentences was over four years long, which was probably why Howdy had become something of a celebrity to those who attended the annual McHenry Penitentiary Rodeo.

The event, the longest-running prison rodeo in the country, was held on the prison grounds and drew tourists from as far away as Europe and Japan. Howdy's specialty was the ribbon-snatching event. He never lost. Contestants were required to run into the arena, snatch a bandanna tied to the horns of a Mexican bull, and climb back behind the fence. Howdy was so fast, and he'd had so much more practice than the other inmates, that the bulls' horns had never so much as scratched him.

But Howdy's speed and luck were not always dependable on the outside. On his last trip beyond the prison walls, Howdy had escaped from county jail after a forgery charge. But then, in a masterful stroke of the worst of all possible bad luck, he randomly chose to burglarize, of all places, the district attorney's home.

He had been paroled on three previous occasions but had not left the penitentiary in the last ten years. He was simply paroling from one sentence to the next.

Wyndott asked, "Well, sir, what do you have to say for yourself?"

Howdy grinned, ducked his head, and shuffled his feet like an embarrassed adolescent. "With my record, sir," Howdy replied, "I can't imagine you people would believe anything I said."

Wyndott cleared his throat and asked about the man's crime. Howdy's response was a long dissertation that made Eric feel like a United Nations delegate badly in need of an interpreter.

"Well, folks," Howdy drawled, "ah started shooting cocaine at eleven and heroin at thirteen and, 'course, ah used speed off and on. But ah've laid all them aside, and now ah wanna do the rest of my time on paper."

Finally, Howdy got to the crux of the matter.

"Folks," he said with a shrug of his narrow shoulders, "Ah've just reached the tailgate of my life. Besides that, ah've got two grandchildren that are carrying me fast. Ah also got an eighty-year-old father out there what needs my help. Ya know, he's been married fifteen times and now he's got back trouble. So ah need to help him get around."

By this time, every member of the board, including Eric, was gasping for air and choking back laughter. When asked by Wyndott if they didn't want to take a short break, Eric replied that he didn't think the board could stand it. George Davis had given up trying to write anything, his shoulders shaking with laughter. Howdy just grinned and continued.

"Now ah want you folks to know, ah'm not just ticklin' ya with a feather. Ah'm tellin' the God's honest truth. You know, another thing ah know you folks look at is the write-ups ah've had. So ah'm gonna lay it on the ground for ya. Ah'm just right up prone. See, ah'm like the dude what got struck by lightnin' four times. Only one in the world. Seems like ah jest think 'bout doin' wrong and the fellas write me up. But ya know, ah've been here an awful long time and ah know there are only two kinds of people in this world: taxpayers and tax users. They tell me it costs twelve thousand dollars per year fer the government to take care of me, and ah b'lieve ah have, as you can see, taken full advantage of that fact."

Ethel Wilson sputtered out a question that stopped Howdy's stream of conversation. "Mr. . . . uh . . . Howdy, would you promise never to come back here if you got out?"

"No, ma'am," the redheaded comedian answered. "Ah never make a promise I cain't keep."

Eric and the other board members exploded into laughter, and all semblance of organized formality disintegrated. Eric, wiping his eyes with his handkerchief, noticed that Howdy looked a bit bewildered for a moment. But then he seemed to decide his best bet was to join in the fun, so he tilted back his head and guffawed along with everyone else.

Eric voted with the other members of the board to parole John Jacob Adams. Still, as Howdy was escorted from the room, Eric whispered to Earl that he wasn't so sure Howdy wouldn't be back for his eighteenth turn on the dance floor.

Earl laughed and said, "Well, I reckon he's earned it. Hell, he's a friendly sort of guy. Probably find a good, steady job on the outside, too. Maybe learn to install burglar alarms!"

Earl's comment reignited the laughter. Wyndott finally called a halt to the proceedings, and the board disbanded for the day. For once, the board filed out with a smile on their faces.

Earl motioned to Eric, and the two of them slipped down the hall into Earl's office.

"Well," the big man said, reaching into his small refrigerator for two bottles of soda, "they've done it."

"What?" Eric replied, his head too full to try and puzzle out what his friend was talking about.

"Horton and leaders of the House and Senate have passed a bill to remodel the utilities here."

"Great!"

"Yeah, sure," Earl said, walking over to the tiny barred window that overlooked the exercise yard. "And, on top of that, in spite of his own problems with the feds, Tobias managed a last-minute amendment that requires that all the work be done by convicts."

"Should save some money," Eric murmured.

"Hell, yes! And who knows," Earl said with a laugh, "might be a chance for some of these guys to learn a real valuable trade, huh? Get rehabilitated real good, right?"

Eric could see that Earl was upset about the news, but he wasn't sure why. He didn't answer because he didn't quite know how. Instead, he let his thoughts drift to something he could change. Then he drained his soda and straightened his tie.

"Ready to meet the little lady formally?" Earl asked.

Eric nodded, and Earl led him toward his meeting with Kim.

The news of the remodeling was a cause for celebration elsewhere, however. John Jeffries rejoiced by getting high on a few joints of contraband pot, something he didn't normally indulge in. But what the hell. After all, his moment had finally arrived.

13

TWO INTERVIEWS

"Wish you'd have agreed to come back on another day to do this," Earl murmured as he and Eric drove around the lake toward the women's facility. "I hate the way Wyndott gawked at us in the parking lot."

Eric shrugged. "Well, maybe I'm too damn rebellious for my own good, Earl, but I don't see any reason to hide the fact that I'm doing research on convict rehabilitation."

Earl sighed. "It's just that you're buckin' procedure by not clearing this with the warden, that's all. Makes me nervous."

Eric turned sideways in his seat and gazed at his friend.

Earl stretched his neck and loosened his tie and collar. "Someone besides me ought to know what you're doin', man. Otherwise—"

"Listen, Earl, do you believe me when I tell you that my interest in this girl is purely professional and humanitarian?"

"Yeah, sure, but—"

"Then what's the problem?"

"Eric," Earl began, then he steered the car to the side of the road near the small lake and parked. As Earl sat silently gathering his words, Eric looked past him for the old man in the boat. But he wasn't there, and small waves were beginning to ripple across the glassy surface of the lake. With the windows down, the breeze moved freely through the car, carrying with it the smell of rain. Dry leaves rustled beneath the trees as the sun disappeared behind a curtain of gray, moisture-laden clouds skating across the prairie from the west.

Finally, Earl turned in his seat to face Eric. "Listen, pard, you haven't been here long enough to understand, but I have. So have the people upstairs. True, the rule against board members visiting individual prisoners isn't a hard and fast one, it's more a matter of—"

"Propriety?" Eric asked seriously. But he couldn't help grinning, thinking about Earl's scandalous behavior with the buxom waitress in the steak joint the night of the first board meeting. Earl caught his expression and read his mind.

"Shit, Eric, don't mess with me, please? What we do outside the walls is our own business. For the most part. But this unwritten rule exists for damn good reasons."

Eric sighed and shook his head. "Earl, I—"

"Now just you listen to me a second. I like you, Eric. You're a smart boy with a lot of heart. I'm only agreeing to help you do this because I think you got brains and heart in equal proportions. Understand?"

Eric smiled. "Well, you know, this girl isn't the only one I'm interested in interviewing."

Earl's eyes bunched into an angry, disbelieving squint and his broad face flushed bright red. He turned back to face the road, slammed the car into drive, and mashed the accelerator. The car fishtailed, laying rubber for a short distance down the blacktop. Eric decided it was time to lay out his cards.

"Calm down, man!" he said. "I'm trying to put your mind at rest, not get us both killed! I talked to the warden."

Earl turned to stare at Eric and nearly drove off the road. He jerked the steering wheel, brought the car back into line, slowed to a crawl, and swallowed hard. "You did?"

"Yeah, I did." Eric grinned, loving the effect his surprise was having. "I told her exactly what I was planning to do, and she suggested I give George Davis the whole scoop and let him interview me for the convict paper as soon as I finish with Kim. I told her I thought George ought to be allowed to interview all the board members."

Earl snorted once, then tilted his huge head all the way back and laughed. His broad shoulders shook as though he were sobbing. "Jesus, I can just see old Wyndott agreeing to that!"

"She can't force them to do it, of course. But she did say she would send them all letters. And she said she is 'vitally interested' in the rehabilitation report I'm writing."

Eric was glad he'd decided to write the report after all. It really wouldn't take that long or be that difficult. Guilt over his attraction to Kim still nagged at him a little, but at least he felt better about involving Earl.

"Well," Earl said, pulling into a parking slot in front of the women's facility, "I'm proud of you, son. Now, let's go on in and get this dog and pony show on the road."

Having cleared the air, Eric felt at ease as he trailed along behind Earl into the small room inside the women's facility that served as the shakedown area. He actually looked forward to bantering with the key man, who had given him such caustic advice on his first there. *Watch the whores. Dopers are next. The rest are shit.*

After passing Earl through, the key man faced Eric. Her black roots were still visible in the murky depths of her beehive hairdo. In uncharacteristic silence, she motioned impatiently for Eric to hurry.

Once face to face with him in the narrow space, the key man's usual friendly smile faded into a straight line. When she spoke, her voice was an octave lower than usual. She was angry.

"Empty your pockets and take off your shoes," she growled. "You know the routine."

"Hey, I—" Eric's attempt at light conversation was cut short as the key man shoved him around and did a quick patdown. *Up against the wall, motherfucker*, he thought, and broke into a sweat.

After the patdown, she turned him from the wall and stared into his eyes for what seemed like thirty seconds. At last she stepped to the side and opened the gate to the inner hallway. As Eric tried to slip past her, she caught him and, in a voice more a hiss than a whisper, said, "Took you for a smart one, Williams. Ya shoulda listened."

The visitor's area of the women's penitentiary lay just down the hall, near the dining room. On nice days, the women convicts and their visitors were allowed to sit outside on park benches in a small garden area fenced off by razor wire and visible from the guard tower. Inside or out, however, female guards patrolled the area, ostensibly to prevent inmates and visitors from passing contraband and engaging in sexual activities. Eric knew that, in theory, conjugal visits were verboten. Cameras were supposed to monitor all activity. But given the nature of human beings, and the nature of society within the walls, where there was a will, Eric figured, there was probably always a way.

Earl led Eric to the guard in the visiting area. Eric passed her a letter requesting that he be allowed to visit privately with Kim. The guard seemed to want to pore over the letter forever. Finally, however, she nodded and said, "Ain't much privacy in the visiting room. Best you wait in the dining room."

Eric hadn't even thought to hope for the use of this more private setting. Although he kept telling himself the meeting was strictly for research, his heart rate soared through the ceiling. Jesus, calm down, he thought to himself. As they walked toward the arched doorway, Earl cleared his throat and spoke.

"Think I'll go on up to the assistant warden's office for a while and shoot the breeze. See ya later."

Eric nodded. Earl tried out a smile, discarded it, and lumbered away, leaving Eric alone in the dining room.

He stood at one of the large windows in the dining area, near the door to the visiting room, gazing out at the bleak, wind-tossed scenery. The room was usually well-lit during the day by the sunlight flooding in through the tall, narrow windows. But today, the corners of the large, empty room faded into shadows.

When he heard the sound of her footsteps coming across the dining room floor, the physical evidence of his sexual excitement both surprised and embarrassed him. He began to feel as though he should never have planned this, that he had no business anywhere near this woman.

"Mr. Williams?"

He knew, before he turned around, who was speaking. And then, suddenly, there she stood, in a soft pool of light not ten feet away, slender hands crossed demurely in front of her, her head only slightly bowed. Tight white jeans stretched up her long, lovely legs to meet a matching white tank top that accentuated the creamy chocolate of her skin and drew his attention to the soft fullness of her breasts. The red bandanna tied at her neck and the natural scarlet color of her full, sensuous lips were the only touches of certain color. Her small, pink tongue licked her lips and made them shine. The mass of ebony hair tumbled down in long, sweeping curves that flashed silver around her shoulders and high cheekbones. In partial shadow, beneath her perfectly arched brows and the thick, black fringes of her lashes, Kim's unusually sapphire eyes took on the sky's pewter hue. *Like Mary Jane's—damn her*! She did not blink but gazed steadily at him.

Heart pounding, Eric stepped forward and extended his hand.

"It's good to see you, Kim."

She did not reach out to him but whispered, "I'm sorry. We're not allowed to touch visitors."

Eric jerked his hand back. "Sorry", he smiled, "still getting used to the rules. Pretty stupid of me, wasn't it?"

A slight smile lit Kim's face.

"Shall we sit down?"

Eric walked over to a table, pulled out a chair, and held it as Kim gracefully sat down. Her natural perfume rekindled an old backlog of fantasies and memories. Once he managed to seat himself across form her at the table without any further embarrassment, he silently congratulated himself.

Over Kim's shoulder, he noticed the key man and two guards staring at them, whispering and smirking. Her head bowed, Kim asked, "Have I done something wrong, Mr. Williams?"

Eric realized he was frowning. He coughed, managed a smile, and sat back in a more relaxed posture.

"Of course not, Kim," he assured her. "I just wanted to reply in person to your letter. I need a little more information about you, in regard to rehabilitation, so that I can perhaps consider you for an early parole." He felt as though he was on the verge of rattling on and on like a total idiot. It was unlike him and vaguely disturbing. She's just like a client, he told himself.

"I know you're a lawyer," Kim murmured, "so I can understand why you would like to have as much information as possible." Her voice flowed like a satiny stream of cool, clear spring water. "I can't remember when anyone has ever been this nice to me. It means so much."

Eric was grateful, but caution nagged at him. *Be easy boy*, he thought. Eric thought her the most beautiful, desirable woman he had seen since Mary Jane. He was acutely aware of the continued striking similarity between the two women. Also, Kim was an inmate. He quickly shoved those thoughts aside. He swallowed, but his throat still felt dry. "Kim, I found your story quite touching and thoughtful. Of course, I'm familiar with the history of the Seminoles and can sympathize with their plight. But what bothers me is—"

Eric stopped talking when Kim's head suddenly snapped upright and her eyes bored directly into him.

"What bothers you, if I'm not mistaken, Mr. Williams, are the so-called facts of my crime."

"Well, yes, I—"

"Let me be very honest with you," Kim said. She paused, folded her hands into a clenched knot of supplication on the surface of the table, and leaned forward, lowering her eyes. "I am neither an angel nor a demon. I am a human being. I became involved in drugs because drugs eased my pain. I sold my body because, at the time, I believed my body was all I had of value. When I killed that man, I was trying to protect myself. I have done many things in order to survive in this world. But I have never lied."

When she looked up at him, Kim's eyes were swimming like dark saltwater pearls. He instinctively reached out and clasped her hands in his. Kim lay her head on their combined hands, her soft hair and tears bathing his knuckles.

"I don't care if they see us," she whispered, "I need your help. I need your touch."

Slowly, Eric withdrew his hands from hers and placed them on either side of her tear-drenched face. When she spoke, her voice was tight and thin.

"I will do anything for you, be yours forever in this life

and beyond. You are the only one, Mr. Williams, who has ever believed in me, ever tried to help."

Kim slid back her chair, stood up, and ran from the room, leaving Eric stunned and embarrassed. As the echoes of her footfalls died, a swift, unexpected sorrow filled his heart and sharpened into an instant stab of pain. He remembered hurting. Kim was trouble, he knew it, but it made him feel good for someone to need him. He needed to feel the power and happiness that comes from helping someone. She was beautiful, and he even fantasized he could sweep her into his arms and satisfy the almost overwhelming desire that came over him in that brief moment of contact. He shook his head. Hell, he needed a woman's heat more than he realized. He rose and quickly walked to the gate to get away from those lusty thoughts and needs.

Although Earl met him in the hallway and accompanied him to the car, Eric was barely aware of his presence or their surroundings. He stared down the key man and talked and laughed with his friend, but his brain was still burning. Maybe he better get Jolene to fix him up.

During the drive back to the men's prison, Earl didn't press Eric, for which he was grateful. He needed the time to come down off the unexpected high produced by his brief contact with Kim. Until they pulled into the parking lot of the men's facility, he'd almost forgotten about his interview with George Davis.

"Well," Earl said, "why don't you go on up to my office. I'll go get George."

Eric nodded. Fifteen minutes later he was sitting on the battered black Naugahyde couch in Earl's office hastily composing his thoughts. At last Earl stepped in, briefly introduced George Davis, excused himself, and shut the door.

Eric noted that George Davis hadn't changed all that much since the photo had been taken of Coltrane's company in Vietnam, the one Eric had seen on the colonel's wall. His sandy hair was still clipped short, military style. He was older, had a few more wrinkles, and looked a bit less wild eyed. But other than that, Eric decided, he looked much the same.

"How do you do, sir?" George asked, extending his hand.

"How do you do?" Eric shook Davis's hand with a smile. "It's good to finally meet you, Mr. Davis."

Confusion and a touch of resentment seemed to lie just beneath the surface of Davis's smile. The firm, friendly handshake ended abruptly as Davis let his own hand drop to his side. Eric cleared his throat and spoke.

"I recently had the pleasure of meeting and talking to a couple of your very good friends: Colonel Ted Coltrane and Clint Morris."

"Oh?" Davis said in obvious surprise and with not a little suspicion in his gaze.

Eric, noticing Davis's expression, felt compelled to offer an explanation. "Well, yes. I developed an interest in you when I first read your file. Your self-rehabilitation efforts were very impressive. So I took the liberty of contacting Ted and Clint. Both gave me glowing reports. In fact, when you're paroled they very much want to see you."

An uncomfortable moment of silence descended as Davis stared deeply into Eric's eyes. The word *liberty* echoed crazily inside Eric's skull, and suddenly he felt a deep sense of shame. For the first time, he realized what he had done, what he was attempting even now to do. He had gone beyond the usual reports provided to board members by corrections officials, law enforcement, and the courts. He had intruded himself into George Davis's life without his permission and solicited information that, luckily, turned out to be helpful and, for the most part, positive. But what if his sources had possessed their own, separate agendas? He loathed the power-hungry political machinations of a man like Tobias, the Dark Prince. But what of his own? What made Eric think the ends would, in Davis's mind, justify the means?

Miraculously, Davis smiled broadly and said, "I'm just surprised, that's all. I'd, uh, lost contact with them. You never know how people are going to react to the changes you make in your life. And you have to admit"—Davis's expansive gesture seemed to embrace himself, the room, and the entire prison system—"this is a major change."

Eric felt grateful and relieved. He was beginning to like and trust this man. "Well," he said, moving toward the center of the room and changing the subject, "we need to get on with this, I think. I have questions, you have questions. Why don't you start? Want some coffee?"

Davis nodded. "Sure." Then he walked over to the couch, sat down, opened his reporter's notebook, and withdrew a pen from behind his ear. He accepted the steaming Styrofoam cup from Eric, sipped at it gingerly, and said, "I guess we could sort of start by taking turns and see where things go from there. How's that sound?"

Eric nodded, sitting on the opposite end of the couch with his own cup. "Fine with me. You first."

Davis chewed on his lip for a moment before speaking. "Okay, this interview of a board member is a first for me. I think if you can get me a copy of your résumé, I can take biographical info from there. That should save us both a little time. What I'd really like to do is ask you, since you're a new member, about your philosophy, your impressions of the board and its purpose, the facility, things like that."

"Fine," Eric said, wondering how far he should allow himself to be drawn into this interview. "In fact, you've already answered one of my questions."

"Oh?" said Davis.

Eric laughed, then said, "It's just that you seem fully rehabilitated and ready to go to work."

"I am," said Davis, then he sighed. "No one who has never spent time in prison could possibly know what it's like, day in and day out, to have his or her freedom taken away. I needed to be here when I came here, for sure. But I'm ready, now, to go back out there."

"Damn, George, if this were the army we could use that on a recruiting poster!"

Davis laughed. "No way, man!" Then, more quietly, he added, "To be honest, the army was good for me in that it gave me a chance to develop self-discipline. It wasn't the military's fault I got into the drug scene. But I couldn't have told you that, and believed it, before spending time here. Maybe everything that happens does so for a reason, ya s'pose?"

Eric smiled and nodded.

"Anyway," George said, "let's talk about you. Your job is part-time now. Do you think that you could do a better job if it was full-time?"

"God, no!" said Eric, then added, "I think a part-time board might be the best way to prevent members from becoming too wound up in the system within the walls. Full-time members might forget there's a real world outside the walls to which most inmates should, at some point, return. Besides, I couldn't take this job without having something else to do. I like being an attorney."

"Uh-huh, well. . ." Davis's face reflected an obvious distaste for the profession in general, Eric thought, but not a personal dislike for Eric himself. Then Davis asked, "What about the governor? He can override your decisions. Is that okay with you?"

Eric answered quickly. "No, it isn't. I don't think governors have any business making decisions regarding parole."

"Say what?" Davis asked incredulously, a hint of humor behind his wide eyes. "I mean, haven't you seen all those old movies where the governor calls at the last minute and saves the innocent inmate from wrongful execution?"

"Yeah," Eric said, "But movies aren't reality. In the real world, the board reviews each case and makes its decisions without worrying about what the governor will do. The governor makes political decisions, not executive ones."

"That's a pretty heavy accusation," Davis said.

Eric shrugged. "It's a fact. And he isn't the only one. An upcoming election brings out candidates willing to manipulate the public's fears in exchange for votes. Too often the facts are distorted or misused."

"Then let me ask you this," Davis said quietly. "Within the last couple of weeks, the attorney for the most populous county in the state appeared on television saying that murderers are paroled out of McHenry in seven years. Did you hear that?"

"No. But I'm not surprised. He's probably either running for office now or will someday."

"You've heard statements like this before?" said Davis.

Eric nodded. "Sure. In this country, one effective way to get elected is by frightening the public with misinformation about crime and criminals and then promising to protect them by putting more criminals in prison and keeping them there. The fact is, our state statute requires that no one convicted of first-degree murder can even be considered for parole until after they've served fifteen years in prison. Minimum sentencing."

"Right," Davis said. Then he narrowed his eyes. "But

 there's a guy in here who committed a murder when he was seventeen and received a life sentence. He's been here for nineteen years and would like to parole to a fifty-year sentence. What possible justification is there for not paroling a guy who made a lousy mistake when he was a kid but who has since made something of himself?"

Eric knew who Davis was talking about and, although the young man had made exceptional progress toward rehabilitation, the board had voted to give him two or three more years because the victim's family had filed a protest through Senator Tobias.

"Well," Eric said, "in this case, a protest was filed."

"You mean all it takes is for someone down the line to protest and everything an inmate has done to rehabilitate him- or herself is forgotten?"

"No. Once I vote in favor of parole, and if no further serious misconducts accrue—breaking into the chow line is not a lethal offense—then I will not change my vote."

"But you're only one member of the board."

"That's right. Overall, however, I think the system we use to determine whether or not to parole someone is pretty good. We have a list of criteria to use in making our decisions." Eric ticked off his fingers as he recited his list. "First, we categorize according to the severity of a crime. Murder versus unarmed robbery, for instance. Then we look at whether or not the situation in which the crime occurred is likely to occur again, whether or not drugs or alcohol were involved, whether or not the inmate's family environment and education are part of the problem, and finally, whether or not any of these factors have changed over the course of incarceration."

Davis nodded. "So, when you look at an inmate who's coming up for parole, what do you look for?"

"Well, as you know," Eric said, leaning forward, his hands clasping his knees, "prisons are already overcrowded. We definitely don't need repeat offenders. If we put people who still have the same problems into the same set of circumstances that helped produce their problems, statistics show they will be repeat offenders. However, *if* that person rehabilitates him- or herself while incarcerated, and *if* we can see that he or she will not go back into the same set of circumstances, then we figure the inmate is a good risk for parole."

"Well," Davis said, scratching his head with his pen, "sounds simple enough. But what about when prison budgets are cut and rehabilitation programs and services disappear, as happened during the Reagan years?"

"Then we end up with exactly what we have today. A massive backlog in the courts and in the prisons, more crime on the streets, and badly designed, poorly executed early release programs."

"So what's the answer?" As he waited for Eric's response, Davis drained the dregs of his coffee, crushed the cup, and tossed it into Earl's trash can.

"Well, it's like this," Eric said, standing up and pacing about the small room. "Society outside the walls can vote to spend the money to build facilities in which violent criminals are separated from nonviolent criminals, create true minimum, medium, and maximum facilities instead of lumping everyone together and treating them as though they are the same. Society can vote for funding that will aid inmates with a desire to rehabilitate themselves. That includes drug and alcohol programs, psychological counseling, vo-tech, GED and college courses, and social work. Or we can cut the budget and be absolutely assured that a kid sent to prison for robbery is learning trade secrets from seasoned professionals. And we can accept the fact that, once released, this kid will still be an illiterate drug addict liable to prey on society instead of contribute to it."

Davis scribbled furiously. When he'd finished, he

 looked up at Eric and said, "In other words, Mr. Williams, society will have to either pay now or pay later."

Eric nodded and sank back onto the couch. George Davis shook his head.

"But with all the politicians running for office, scaring the public with their version of the facts, how can we expect them to vote for these sorts of improvements?"

"The answer is education, which is what your newspaper is all about, and a return to the idea on which this nation was founded: namely, that people deserve a fair chance to effect changes in their lives. Most people who make mistakes are capable of learning from them. You and I both know that there will always be those who will not or cannot change, no matter what help is made available to them. These people are a danger to society and must be locked up because they insist on playing the game their way, no matter who they hurt, till the day they die."

Davis nodded as he took notes. "Hard cases. But all of life's a game, Mr. Williams," Davis said. "Aren't you just advocating that inmates give up control over their own lives and play by society's rules?"

Eric leaned his head on his palm and stared straight at Davis. "What I think we are asking, Mr. Davis, is for inmates to take *more* control over their own lives by conforming to society's rules—the same rules, by the way, that also protect them from predation by criminals—in order to receive *more* freedom to control their own destinies. But the answer, as far as prisons go, is to concentrate on teaching inmates the techniques of play as well as the rules of the game." Eric leaned forward once more. "Give inmates a chance to return to the board with a more complete overview of the game and a belief in their ability to win without doing so at the expense of other players."

Davis wrote for a moment,then tapped one long index

finger against his forehead for a moment. Eventually, he looked up with a smile. "Whew! I apologize for lumping you in with the worst of your breed. If I ever need a lawyer again, I hope you'll take me on."

"Only if you get a divorce," Eric said, grinning.

"Well, guess I'd have to get married first, huh?"

"Had enough?" Eric asked.

"Yeah, at least for now."

"Good. Then it's my turn, right?" Eric said, putting his arms behind his head and stretching back against the corner of the couch. He'd crowded Davis into the other corner, but Davis flashed a wry smile that said he didn't mind. He put his notebook on the couch beside him.

"Shoot."

"Okay," Eric said, shutting his eyes. "You're a shining example, in my opinion, of someone who has done just what I'm advocating." Eric opened his eyes and stared at Davis. "Why?"

Davis looked perplexed. "Why what?"

"Why did you take hold and go for it, George?"

"Probably because I grew up in a loving, supportive family and once I quit wanting to die, I found the will to live."

Eric nodded. "Where did you find it?"

"Well. . ." George sighed. "I had to get straight first. Number one. The recovery program I started in after going cold turkey—which, by the way, is the closest I want to come to death for a good long time—was cut after I'd been here for a while. I got the benefits of it, though. I worked hard to forgive myself for doing what I'd been trained to do, for not being able to change some things, and then I took control of changing what I could change—not the past, by my reactions to it."

"Do you still have nightmares?" Eric asked quietly.

"Yeah. Sometimes. But, hey, I've even learned that to

some extent I can control my dreams. Now, when I can't control a situation, I can usually control my response to it."

"Usually?"

"Yeah. There are still times when I find myself feeling down or angry. But I look at all I've got going for me, and I don't want to blow it. I have things I want to do now, so I'm not just a giant wad of pain floating around. Mainly, I want to make restitution to all the people I've hurt in the past. I've written lots of letter, but—"

"To the family of the man you shot?" Eric was surprised. There was nothing in any of the reports to indicate Davis had taken this action.

"Sure. They didn't answer, but that isn't as important to me as the fact that I wrote the letter, that I made the effort. I don't know, if I were them, if I would have been able to forgive me."

"Really?" The comment worried Eric a bit.

"Damn right. I think that at one time I'd have been mad as hell, I mean, very torn up about it, if my father or brother or uncle had died because some punk kid with a drug problem and a death wish had flipped out. But to go on with my life, I have to forgive a lot of people for a lot of things. Especially myself. Like I told them in the letter, the only way I can pay that man and his family back is to use my talents to contribute to society. If I keep blindly striking out, someone, somewhere, will eventually put me down like a sick old dog."

Eric sat silent for a moment. Then he nodded. This, he thought, was why George Davis and Kim Whitlock no longer needed to be here and why he, himself, had joined the board.

14

THE OLD OAKEN CHAIR

Senator Glen Tobias's amendment requiring the use of inmate labor fit squarely within the federal prison reform mandate. The job of reworking the electrical and plumbing facilities around the electric chair was given to a master electrician and plumber, John Jeffries, whose plumbing and electrical company had been more than just a front for his criminal activities while he was on the street. He'd kept up his license because, as he told the warden, "The shit you deal with in plumbing is always better than the shit you deal with in the real world."

John relished the idea that his new job was near the old oaken chair. During John's time in plumbing and wiring the east and west cell blocks, he had come across old architectural drawings that indicated that there might be a tunnel near the location of the electric chair. That, and prison legend, was enough to pique John's interest and to convince him that if there were a tunnel, the chair location was the key to its entrance. He also knew that the old sewer tunnels leading to the cisterns outside the prison had to be from that location, since the electric chair was the very center of the penitentiary when it was first built in the teens.

John met Al in their usual conference area beneath the guard run at least once or twice a week. During one of those conversations, John gleefully told Al, "The plan is coming down perfect as two dogs in heat."

John worked the key man to allow one of his own punks to be his helper. He chose Mean Boy Miller. Undependable, unpredictable, and twenty-one years of age, Mean Boy had been on death row for the brutal murders of an elderly bedridden man and his nurse during a burglary. In the ensuing struggle, he had almost decapitated the nurse with a saw-toothed fishing knife. He then proceeded to cut the heart out of the old man in a rage when he discovered there was only two dollars in the house. His troubles had started when he was twelve years old. He had bounced around every juvenile detention center in the state. By the time he was sixteen he had been arrested for multiple burglaries, car theft, assault and battery, attempted rape, and armed robbery. On his sixteenth birthday, during one of the periods he was between juvenile facilities, he was attacked by three members of a rival gang. In the ensuing melee, Mean Boy lost his vision in one eye from a knife wound. He killed two of the gang members and despite his record was given a lenient sentence when it was decided that he was fighting in self-defense. Six feet tall and weighing 210 pounds, he was all grit and muscle. Both arms, chest, and back were covered with tatoos. Since arriving on death row, he had shaved his head. An angry scar ran from midway on his forehead straight to his jaw, broken only by the permanent stare of a glass eye. His frightening appearance made it easy to intimidate most other inmates. After he had come off death row, thanks to a new Supreme Court decision commuting his sentence to life without parole, he had become the main hit man for John Jeffries. It was a position he relished.

The key man also put on the crew a young inmate over whom John, as yet, had no control. The new punk, Chavez Ramirez, had been in for about a month, but apparently he'd been clever enough to have kept to himself and somehow avoid being forced into slavery with one of the inmate groups. According to the grapevine, something about him made the other inmates uncomfortable. Without meeting him, John knew Ramirez was trouble. Since he had to have a crew he could trust, John sent the word out that he'd pay for information on the kid.

A guard had been assigned to watch the crew. This didn't bother John, however. As he told Al, "The jerk's I.Q. will probably be about ten points lower than most of the cons. Why the fuck else would he accept a measly three hundred bucks a month to spend all his time around people who kill and maim and steal for a living? I just love the government. Assholes pay just enough money to hire people with not quite enough brains to deal with us, so we can use them to get the hell out of the joint!"

During his stay at McHenry, John had done repair work from time to time in the east and west cell house, so it was logical to use him down in the chair area. The chair hadn't been used since 1966, when Larry Baker rode the lightning. The utilities in the area surrounding the chair had deteriorated and were causing electrical and plumbing problems in other areas of the facility. Besides, there was hope among some of the officials that Ole Sparky might be rejuvenated, since two members of the court of criminal appeals who didn't believe in the death penalty had recently been replaced.

John had just stepped out of his cell on the second tier and was directing his punks as they put his tools in a canvas bag, which Mean Boy Miller was to carry, when the guard assigned to accompany the work detail sauntered up carrying a scattergun and introduced John to his new helper. John wasn't impressed by the puny-looking Latino boy. The scattergun, however, was a nice surprise. Ordinarily prison officials avoided arming guards because inmates could too easily disarm them. John smiled to himself at the prospect of such a bonus.

When John offered his hand to the young inmate, the

 boy didn't take it. The look in his eyes sent chills down John's spine.

"Nice to meet ya, son," John growled.

Ramirez didn't speak, didn't even nod. Although he probably didn't weigh 130 pounds soaking wet, he was well built, and his eyes had a dead, cold look that spoke volumes. The older man coughed, shrugged, grinned at the guard, and determined silently that he would absolutely have to replace Ramirez. Fast.

As they moved along toward their work detail, John noticed that, while Ramirez never spoke, he seemed to understand enough English to follow simple directions.

After descending the stairs to the rotunda level, John spotted George Davis walking between the red lines on the opposite side of the rotunda. When John called out to him, both guards and the two cons on the crew stopped and watched him cross over the red lines to meet Davis on the opposite side of the rotunda. The guards made no move to interrupt his journey. They sauntered over to the cage that protected the guard who controlled all of the gates to the rotunda, shook out two cigarettes, and started to smoke and chat with the guards inside the cage. The clear breach of the rules by Jeffries was ignored. The other inmates remained standing between the red lines waiting for the head con to return.

John shook Davis's hand and clapped him on the back. "Glad to have you here, George," he said loudly. "You can certainly help us with that paper of yours. It'll make the guys in here feel real good." John lowered his voice and whispered without moving his lips. "Did you get my message?"

George nodded. John raised his voice again.

"I sure was glad to hear 'bout your parole board appearance. When do ya go up?"

George replied, "Next regular meeting. Saturday."

"Ain't that great!" John exclaimed, thumping Davis heartily on the back. "Well, gotta go, George," John said loudly. Then he smiled and whispered, "We'll get you out one way or another."

John walked off before George could respond. On his way across the rotunda floor, John enjoyed imagining George's startled expression as he watched him return to his work crew unmolested. *George probably thinks he's already got it made,* John thought. *Probably thinks he won't have to fuck with the likes of lil' ole John Jeffries anymore.*

John was in high good humor as he and his crew made their way toward the stairway that led to the underside of the prison. They met up with a guard carrying a handful of ancient, rusty keys. The guard with the scattergun took up the rear as they descended into the darkness accompanied only by the dim light of two flashlights.

The stairwell, built as part of the original facility in 1917, was filthy, massive, and damp, with very low ceilings. Even Ramirez, who stood only about five feet, six inches tall, had to duck.

On the first landing, the lead guard brushed aside a cobweb and switched on a wall fixture. The light cast a dull yellow circle on the floor. Rats had chewed through the wiring after the electric chair was no longer in use, and since then the repairs had been infrequent and patchy at best.

The first passageway at the bottom of the stairs was damp and puddled with water that had either seeped up from underground or dripped down from leaky pipes. The air was thick with the smell of mildew and rat droppings. The splashing of their footsteps echoed off the walls.

Suddenly, Mean Boy let out a piercing whistle that

reverberated throughout the passageway. The rear guard jumped a foot, slipped on the slick floor, and almost dropped the scattergun.

"Damn you, Miller!" the guard shouted. "You do that again and I'm gonna let this loose on you."

John and Mean Boy laughed. Ramirez remained silent.

At the second iron door, the lead guard fumbled with three or four keys before he found one that unlocked the heavy door. The next passageway led into outer rooms with windows just above ground level. Bars were fitted into the outside openings, and the windows themselves had been painted over with peeling layers of dingy white paint.

John knew why, even if the rest of his crew did not. Death had once been a major spectator sport in the early days of the prison, and this was where all the excitement took place. The paint foiled the plans of nosy reporters who had crowded around the windows trying to get a free peek or take a photo they could sell later for big bucks.

The lead guard called Mean Boy over to help raise the windows. Although they were as old as the locks and keys, once the rust was scraped off, they opened smoothly. Sunlight flooded into the room from between the heavy iron bars.

So this, John thought, was the preparation area—a ten-by-twelve-foot room, separated only by a false plywood wall from the viewing area that surrounded the electric chair. Behind the wall was a standing area for execution witnesses. Immediately to the right of the window, sitting in a corner where the stone walls of the foundation of the penitentiary came together, sat Ole Sparky.

All the implements and straps were still in place. But an inch-thick layer of dust and grime covered the seat, the chair, and the head conductor that had once fit like a skullcap over the hapless occupants of the chair.

To the right of the chair was a small door to a closet that, John knew, housed the central fuse box and main water valve that served this portion of the prison and connected it to the utilities in the more modern areas of the facility.

If the old plans he had seen were accurate, and John believed at least parts of them were, the tunnel had to be behind the wall of the utility closet. Supposedly it stretched outside the facility to the old cesspools that once served the prison population. The system had been bypassed in the 1920s when cell houses were expanded and the canning and license manufacturing areas were built. John believed that, over the years, the tunnel had simply been forgotten.

With another of the ancient, rusty keys the lead guard opened the dust-encrusted closet, and John set to work replacing the fuse box. In spite of the temperature—the sweating gray stone walls kept the basement twenty-five degrees cooler than the outside air—he was drenched with sweat by the time he disconnected the old box. Mean Boy helped him pull it from the wall.

John called for a flashlight and, while ostensibly checking for stray wires, aimed the beam into the gaping hole in the wall. His heart raced for an instant, then fell into the pit of his bowels. The light reflected off an older, rock wall just two feet from the plastered board of the wall that had held the fuse box.

"Shit," John muttered, wanting desperately to vent his frustration by ripping out the false back wall of the closet with his bare hands or kicking it in with his boots. Instead, he whistled tunelessly as he carefully set to work replacing the old fuse box with a more modern, plastic version.

Since he was smaller and could fit more easily into the closet, John directed Ramirez to hand him tools and pass him clips and tape. The Latino watched the procedure attentively. He seemed at ease, so John decided to chance a little conversation.

"What you in for, son?" he murmured.

Ramirez kept his silence, but the lead guard, who had overheard the question, laughed.

"Jeffries, the spick don't habla no English." The guard's loud remark bounced off the walls of the larger room. "But I'd wager he's a real bad motherfucker. Ain't that right, Ramirez?"

Ramirez still did not speak, but John could smell the Latino's anger rising like musk in the close space, feel his muscles tense as he turned and fixed his cold glare on the guard.

"Done!" John exclaimed as he backed out of the closet and shut the door.

Mean Boy and John were gathering up and stowing away their tools near the windowed wall of the room when the lead guard stumbled over an old, discarded soda can and sent it clattering across the stone floor and under the chair. A high-pitched squeal erupted as a terrified twenty-pound rat ran out into the room.

Everyone jumped backward except Ramirez, who leaped forward, stepped on the rat's tail, picked it up, and snapped its neck in one smooth, blurred series of motions.

The rat died instantly. Ramirez, holding the vermin by its long tail, turned to the rest of the crew with a broad, ghastly smile that revealed two gold front teeth and wrinkled the brown skin around his eyes. "Anyone for lunch?" he asked in pleasant, perfect English. The smile disappeared as the carcass of the rat flew through the air and landed with a sick thud on the seat of the chair.

The guard holding the scattergun stumbled back and fell on the seat of his pants, discharging the gun and sending shot ricocheting in all directions. Everyone on the crew but Ramirez hit the floor with his arms over his head.

With his face pressed in the filth on the floor, Mean Boy looked over at John with tears in his one good eye and terror written in giant letters across his face. "Jesus!" he exclaimed. "I think I pissed my pants."

The guard rose quickly, still holding the scattergun. Shaking like grass in a strong westerly, he croaked, "Okay, boys. Fun's over."

John picked himself up, hauled Mean Boy back up on his feet, and ambled over near the false plywood wall.

"Ramirez," he growled at the boy still standing near the chair, "that was lots of fun, but we got work to do. Since you got so much energy, grab that crowbar and get busy over here."

Ramirez turned and fixed his dark, dead stare on the older con. John forced himself to smile broadly, make eye contact, and return the stare with his own, equally threatening gaze. Then, in a voice oily with sarcasm, John asked, "Please, Mr. Ramirez?"

Now Ramirez moved in slow motion, turning, reaching down, picking up the crowbar, and walking first toward John and then past him. Finally, standing before the wall, the Latino placidly began tearing it down.

The guards had not uttered a sound during the exchange between the two cons. Both men, once Ramirez started to work, relaxed and eventually leaned against the walls with their booted feet crossed.

John grinned to himself. *Lucky bastards oughta be damn glad someone's in charge down here with this crazy son of a bitch.*

Mean Boy shuffled over and tapped the conduction cap on Ole Sparky, turned to John, and giggled nervously.

"Hey John! S'pose we'll find Larry Baker's ghost down here?"

John's eyes were still on Ramirez, who was patiently tearing the wall apart, bit by small bit. It was a few seconds before John responded to Mean Boy's question. "He may already be with us, Mean Boy," John replied.

III That night John returned to his cell tired and frustrated. He'd been 99 percent certain that the tunnel existed and that it lay behind the wall of the utility closet. But during the remainder of the time he and his crew had spent in the execution room, the tension remained too high—what with Ramirez's little stunt and the idiot guard's stupid reaction—to risk any further exploration. John was feeling like throwing his meager belongings against the cell walls when the barred gate to his cell scraped and clanged shut behind him. A white plastic tube he had been waiting for was tossed onto his bunk.

John snatched up the tube, carried it to the far corner of his cell, and with his back to the run, carefully peeled back the plastic outer layer. Inside was a fragile, yellowing roll of papers that appeared to be blueprints. He worked slowly, carefully peeling back the plastic and gently unfurling the sheets. The blueprints were dated 1909, the year the foundation of the prison had originally been laid. Included in the plans were layouts of all sorts that involved every nook and cranny of the original building. John grew more and more excited as he glanced over the sheets. Finally he found what he'd been hoping for. The layout for the plumbing and electrical systems. And there, as clearly defined as the lines on his own face, lay a drawing of the execution room utilities tunnel.

By going through the back wall of the current utilities closet, he'd missed the tunnel by less than six feet.

John hurriedly rolled the plans back up, tugged the plastic down over them, and stuffed them between the mattress and springs of his bunk. *Now,* he thought, *we're cookin' with gas!*

Just before lights out, the prisoners were allowed an

evening exercise period. John knew Al would be waiting for him in the yard.

Sure enough, Al strolled over toward John and took from his shirt pocket a thin paperback book with a folded sheet of paper sticking out between the pages. He handed it over and said, "Happy Independence Day, ole buddy."

"Thanks, but you're a month late," John muttered. "What is it?"

"A reduced copy of the Ramirez kid's rap sheet. But don't thank me. I have no idea where it came from. I just put the word out and it appeared in the pages of a book I was checking out of the library.

"Don't worry, whoever sent it will let us know what he wants."

Al laughed. "Yeah. Then we'll have to decide when and how he gets it, huh?"

John laughed his first genuine laugh in a long time. He pulled the rap sheet out and tossed the book back to Al. When he glanced over the paper in his hands, however, his mirth died. When he'd finished, he wadded the paper into a tight ball, popped it in his mouth, and swallowed.

"Well," Al asked, "bon appétit?"

John lit a cigarette. "His daddy's one of Castro's Cuban rejects. His mama's a wetback. He's been drinking and doing drugs since he was small. Killed a guy and his kid during a robbery."

"Armed?"

"You might say that. Used a screwdriver on one, a hammer on the other."

"Jesus, sounds like a real handy sort of guy."

"Just the kind of help I need on a fucking work detail, right?"

Both men laughed.

"Well, other than his choice of weapons, he sounds like a lot of other guys in here, John."

"Yeah, but most guys in here wouldn't cut a guy's dick off and eat his balls for lunch."

Al raised one bushy eyebrow and whistled long and low. "And to think, the evidence was circumstantial, that's why he isn't on death row. He's servin' ten to life."

"Scary."

"Yeah, and lucky."

"Real scary. Real lucky too. Report says he's a sociopath or psychopath or both."

Al scoffed. "That's what shrinks always say about someone who's pure-dee evil."

"Uh-huh. But we're safe, now. We know his weakness."

"We do? Shit, John, he sounds like one uncontrollable son of a bitch to me."

"Yeah, but he's a glue sniffer. And that, my friend," John said, slapping his old friend on the back, "is the handle we can use to steer this poor misbegotten soul down the path to righteousness." With that, he strolled away from Al humming "Love Me Tender," a sure sign to everyone within range that Mr. John Jeffries was a very happy man.

15

DECISIONS

The temptation to chew her nails was almost more than Chili could bear. Sitting outside the parole board room for an hour without a cigarette, her hands carefully arranged in her lap to hide the head of the tattooed snake and thus project the image of demure innocence—when she couldn't remember ever having been either demure or innocent—wasn't the hardest thing Chili had ever done. But it came damn close.

To quell her anxiety, Chili counted off in her mind the insurance policies she had painstakingly stacked away against this rainy day when she would have her chance to secure a work release. First, there was the valuable favor owed by the guard that she'd exchanged in order to cover her indiscretion with Kim. Then, there was the glowing personal recommendation from her kitchen supervisor, a weak woman whom Chili had managed to terrorize into a state of weak-kneed obedience. Finally, and most difficult and disgusting of all, there were the months of ass kissing necessary to purchase the approval of the warden, a sticky-sweet fat bitch whose only sexual release probably came from fantasies of being handcuffed and beaten by the women over whose lives she had exercised complete control.

At last, the door to the getaway room opened. A guard stuck his head out and called, "Gloria Benning."

For a moment, Chili did not respond, so strange did her real name sound after years of being either Chili or a number. When she did stand up, she was surprised to feel her legs shaking. *This is it,* she told herself. *Get your act together.*

Chili took a deep breath and walked with measured steps into the hearing room, stood smartly behind the chair, and raised her right hand. The ugly old fat man sitting behind the table, whom she knew to be the chairman of the board, Chester Wyndott, swore her in:

"Swear to tell the truth, the whole truth, and nothing but the truth?" he asked without even looking up at her.

"I do, sir," Chili answered, and took her seat.

As she listened to the official version of her life and crimes being read, Chili watched the faces and postures of each of the board members. She immediately sensed which members were revolted by the tale, which were bored, and which were the most sympathetic. The pupils of the new guy Kim had been working on, those of the black bitch, Wilson, and of the newspaper guy, Hurst, all seemed to remain about the same size. Willie Jacks and Wyndott, however, were something else. But since one was a sex pervert and the other an idiot, Chili knew better than to even try to appeal to them.

When it came time to answer questions, Chili concentrated on presenting herself in the best light. Not that she tried to act as though she'd never done anything wrong. That wouldn't have worked and she knew it. She merely presented herself as honest, forthright, and well-spoken. In essence, a carbon copy of the high-dollar sluts she'd watched on TV.

Like the woman lawyer who'd busted all the politicians' asses on national television when she testified about the jerk who wanted to be a Supreme Court justice. Chili had followed the hearings closely. Not because she believed either the woman or the man. Any silly bitch who'd put up with shit from a dick-for-brains who didn't know how to control himself, let alone a woman, didn't have much upstairs. In the end, of course, the dickhead lied better and got the job. But the woman hadn't done badly. Chili was most impressed by the woman's self-control and her overall control of the situation. And that, she thought, was exactly what she wanted. Control.

"The board has received several letters of support from individuals within the institution," Wyndott intoned as though he were talking in his sleep, "and Senator Tobias, from your own hometown, has also lent his favorable recommendation."

Chili smiled graciously.

"Ladies and gentlemen, let's get on with the vote."

Chili tried not to hold her breath as the tally was taken. When the vote was split, with Wilson and Hurst on her side and the bastards Willie Jacks and Wyndott against her, Chili knew she had it made. The tie had to be broken by Williams, Kim's easy mark. His recent divorce had made everything a cinch. It was all Chili could do to keep from jumping out of her seat and shouting before the man actually cast his vote in her favor.

When he did, Chili went into scene two of her performance, which was based on her absolute certainty that nobody did anything for nothing. Those who had voted for Chili expected some kind of bang for their buck, some kind of return on their investment.

So Chili gave them tears, smiles, and gushy thanks all around—in general, milked the situation for all it was worth. Then, just before making her exit, she made a little show of regaining her composure. No inflection, no gesture, was left to chance. This was, after all, the most important role she would ever play.

As she returned to her cell, Chili congratulated herself and planned her next move. While she had to admit that John's plans seemed to be working out, she also knew better than to put her life solely in his charge. When things went bad, as they always did when she let a man get involved in any aspect of her life, Chili wanted all the aces in her own hand.

Eric had been impressed with Chili. Her demeanor and behavior proved she was intelligent. A born leader. For some reason, he could picture this woman going back to college someday, maybe even heading up a large company somewhere or—hell, who knows—becoming a lawyer herself. She had taken college classes in psychology during her incarceration and had done very well.

What irritated Eric, however, was the slick way in which Wyndott had maneuvered him into casting the swing vote. Not that he would have voted any differently. He felt Chili deserved a chance to show what she could do. Still . . .

Last on the docket was George Davis. Eric smiled at him as he rose from his desk in the corner of the room where he'd been sitting all morning taking notes on the proceedings. He stood in front of his chair and was sworn in just as he'd listened to others being sworn in. Finally, face flushed and his eyes shining, George took his seat before the board.

What happened after that, although it began innocently enough, was like a nightmare.

At first, Wyndott seemed to be taking a rather hard line. But Eric had expected that.

"I want you to know, Mr. Davis," he began, "that even though you write for the convict newspaper, have covered these meetings as a reporter, and have therefore been privy to much of what we've done and said, our decision will not be influenced by that fact. Is that clear?"

George looked somewhat taken aback and shifted slightly in his seat. "Yes, sir," he answered.

Wyndott then performed his usual task of reading the inmate's history. After that, Eric was allowed to elicit from Davis the information concerning what he intended to do with his life once released. None of it was news to Eric, but he was glad he could give George an opportunity to speak for himself. His goals were realistic and well thought out, which was not always the case among the inmates seeking parole. What's more, George eloquently expressed the longing of a man who seemed to have truly found himself and who was ready to put into living all that he was as a man and as a member of the human race.

Finally, the time came to vote. As usual, Willie Jacks and Wyndott voted no. Then the bomb dropped. Both Ethel Wilson and Hurst voted against parole. Stunned, Eric found himself casting the only affirmative vote.

As much of a shock as the rejection caused Eric, the effect of the vote appeared to devastate George Davis. His face blanched as the prospect of three more long years behind bars crash-dived into his consciousness. He stood slowly. He opened his mouth but seemed unable to speak. The pain was so obvious that no one on the board except Eric seemed able to look him in the face. The question written there was plain: *Why?*

As the rest of the board members busied themselves shuffling and gathering up papers, rage rose up inside Eric. George Davis walked like a robot to the door and let himself out. His green spiral reporter's notebook still lay on his desk in the back of the room. The sound of the door closing lit Eric's fuse, and he exploded.

"What in hell was that?"

Wyndott gazed up at him, his eyes blank. Ethel Wilson sucked in her lower lip and went on organizing her files. Hurst, his face a mask, spoke up.

"While we all enjoyed reading the interview with you that Mr. Davis recently published in his newspaper, and while we understand that during the course of the interview you might well have received insights into his personality that we do not share, we must base our decisions on the facts of the case. After all, Mr. Williams, the man did kill someone. And he has only served ten years," Hurst said. "I am particularly aware of the pressures that his chosen career will place on him, and I truly believe the man needs a bit more time."

Eric slowly ran both hands through his thick, dark hair from his forehead to the nape of his neck. Then he looked up at Ms. Wilson.

"Besides that, Eric," she said softly, "we received a call from Senator Tobias. Many relatives of the man George killed live in his district."

"What?" Eric exclaimed. He'd been irritated by the way Glen Tobias's name kept cropping up during hearings. Now Eric was dismayed and furious.

Hurst seemed to read his mind. "You know, Mr. Williams, that from time to time senators do consent to speak on behalf of friends and relatives of inmates in their districts. Sometimes they give us valuable information concerning inmates themselves."

Wyndott's smirk was not nearly as irritating as his comment. "Senator Tobias, of course, has put no pressure on this board. However, his concern is that Mr. Davis might still be harboring a drug problem. The senator feels that more time is warranted for a thorough investigation of Mr. Davis's background and treatment status."

As Eric stood up, his chair hit the floor with a startling slam that brought him back to his senses before he said what he was feeling, what he knew would be repeated into the ears of both the governor and the Dark Prince within minutes.

"Eric," Ethel Wilson said, hurt and indignation thickening her voice, "surely you understand that our concern is only for the welfare of Mr. Davis."

Eric nodded, thinking. Why was he the only board member who had not been called?

On the way home that evening, Eric ran the Davis hearing over and over in his mind. He still could not come up with a plausible reason why Tobias would be out to get George Davis.

Meanwhile, John Jeffries had no such haunting puzzle to work. His plans were going down as smoothly as the whiskey Al had passed him during evening exercise. He knew what the signal meant. To celebrate, he figured he'd watch Mean Boy break in a new punk at midnight in the shower run.

Although George hadn't been there long, he had made several friends among the guards. One of them, an African American who had also served in Vietnam, spoke quietly as he escorted George to his cell.

"Take it easy, man. Don't blow it. You hear me?"

Davis spoke between clenched teeth. "Yeah. Right."

"Just got to keep on keeping on. You hear me? It don't mean nothin', right?"

"Sure, man. I hear ya," Davis murmured his face displaying anger, frustration, and disappointment.

Several hours later, Davis was lying on his bunk with his back to the cell gate when two shadows fell across his chest.

"George, can we come in?"

"Sure, why not?" George answered. He recognized John Jeffries's gravelly voice. *A visit from the terrible twins,* he thought. *Now it begins.* Sitting up, George noticed that Mean Boy had stayed in the run, acting as a lookout.

"Sorry to hear about your hearing," John murmured.

George nodded.

"Seems to me," John said, "you got screwed without gettin' kissed."

George fixed his gaze on the wall across from his bunk, about a foot to the left of John's face.

"You remember what I said to you in the rotunda?"

George shrugged. "I got your message."

"I said we would get you out of here one way or another."

George let his gaze drift until it caught on John's sharp stare. "Spell it out, man."

"I was afraid you might get your parole. But since you got the shaft like we all do, it's time to start moving on the rest of the plan. You ready?"

George nodded with just a hint of a smile.

16

THE DAY

During the month between the August and September parole board meetings, Eric threw himself into his work at the firm. Several important cases were reaching fruition at once, and he still had to eat and pay bills. Yet he made time to think about Kim.

He had decided that her best bet for work release was to be moved first to a minimum security prison. In order for that to happen, someone within the corrections department would have to request that she be transferred. Eric's first thought had been to discuss this with Earl. His second thought was that he'd be wiser to work this one out on his own.

Soon after taking his position on the parole board, Eric had begun receiving complimentary copies of various trade publications. He had seen an announcement in *Corrections World* that a nationwide conference of prison wardens was scheduled to take place in San Antonio during the third week of August. Knowing that the wardens of the men's and women's facilities at McHenry preferred not to attend such events, Eric arranged to be in San Antonio by scheduling a deposition in a case he had pending. The timing worked out just right. He booked a room in the motel directly across from the Alamo and, when the day arrived, caught a late afternoon flight.

His plan was to approach a female warden whom he'd had Jolene research. Ms. Lydia Steele, the warden of Bertha Masset Correctional Center, another of the state's facilities, never missed a meeting of the type scheduled for San

 Antonio. She also had a reputation for working hard to promote the rehabilitation of female inmates in her facility and others. He wanted to talk to her about the possibility of work release for Kim. Eric felt rather pleased with himself as he sipped a beer in first class.

Once he arrived, however, nothing went according to his plan. Although he made a point of being in the tiny hotel bar during the cocktail hours on both Friday and Saturday and paid his way into several boring meetings and two bland luncheons, Ms. Steele was not in attendance. He began to think that she'd canceled out. No one he spoke to seemed to have seen her. Eric finally gave up his search at five in the evening on Sunday and decided to walk off his frustration before catching a late flight home. His wanderings led him across the street and down to the famous Riverwalk.

Spanish moss hung from the live oaks along the river's winding banks, casting long, soft shadows on the walkway and the river. The shops and restaurants were closing down. The plaintive strains of an Irish folk song emanated from a pub somewhere along the walkway.

Then he saw her, standing alone on one of the limestone bridges built across the river. The sun was setting and the shadows were deepening, but the light where she stood shone gold-tinged and strong. He kicked himself for not having looked more closely at the photo Jolene had scrounged from the files, a photo of a woman just entering middle age. The woman on the limestone bridge was obviously in her sixties or seventies and, although well preserved, her air of frailty made her seem almost transparent.

"Ms. Steele?" he queried as he walked slowly up to her.

"Yes?" she answered, turning her gray head and eyeing him warily.

"I thought I recognized you. My name is Eric Williams. I'm a new member of the parole board."

They shook hands, and Lydia Steele peered into Eric's face as though studying him in preparation for the execution of a sculpture like that of Saint Anthony, the patron saint of the city, which stood only a few feet away. Her voice was somewhat frail. Eric was forced to listen carefully.

"I read the interview you did for Mr. Davis's newspaper," she said.

He knew he was blushing with both pride and embarrassment.

"You seem very bright, very caring," she went on. "Which is exactly, Mr. Williams, why I am afraid for your soul."

Her remark sent chills down Eric's spine. He barely managed to even out his voice enough to ask her why.

"You seem to be a model of the level of involvement to which all parole members might aspire. My concern is that perhaps you are unaware of how vulnerable your power as a member of the board renders you."

Eric was unsure how to respond. He'd pictured a completely different woman, imagined a totally different conversation.

"I suspect," Ms. Steele said with a small, delicate smile, "that your presence on this bridge is no accident. So before you have a chance to immerse yourself in any more hot water, I'll offer you a piece of advice based on my many years of experience."

Eric shoved his hands down into his pockets, leaned against the cool stone railing of the bridge, and swallowed hard.

"Regardless of your strong desire to help others, you must constantly be aware that you are working with people whose main concern is to regain control over their own lives at any cost. They do not care, for the most part, about your life—no matter how much you care about theirs. So you must arm yourself."

Eric had not come for a lecture. In his indignation, he turned toward Steele with the thought of telling her so and walking away. But as his hot gaze met her cool one, the compassion he found there extinguished his anger.

"I probably know as much about you as you know about me, young man," Steele said. "Your mother, Irene, raised you by herself after your father died. I doubt that you remember, but after you went away to college, she became a volunteer at the facility where I worked at the time. She was a wonderful woman, Eric, strong yet caring, and she loved you and your father with all her heart. She was very proud of both of you. And I know you loved her deeply. In a way, you are much like her."

Eric's heart swelled with the grief he'd been unable to express since his mother's death. He took deep breaths and shut his eyes as Steele continued.

"Any young man raised solely by his mother develops a close affinity with females, but especially with seemingly helpless ones. I have a great wealth of experience, Mr. Williams, so allow me to share something of value with you that may well save your soul, if not your life. Very few women, especially those within the prison system, are truly helpless."

"But Kim's is a totally different story!" Eric exclaimed involuntarily, the strength of his assertion surprising him but, apparently, not Steele.

"Ask yourself this. If the young woman in question is truly deserving, why do you find it necessary to risk losing your position on the board by seeking me out and asking me for a favor? Think about the male prisoners whom you admire. Mr. Davis for instance. How has he helped himself?"

Eric ducked his head and thought for a moment. Davis had, to his knowledge, never manipulated anyone. The closest he'd come, perhaps, was while interviewing Eric, and the interview had been Eric's idea. Kim, however, with tears streaming down her face, had torn at his heartstrings.

Steele spoke softly, as though she were able to see deep inside him, into the recesses to which he, as yet, had no access.

"Why," she asked, "does this woman need you? The answer, Mr. Williams, is that she does not. Not really. That in itself may be the most difficult thing for you to face. Do not confuse need with love. Do not confuse pity with love. Above all, do not seek to do for others what they can, and should, do for themselves. Then God will bless you, and them, young man."

With that, Ms. Steele reached out, touched Eric's cheek with a gloved hand, and walked away, leaving him alone on the bridge.

Eric packed his bags and caught a taxi to the airport. He left San Antonio with mixed emotions. During the flight home he determined to help Kim get on work release status. She qualified, so why not? If she failed, he rationalized, she was still under supervision and could be brought back within the penitentiary walls. Yet despite that determination, Lydia Steele's advice still nagged at him.

A week later, at their September meeting, as he dug through his box searching for the file on the next case under consideration by the board, Ethel Wilson smiled at Eric and leaned over to whisper.

"I know you've probably noticed that this batch is mostly old-timers and some of the more violent criminals, Eric. It may seem strange to you that we should even be seeing them, but the rules call for them to appear whether or not they have much chance of actually being paroled."

Eric nodded. While to some extent seeing so many of these men and women had seemed like a waste of time, he knew that their opportunity to appear before the board was guaranteed by law.

Prior to the appearance of the inmates themselves, family members were given an opportunity to address the board. Relatively few convicts actually had any family to speak of, however. Those who did seldom heard from them. Consequently, only a few family members were ever scheduled to testify as to why their loved ones should, or should not, be released.

During his short time on the board, Eric had heard testimonials of both types. But nothing he'd heard previously prepared him for the last case of the day—a small, unassuming Plains Indian man who had asked to speak on his son's behalf.

Dressed in khaki pants and a blue work shirt open at the collar, the father's leathery face and hands revealed the ravages of hard outdoor work. His sad, jet black eyes were set off by strands of silver hair at his temples. He refused to be seated, not out of belligerence, Eric felt sure, but in an attempt to salvage some sense of pride. The man began speaking in a slow, deliberate way that captured and held the attention of board members in a way no candidate for public office could ever have hoped to achieve.

"First off, I appreciate you lettin' me have this chance to talk about my boy, Sonny," the man began. His work-roughened hands lay folded carefully in front of him. "You should know that he was born when we was havin' a rough time and . . . well, Sonny, he's had a rough time ever since. We've never rightly known why he is like he is, but he's ours and we love him. Always have. Maybe we shoulda sent him off someplace when he was born, but that didn't hardly seem right. Even now, I don't know that we coulda felt good about doin' that even if we'd known what was gonna happen later. Besides, for a long time we didn't have no money. We didn't want to go on no welfare, 'cause me and mine believe in helping ourselves and each other and not in askin' strangers for handouts."

The man paused, pulled a blue bandanna out of his hip pocket, wiped his brow, and clutched the bandanna as though it was a lifeline. "I'm sorry," he continued. "I don't talk so good, I know. And Sonny's mama, she's had a real hard time. Since it happened, she don't hardly talk at all. Just sits by the winda and stares outside. She'd be here too, if she could, but . . ."

The man shifted his weight from one foot to the other and battled to make eye contact with one after another of the board members. "Anyway, when Sonny was about eight, he just wasn't actin' right. They didn't want him in the school. Teachers told us we oughta take Sonny somewhere and have tests done. So we saved up and took Sonny to a big hospital out west. The doctors there, they told us Sonny was sick. He looked healthy, but they said he was sick in the head, that he had skits-uh, skit-uh . . . something. Said he needed to be on medicine. That we should leave him there and they'd take care of him."

Eric's stomach contracted in a physical reaction to the man's painful recitation. The man paused and took a deep breath before going on with his story.

"Well, we didn't want to do that. Sonny is our son. But we finally had to admit we couldn't do nothin' but love him. So we took him back to the hospital and left him there. Sonny cried till it like to broke his mama's heart. He was still just a little boy. Doctors said we shouldn't come back to see him for a while, said he wouldn't get used to the place if we did. Well, the doctors finally called about a month later and said Sonny was cryin' all the time and wouldn't eat nothin'. Finally, we couldn't take it no more. We drove up there and took him outta that place. See, even though he tore things up and got mean with his mama and me sometimes, he was our boy and we loved him. We knew he was sick. That was why he done what he did. He didn't mean to hurt us. When he got home, Sonny tried extra hard to be good 'cause he didn't never want to go back there. For a long time things were just fine. The medicine he was takin' cost a lot, but it seemed to work pretty good."

The father paused, shuffled his feet, and stared at the floor for a moment before going on. "Then his brother, Billy, was born. I worried, at first, could Mama deal with the two of them. But Sonny was a real help to his mama and took good care of his little brother." The father looked up with a smile. "Sonny got more pleasure outta bein' with Billy and playin' with him. See, Sonny was a might slow, but Billy was real bright. So after a while, it got to where they almost seemed like they was the same age. We thought things was gonna turn out fine. Then, one day when Billy was about six years old, Sonny hurt him some. Not bad, really. But Billy, well, he knew his brother loved him and he didn't understand. Sonny was so much bigger than Billy. Mama and I got scared and thought we'd best take Sonny back to that . . . place."

The tortured look in the father's eyes was almost more than Eric could stand.

"Sonny purely hated bein' there. He was real bad homesick, especially for Billy. The doctors told us not to let Sonny around Billy for a while. 'Give him some time,' they said. 'Maybe someday, after a year or two, Sonny can make a few short visits home.' So for a year I rode the bus out west to see Sonny every weekend I could. But he got to where he hoped around more and more and wouldn't hardly talk to me. Every time I'd go, he'd ask why he couldn't be with Billy and us. I hated seeing him cause he was so miserable, but I couldn't quit going 'cause I felt so miserable for him. I kept on goin', though. He's my son. I'm his daddy. He needed me like I needed him. Finally, one weekend I packed up his bag and brought him on home."

When the old man paused, Eric shut his eyes in a futile attempt to regain his own emotional equilibrium. Instead, he felt himself as a lonely, guilt-ridden child, waiting in vain for his father, the brave soldier, to come home. In spite of all his mother's reassurances, in spite of his father's warm letters to him, Eric had become convinced he'd done something terribly wrong to make his father want to stay away so long. Gradually, the guilt turned to anger. Why wouldn't his father come home?

Then, when his mother told him his father had been killed, Eric came to believe that, somehow, his anger with his father had caused his father to die. Now, years later, all those horrible feelings washed back through him like a tidal wave and then suddenly receded. Now he knew. His father had loved him just as Sonny's father loved Sonny.

When Eric finally opened his eyes, tears were dripping onto his stack of files. He dried his face with the back of his hand and looked up.

Untended tears tracked down the silent old man's rough, brown cheeks. In the grip of a pain too deep to soothe, he, too, fought for control, moving his head from side to side. His hands seemed detached from his arms as they slid in and out of his pockets. Finally, he stood spread-legged, determined to finish speaking in spite of the emotions threatening to overwhelm him.

"To this day, I don't know why Sonny done it. I tried to watch him real close. That day I had to work out in the fields. Mama was diggin' up potatoes in the back. The boys had been havin' a good time together playin' in the yard. They loved each other so much. We'd got to where we thought everything was gonna be all right again."

The man shut his eyes for an instant and took a deep breath. When he opened his eyes, his gaze seemed fixed on the wall behind the board members. But Eric knew he was looking back into the past and down into himself.

"I heard a scream and I thought—well, I reckon I prayed—it was a hawk gettin' a field mouse. Even though I was sweatin' like everything, this cold pain hit me in the stomach and I broke out runnin' for the house. All the way there the screaming went on and on. When I got there . . . well, I knowed for certain it weren't no hawk with a mouse.

"Mama was sittin' on the ground, holdin' Billy and swayin' and rockin' him and screamin'. She was tryin' to remember the words to a death song in the old tongue, but the words wouldn't come. I'll never forget Billy's face. He was all pale and his eyes was still open, like death had caught him by surprise. There was blood all over him and Mama and the grass. Everywhere. Red."

The man's voice had become a monotone. "Sonny was kneeling on the ground, holding himself real tight, sayin' 'No, no, no, no,' over and over again, like he couldn't believe he'd done it. We ain't never figured out why he stuck that knife in his brother's throat.

"Sonny loved Billy and Billy loved him. You shoulda seen 'em. Laughing and running in the sun. They was such handsome, strong young boys—just like ponies. Wild, free ponies. Then, all of a sudden, Billy was dead and part of Sonny died too. I knew Sonny didn't mean to do it. Maybe if we hadn't took him to the hospital when he was little. Maybe if we'd took him sooner. If we'd left him there and never brought him home again, maybe none of this would have happened. I don't know. I'll never know. But please, y'all. Sonny's been locked up for two years. He's all we got left now."

The old man's eyes pleaded, but his voice strained with quiet resolve. "He won't get into no more trouble. I know he may need to be locked up somewhere from time to time. But if you'll let him come home, I promise I'll watch him real close. Thank you for listenin' to me. I'm sorry I don't talk so good and I'm sorry this all happened. But I had to do somethin'. I just had to do somethin'."

With that, the man turned around, shuffled to the back of the room, and sat down. He hid his face in his hands for a moment and his shoulders shook. The silence in the boardroom was punctuated only by his muted, stifled sobs. Not until the old man stood up and quietly left the room did anyone speak.

Eric opened the file in front of him and glanced over the pages he hadn't had time to read. The reports said Sonny was serving ten years to life for manslaughter, isolated in the psychiatric unit. Billy, an honor student and a budding star athlete, had lived only ten years and three days.

Eric cast his vote to deny parole, but he wondered who would parole the boy's father, whose guilt and grief were every bit as incurable as his son's paranoid schizophrenia.

III John Jeffries, his hands wrapped around the window bars in the execution room of the facility's basement, watched the old Indian man shuffle out to his battered pickup and leave the penitentiary. John and his crew had been working in the old electric chair area for over a month, and now their work was drawing to a close. Much of the old electrical and plumbing systems had had to be replaced. Finding and matching up the wires leading from the electrical boxes had been tedious work. The water pipes were in many instances collapsed. *We've really done a Hell of a job,* John thought. *Too bad some poor son-of-a-bitch con is going to have to do it all over again after we leave.*

They had been under close security with two to four guards during most of their workdays. Now the guard shift was down to one or two at a time. John chuckled to himself. *Guess they trust us.*

Mean Boy was busily engaged in conversation with the guard. John offhandedly addressed Ramirez.

"Kid, you been doin' such good work, I brung you a present."

Ramirez looked up from where he'd been working on a length of PVC pipe as John dropped a Ziploc bag between the toes of his boots. In the bag were all the apparatus necessary for a good high, including the glue. The Latino quickly pocketed the bag and glanced up again at John, a question in his eyes.

"You don't owe me nothin', kid," John said. "Matter of fact, I'm gettin' you off the detail. You can go back to your cell and, while the guards ain't looking, have a big ole time on me. Oh. Here's an extra, case you got any buddies you want to share with." John dropped another bag between Ramirez's toes.

As he stood up, Ramirez flashed the same death's head grin he'd shown the day he'd killed the rat. John figured this was the closest Ramirez ever got to being friendly.

"Hey! Guard!" John called, "Ramirez here ain't feelin' too good, so I told him he could go on back to his cell. Mean Boy and I can finish up down here without him."

The guard, however, seemed reluctant to leave the two inmates alone in the room.

"Okay. I'll just go call someone to come get him."

"That's all right," John reassured him. "Where the hell would we go, anyway? Why don't you take him down to the end of the hall?" John asked mildly.

The guard stood with his hands on his hips, obviously trying to decide whether or not to take the risk. Finally he said, "Well, I reckon you got a point there, John." Then he started over toward the windows.

Ramirez bent double and started moaning. "Jesus Cristos, my stomach is crampin', man!"

The guard moved back toward the center of the room, put an arm around Ramirez's shoulder, and started walking him up the passageway. John and Mean Boy listened to the guard fumble with the keys to the stubborn lock. It finally opened with a clang, and footsteps died away down the passageway.

Mean Boy and John took the acetylene torch they'd been using on the pipes to the bars behind the windows, cut through two bars, and set them back into position just as the guard's returning steps echoed in the passageway.

"Now," John whispered, as he dusted bits of metal off the sill and tossed a handful of dust at the still-warm bars, "when the time comes, they'll think we went out through here." John grinned at Mean Boy. "It is almost party time, my man, it's almost party time." Mean Boy bobbed his head and grinned.

Ramirez rounded the corner to his cell and nearly ran into Al McDougal.

"I heard you was gonna lay off work this afternoon, Ramirez," Al mumbled around his nonfiltered cigarette. "John asked me to help you with your little party."

Ramirez shrugged his shoulders and walked on past McDougal, far more interested in the contents of his shirt pocket than with some mumbling, shit-for-brains gringo.

"I've fixed it so you won't be bothered by any of the guards," Al added, struggling to match his steps with Ramirez's. "The lieutenant is up at the end of the run and will be for the next two hours. Bunch of the boys down here are getting kinda antsy and are up for a party. Thought you might like a little company."

Ramirez said nothing. He didn't care one way or the other. As long as nobody got in his way.

A group of young men were waiting at the end of the run near Ramirez's cell. Several had already been toking up, and a few were passing a joint around and drinking what smelled to Ramirez like the worst kind of home-made brew.

Without acknowledging anyone, Ramirez walked into his cell, sat down on the bunk, and pulled both bags out of his pocket. With trembling hands, he squirted the glue into the bag, put his face down inside and, holding the top edge tight against his face, inhaled deeply.

A few seconds later, Ramirez stood shakily and weaved over to the metal mirror on the wall of his cell. Two black holes stared back at him from the center of his face. Then Al's face appeared over his shoulder out of nowhere. He guided Ramirez back to his bunk, fixed him another hit, and murmured in a low voice. The noise outside his cell seemed to be getting louder and louder.

The voice of God, Ramirez thought, as Al's words played through his head. "Don't let the guards fuck with you, man. They want to see you dead so the rats can eat you. Remember the rats? Sure you do. That's all guards are, you know? Big fuckin' rats with boots on. Bet you'd like to skin you a few of 'em, wouldn't you, son?"

Ramirez's heart leaped. His breathing became rapid. He didn't notice and didn't care who handed him the shank that slipped so smoothly into the inside of his right boot.

Al stepped up the sleeping, middle-aged guard who had his feet up on the rail. He smiled for a moment, then knocked the man's feet to the floor. "Hey! Lieutenant! That crazy spick is causing problems. Boys are gettin' a little rowdy. Might check it out before they get out of control if you want to get your full retirement in three months."

The lieutenant frowned, stood up, stretched, and

turned toward the source of the ruckus. As Al slipped past him unnoticed, the lieutenant murmured "Don't you worry, McDougal. Me an' the boys'll straighten their little asses out but good."

But Al had already left and was on his way into the rotunda. He walked to the door leading to the parole board room. The guard, who was too low on the totem pole to have a list of individuals appearing before the board, figured Al's I.D., which identified him as a trustee, was sufficient. He passed Al through.

Al had just reached the floor where the parole board meeting was taking place when a bloodcurdling scream erupted from below. Al smiled. The voice sounded like that of the lieutenant. He pictured the sharpened shank buried in the blubbery corpse by the swift, fevered hand of Chavez Ramirez.

After taking out the lieutenant, Ramirez quickly dispatched the other two guards. One he caught just below his big western belt buckle and shoved the shank up to its hilt. Blood gushed from the guard's wounds as he pantomimed a scream. The other guard turned to run and was yelling for help when three inmates tackled him halfway up the ramp.

Curled up against the wall, the lieutenant lay dying from a chest wound.

"Please, son," the breathless voice pleaded, "don't hurt me, please. I only got a few more weeks!"

In Ramirez's mind, the man's whimpers became the squealing of rats as they rustled inside decaying walls and the starved, muted cries of his baby brother being eaten alive in his dark crib. Ramirez had learned to clutch a knife in his hands and wait. The rats would come. They always came. This one had two legs instead of four. As Ramirez stepped closer, the lieutenant's whimpers escalated until he was making the same fearful, high-pitched noise that cornered rats always made. Ramirez, smiling in triumph, drew the shank in one lightning-fast pass across the rat's throat and listened as his scream died in a gurgle of blood.

Ramirez staggered up toward the rotunda, convicts swirling into a wedge behind him as, one by one, they emptied their overcrowded cells. They dragged the last guard along with them as a shield.

Guards on the walkways, vastly outnumbered, backed toward the doors as shouting inmates bearing handmade weapons bubbled up out of nowhere and spilled like molten lava into the rotunda.

In theory, the remote locking mechanisms could have closed the gates at the head of each run that led to the rotunda. Each cell house would then have been isolated, and the rotunda, with all its inside gate controls, would have remained secure. In fact, those who ran the controls abandoned their posts, and all control of the facility, to Ramirez and the swirling heat behind him. The guards fired no shots. They simply evaporated. In less than ten minutes, McHenry had been quite suddenly and completely possessed by its enraged inhabitants.

17

RIOT

The board had just settled in for what Eric knew would be an extremely long day of reviews when Billy Bob Bassett appeared before the board.

Earlier, while reviewing his file, the cynicism Eric had felt creeping into his views had suddenly stood up and shook him by the shoulders. While he still wanted to believe in the basic goodness of all people, Bassett's story forced that belief to recede rapidly into the world of myth. Eric felt his objections to punishment in general and retribution in particular fade as he listened to Wyndott's review of the facts he'd already read.

The report showed that Billy Bob Bassett, at the age of twenty-eight, had a long history of juvenile and adult offenses. His latest crime, however, was his most heinous.

Under cover of darkness, after midnight, Bassett had entered an unlocked farmhouse looking for money and valuables. The young owners, recently honored as the Farm Couple of the Year, had just taken over a section of prime farmland given them by the young man's father, a fourth-generation farmer. They were sleeping peacefully until Bassett, who'd already assembled a sack full of loot, woke them and forced them to kneel on the floor near their bed. There, without a struggle, he executed each of them with one bullet to the back of the head.

Then Bassett had walked into the adjoining room and crossed the new, fluffy pink carpet to the Jenny Lind crib standing against the far wall. There he destroyed the face of the couple's four-month-old daughter with two shots from his pistol.

For once, Eric felt no qualms about denying parole. Not this time. In fact, a part of him wanted to exact the ultimate punishment, to be the one to put the smiling man before him to death. Evil, he realized, was alive and living in the hearts of men like the one now being escorted back to his cell. Lydia Steele and Earl Brown were right. May the bastard rot in here until he can rot elsewhere, Eric thought. And this time, he felt not a twinge of pity.

The roar from inside the prison reached the parole board members' ears just as Jimmy Laton was finishing his turn at bat. Even after the vote was taken and he'd been denied parole, the pleasant, clean-cut young man stood vehemently insisting that, as a conscientious undercover employee of a highly classified United States intelligence organization, he had actually been ordered to kill the seventy-five-year-old retired shoe salesman. In reality, Laton said, the old man was a Soviet KGB agent.

Meanwhile, out in the hall, corrections officials who served as security guards for the board meetings broke ranks, scattered, and ran, abandoning the inmates who had been awaiting turns before the board. Amid the confusion, Al McDougal flattened himself against the wall and remained there, unnoticed, until the last, anxious guard attempted to pass by him.

With one quick sweep of his arm, Al caught the straggler around the neck and, with a snap that went unheard beneath the cacophony, broke the man's neck. As the guard's limp body slid to the floor, Al unfastened a heavy ring of keys from his hand-tooled belt and moved rapidly toward the boardroom between the mute, double rows of wide-eyed, shackled inmates who lined the hall.

Eric felt the adrenaline hit his system. He was halfway to the door when Wyndott's voice rang out.

"Williams! Stop!"

Eric looked down at the fistful of papers he'd unconsciously hauled with him to the door. He threw them into the corner of the room. "Sir," he asked hoarsely, "don't you think we'd better find out what the hell's going on out there?"

"I think, Mr. Williams, that we should let the folks who handle these things best deal with the situation," Wyndott answered patronizingly. The lone highway patrol trooper assigned as security for the board members brushed Eric aside on his way to the door while unsnapping the leather strap holding his .44 Magnum in place. "He's right, Mr. Williams. Stand aside, please!"

Eric glanced toward George Davis. The prison editor sat calmly revising his notes as though nothing unusual were going on. In spite of the alarms going off inside his brain, Eric went over to the door and put his head against it, listening.

Hurst, his face flushed, scraped his chair back, stood, and leaned over the table toward Wyndott. "Mr. Chairman," he shouted, "there could well be a riot or a breakout going on down there. If so, we are in very grave danger!"

Ethel Wilson, too, abandoned her files and was following Eric toward the door. She turned her gray head toward Wyndott and shouted, "I don't know about y'all, but my mama didn't raise no fool!" Willie Jacks sat staring in open-mouthed silence.

Wyndott shrugged and began throwing files into a box as the trooper reached out to open the boardroom door. But the knob turned under his hand and he was thrown with some force into the wall. Eric was immediately knocked to the floor with a blow from behind. George Davis had knocked him into the trooper attempting to draw his gun, stepped across him, and smashed his boot on the trooper's wrist, pinning his arm to the floor and causing the gun to spin across the floor and into the waiting hands of the just emerging Albert McDougal. McDougal rose brandishing the trooper's .44 and the guard's .357 Magnum and began issuing orders.

"All right, everybody up against the wall."

Eric peeled himself off the floor and joined his fellow board members, reluctantly placing his sweaty palms and face against the cool wall. Eric began to realize, with a shock, the extent to which the situation had deteriorated when George Davis calmly rose to his feet and caught the heavy ring of keys tossed to him by McDougal. Everything, Eric thought feverishly, is going horribly, terribly wrong.

"George, take the cuffs off the men in the hall and bring them in here. Tell the men to get to the cannery and the license factory. Have them come get this trooper so he can be their hostage, and take Crazy Laton here with you," he added, shoving the bewildered, stuttering man toward the door and locking it behind him. McDougal then turned to the trooper massaging his wrist and kicked him in the side of the head, rendering him unconscious.

This, Eric thought, is not a spur-of-the-moment minor disturbance. Every move has been painstakingly planned and rehearsed. And George Davis is part of it all.

Once outside the boardroom, Davis set about releasing thirty-five of the most violent criminals in the institution. As he worked he tried to blot from his mind the look of dismay and betrayal he'd seen in Eric Williams's eyes. *It doesn't pay,* he thought, *to get too close. Not to anyone.* He'd learned that, once, in the rain forests. All those fancy idealistic words like loyalty, trust, and honor meant nothing when it was your own ass on the line.

As he finished with the last inmate, he relayed to the men Al's instructions. Their docility as they left the hall, bent on carrying out those orders, angered and surprised him. When, he wondered, might his own mental castration take place if he stayed in this hole? Three years? Five years? Ten? He gathered up the cuffs and headed back to the boardroom. When he reentered, Al was standing in the center of the room addressing Earl.

"All right, big boy, you're gonna be our messenger today. George is gonna escort your fat butt outside the walls. When you get there, you tell them press people and cops that we got your little friends here. If they fuck with us in the least way, we can either wound the sons of bitches, off them one at a time, or do a group shoot. Understand? Makes no never mind at all to us. It's however they want it."

"McDougal," Earl growled from the depths of his six-foot-four, 250-pound frame, "you got one chance to give me that gun before I shove it up your ass. These folks ain't goin' nowhere 'cause you ain't takin' 'em nowhere."

Al stepped forward until his face was less than six inches from Earl's and shoved the barrel of the gun up the big man's left nostril. "Don't fuck with me, fuck," he rumbled. "I've killed bigger, smarter pricks than you straight out. Watchin' you die slow would give me no end of pleasure."

Eric shut his eyes, trying to gauge the distance between himself and Earl. He considered stepping between the two men, but then realized that words, which had always been his best tool, were now his only weapon. "Earl, back off," he murmured. "There'll be another time."

McDougal turned and glared at Eric. Everyone in the room knew McDougal had killed at least five men and would think nothing of making Earl his sixth and Eric his seventh.

"Okay," Earl answered, taking the cue, "but I ain't goin' out there. Find yourself another nigger."

"Good man," Ethel Wilson murmured.

"Suit yourself," Al said, shoving Earl up against the wall. "Chain 'em up, George."

Eric watched as Davis cuffed Hurst.

"All but the lady," McDougal added. "I promised her to the Muslims. And save the fucking chairman for last."

Chester Wyndott's face was ashen as sweat poured down out of his thin hair into his unruly eyebrows and bathed his immense jowls. McDougal stepped up behind him and quickly sidekicked him behind the left knee. The big man collapsed with a groan, and McDougal leaned over and spat into his face. "Don't worry, honey," McDougal whispered, "you won't be lonely. You got you a hot date with some of my best boys."

Meanwhile, George was cuffing Eric's hands.

"Why you, George?" Eric whispered.

"Why not, Mr. Williams?" George answered, his quiet voice filled with bitterness. "I know you meant well. But, hey, so did I, right? I did just like my family, my country, and you said. Learned all the rules, played the game well, and played it for keeps. But the fuckin' rules keep changin', man." He shook his head. "Now there ain't no other way I'm ever gettin' outta here."

Eric tried to hide his surprise. So that was it. A breakout.

"Stay calm and keep your mouth shut," George whispered. "Maybe I'll be able to get you out, too."

Eric, Hurst, Willie Jacks, Wyndott, and Earl were forced to sit with their backs against the wall, hands behind them, knees bent, and feet flat against the floor. Ethel Wilson stood near the window, looking out as though she wished she could sprout wings and fly. Acrid smoke from fires being lit in the yard drifted into the room. Shouts mingled with the sounds of mass destruction as inmates raged throughout the prison. Weapons were being fired both inside and outside, most likely not by the guards, who, Eric assumed, were now either prisoners or smoldering corpses. Eric took a deep breath that only made him gag.

Then the door opened and two black men quietly entered the room. One easily outweighed the other, but both were well over six feet tall. The one who seemed to be in charge, the more slender of the two, was a very dark, regal-looking man with gray eyes and a surprising patch of white hair on one side of his closely clipped head. His nose appeared to have been broken at some point and poorly set, if set at all. Eric suddenly remembered what Al had said when he noticed Ethel Wilson watching the man closely from her position near the window.

Muslims. Eric then recalled something Earl had said during one of their early conversations regarding the social structure inside the walls. Eric had commented on an exotic piece of headgear worn by one of the prisoners they'd granted parole, and Earl filled him in on the prison's Muslim population. Apparently this man, their leader, John C. Calhoun, shortly after his incarceration for cocaine distribution, had used his custom-tailored brand of Islam to unite black inmates and encourage them to fight "by any means necessary" against the random violence that all too often resulted in the isolated deaths of individual black inmates. *So,* Eric thought, *this is the famous Muhammed El Amin, guardian of all things truthful. That is,* Eric supposed, *when truth serves his purpose.* Very few true religious or political leaders, he felt sure, could emerge alive from prison unstained by the blood of self-interest.

However, Earl had also said that the man was unusual in that he was well educated, one of the top ten graduates in English literature from the University of Chicago. When he spoke, his background was obvious.

"Good afternoon, gentlemen. Sister Wilson will be leaving with us."

"Don't be givin' me orders, nigger," Al sneered.

The muscular bodyguard started forward, but Muhammad restrained him merely by holding up his left palm. Then, folding both hands elegantly in front of the .38 tucked in his belt, he spoke again.

"Perhaps, Mr. McDougal, you should consult Mr. Jeffries. I don't believe it would help either one of us to have a reenactment of the Civil War. I'm sure you'll find that your esteemed colleague agrees. My interest lies not in you but solely in Sister Wilson."

Ethel Wilson drew herself up to her full five-foot-two-inch height, marched over, and stood directly in front of the Muslim leader.

"Calhoun, I will not be removed," the tiny woman asserted, her hot eyes staring up at her cool, would-be abductor. "I will stay with my fellow board members."

A broad smile creased Muhammad's dark face. White teeth gleaming, he murmured as though to a beloved child, "Sister Wilson, I'm afraid you don't understand. No one is trying to take advantage of your unfortunate circumstances. We are merely here to protect you as one of our own—"

"Your own, my ass," Miss Wilson exclaimed. "You don't care one bit about my safety. You've just found a way to use me and this entire situation to your advantage. Young man, I've never been good at peaceful protest, and if you think—"

Ethel's threat died abruptly when Muhammed nodded to his bodyguard, who hefted the tiny woman over his shoulder, turned, and ducked back out into the hallway. Eric's last view of the woman was of her fists pummeling the broad back of her abductor. Her voice, shouting, "Let me down this instant, you fool!" faded rapidly beneath the riot noise.

Muhammed easily slipped the .38 from his belt and

calmly aimed at Al's head. "We'll be taking our leave now, gentlemen. Don't bother seeing us out," he said, glancing around the room and grinning. "It is quite obvious that you have your hands full as it is."

Meanwhile, in the old section of the prison, Mean Boy Miller and John Jeffries stared into the wide eyes of the guard they had just finished strapping into Ole Sparky. The gag in the horrified man's mouth did not prevent him from trying to scream.

"Don't worry, son," John said, his voice light with joy. "We won't fry you without a fair trial."

Mean Boy, his beefy arms cradling the scattergun, whooped with laughter.

The noise, both inside and outside the prison, indicated that the riot was now in full force.

"You sure was smart to have that spick get the ball rolling," Mean Boy marveled.

"Hell," John answered, "that was the easy part. You keep an eye on our friend here."

The younger man nodded and smiled.

"I've got a wall to haul down," John continued, "and I need to talk to a newsman and see if he can't help us keep folks from gettin' in here. Anybody comes down the corridor without giving the signal, shoot the bastard. Understand?"

Mean Boy grinned and nodded as John turned on his heel and moved rapidly up the corridor to the rotunda. The sound of his happy whistling echoed off the damp walls.

III Word of the riot reached Governor Horton as he was sunning himself in a lawn chair beside the new Olympic-size pool he'd ordered built with a state appropriation for improvement of the governor's mansion. His wife was gone for the day, and Horton had left orders that he was not to be disturbed for any reason. He was mildly high, on his way to pleasantly drunk, and had just popped the top off his fourth can of real, full-calorie beer when the gate guard came running toward him around the hedge at the far end of the pool, his hands cupped around his mouth.

"Governor! Governor!" the man shouted as he ran. "We've got problems!"

"Calm down, Joe," the governor said, steadily pouring his libation into a tall, frosted glass. He frowned, irritated. Too damn much foam. He sipped it off and was sporting a foamy white mustache on his neatly shaven upper lip by the time the guard came to a breathless stop in front of his chair.

"Now," Horton said. "What exactly is the matter?"

"Inmates have taken over McHenry maximum security prison," the guard gasped.

Horton slopped cold beer in his lap as he leaned forward.

"Shit!" The governor jumped up, swiping at the rivulets dripping off his trunks. "Call my aids and contact the heads of all the law enforcement agencies, including the Department of Corrections. We'll meet in my office in five minutes. Also," he continued, walking rapidly toward the open sliding glass doors of the mansion, "get the president pro tem and the Speaker of the House on the phone. Better contact that bastard Tobias. Prison's in his district." Horton drew his hand down his face, squeezing his sun-blurred eyes. "We'll need the adjutant general, too. Where the hell's Reardon?"

The guard shrugged and shook his head.

"Well, son, why don't you just go and find him, okay?" the governor asked, trying to calm himself.

The guard hurried off.

"Have him contact the attorney general!" Horton yelled at the guard's retreating form as he disappeared down the hall. Alone, Horton stood staring at the empty,

native stone fireplace just off the formal dining room.
"Shit!" he shouted. The remains of his beer crashed into the dark, cold space.

III Senator Tobias arrived at the penitentiary approximately five minutes after the governor received news of the riot. The press corps arrived at the same time. To no one's surprise, Tobias delivered the first official statement of the day. With his booming oratorical voice, he took full advantage of his golden moment onstage. For the benefit of voters watching live television reports of the emergency in the security of their own homes, he exuded all the confidence, control, and reassurance that the public sorely needed from the leader of their great state.

"My concern," he said, "is first and foremost for the safety of the hostages. Second, we must bring this crisis to a close as rapidly as possible in order to minimize the damage done to the prison and the resulting shortfall of our legislative dollars. We must consider the taxpayers who are watching their investment in security go up in flames." Not once did Tobias mention the inmates themselves. He ended with a sidelong blast at the governor. "I know that Governor Horton, as soon as he can be reached, will take rapid and resolute action to put this riot down in order to save lives."

In the meantime, the governor had dispatched the National Guard and the state highway patrol. The first troopers, those already in the area, arrived soon after Tobias's speech. The others would be there before midnight, and the National Guard would need about forty-eight hours to mobilize. But the sheriff, his deputies, and the McHenry police were out in full force, milling around with the other law enforcement officers, all of them without direction. Most were nervous and perspiring and seemed at loose ends. None had received any riot training. Corrections officials on the scene, although they had dealt with minor disturbances and had a plan for dealing with escapes of one or two prisoners at a time, had never dealt with a problem on the scale of what they now faced.

A small knot of men and women gathered around the warden, who, luckily, had not been inside the prison walls when the riot began. Video cameras ran and reporters took notes as he explained that he could only guess about possible methods of containment and security, since the riot had sprung up so quickly and was now so all-encompassing.

III As those outside the walls stood coughing in the smoke and contemplating their best course of action, John, Al, and Mean Boy calmly carried out their own plans on the inside.

"Well, Mr. Hurst," John Jeffries said, "this is your lucky day. Since the fat boy here is kinda shy, and since you have experience dealing with cockroaches like yourself, you get to be our spokesman. I've got a message for the press, the bulls, and the bullshitting politicians. You tell them that if they don't back off, we're gonna start killing your friends here, one at a time, until they're ready to listen. If they act in good faith, we'll start sending these folks out one at a time. You got that?"

Hurst swallowed hard. "I think you're making a mistake."

John cuffed Hurst hard across the mouth. "I don't need any advice from you, ya piece of shit!"

Eric watched blood drip from Hurst's lower lip. When he spoke, his voice sounded calm. "He's right, you know. The riot definitely has their attention. But once you start killing people, all bets will be off."

"Well, now, Mr. Williams," John sneered, taking a step toward Eric, "that's not for some pansy-assed, bleeding-heart lawyer like you to decide, is it? Mr. Hurst," John asked, "are you gonna go out and repeat what I said with no additional editorial comments?"

Earl spoke up, "John, don't harm these people, I warn ya. They haven't done nothin' to you. They've tried to be fair and im—"

"Fair?" Jeffries shouted, turning on the big man, "You think fat boy Chester here has been fair?" He walked over to Wyndott and squeezed one of his jowls in his hand. "Do you really think this asshole knows how to be fair?" John kicked the chairman in the balls and smiled as he went down into a crumpled hump on the floor.

Eric moved to help him, but John Jeffries's glare stopped him cold.

"Go on, Hurst," John said, pushing the newspaperman toward the door. "Al will escort you to the front gate and out. The same gate where we'll be leaving the bodies if things don't go so good. You got that?"

Hurst nodded miserably.

John signaled Al, who immediately grabbed Hurst, blindfolded him, and pushed him toward the open door and the stairway beyond.

Al turned back toward the room and addressed the remaining board members. "In a few minutes we'll be moving to a new location. In the meantime, I'd suggest you save your speeches and enjoy every breath. Each one could be your last."

George manacled the board members' legs together and fastened thick, oily smelling rags across their eyes. At first, in this new state of dark confinement, Eric heard only the sounds of destruction rising from within the bowels of the prison. Then, beneath them but closer, another sound surfaced. John was humming "Love Me Tender" slightly off key.

III "That son of a bitch! That lousy, stinkin' son of a bitch!" Horton raged as he stomped around his office in the state capitol. "I wouldn't be surprised if Tobias started the goddamn riot himself."

Reardon switched off the television at the other end of the room. He had rushed over from his house just a few blocks away when an almost incoherent gate guard had called to inform him of the situation. Now, having watched and heard Glen Tobias's speech, he had to admit the man had class. The senator's arrival at the prison had been perfectly timed, his appearance masterfully executed. The speech was so beautifully, cleverly constructed, yet seemingly extemporaneous, and the slam at Horton was so ingeniously woven into the fabric of the speech as to make most who heard and saw it believe that Tobias had been forced to take charge because Horton was neglecting his duties as governor.

Horton stopped in mid-tirade, took a deep breath, and whispered hoarsely, slowly, to one of his aides. "Get the fucking attorney general up here—*now!*"

The aide scurried out of the room. Horton stalked over to his desk chair and sat staring intently out his office window as though he could see the prison going up in flames, and along with it, his political career.

The silence in the room was complete, even though ten people stood waiting for orders. After what seemed like an eternity to Reardon, Horton swiveled his chair to face the assembly and began issuing rapid-fire directions to the assembled representatives of all phases of law enforcement in the state. First on his list was the head of the Department of Corrections.

"Sam, I want on my desk within the hour a contingency plan of how we're going to contain these people. Use all of your corrections officials if you have to. Security will be provided by the National Guard and the highway patrol.

I want you gentlemen stationed around the walls of the prison. No gaps. Above all, there are two things I do not want to see. I want no escapes, and I want no one killed unless absolutely necessary.

The head of the highway patrol asked, "What about tear gas?"

Horton glowered. "What for?" he asked. "To make them uncomfortable? We'd better have a purpose for using it, but that may well be a consideration eventually. First we have to decide whether or not to storm the penitentiary. I hope to God we can negotiate our way out of this mess."

The adjutant general of the National Guard cleared his throat. "That may show a sign of weakness, sir."

"Well, sir," Horton said, glaring at the man, "if it does, then it does. How can you find anything weak about saving lives? Now, if the inmates are killing each other, don't interfere. I want no stray shots. In fact, while the guard is manning the walls, I don't want any ammunition in their weapons."

The adjutant general flushed bright red. "But, sir—"

"No buts about it," Horton shot back. "Or have you forgotten Kent State?"

"With all due respect, Governor," the man responded, "these aren't a bunch of spoiled college students. They're dangerous criminals!"

"General," Horton said, standing up and leaning across his desk into the man's face, "these are people with families, and those families aren't in the penitentiary. I don't want to cause anyone to grieve except the leaders of this riot and any others who might be responsible for starting it. Sam?" he said, turning back to the head of corrections. "Use every snitch you've got, if you can get to them, and find out who started this riot, who we're dealing with, and—"

The red telephone on Horton's desk rang once, and the governor snatched it up. Reardon, knowing it was a direct line to the prison, watched his boss's face carefully.

Horton said hello and then listened silently for a full minute. "I see," he murmured. "Right. Keep him away from the press and chopper him up to my office as soon as possible."

Horton hung up the phone and sat for a moment, holding a heavy, crystal paperweight engraved with the state seal. Then he grinned and looked up at the assembly.

"Gentlemen," Horton said, "I think we have our first break. Two old friends of mine, and of Tobias's, John Jeffries and Al McDougal, have sent a parole board member, Hoyt Hurst, out as their messenger. We know now who's behind this." Horton, the corners of his mouth turning up into a grin, paused a moment before looking straight at Reardon. "Billy, would you kindly check to see if the attorney general has arrived?"

Adrenaline pumped like a tidal wave through Reardon's blood stream. He responded with a salute and a smile. "With extreme pleasure, Governor," he said smoothly.

18

THE CHAIRMAN

The blindfold tied about his eyes plunged Eric into total darkness. Rough hands stripped him of his suit coat and placed metal bonds about his hands, feet, and waist. More metal rattled as they passed through these bonds and he could feel himself being chained to his fellow board members. He and the others were then jerked upright and shoved into a stumbling shuffle. The disembodied voice in Eric's living nightmare undoubtedly belonged to John Jeffries.

"Let's get them downstairs. Mean Boy, you clear a path. I'll bring up the rear. Lead on, Alphonse."

Since they'd been chained together in the order in which they'd sat against the wall, Eric figured he was following Earl and that Chester Wyndott must be directly behind him. Willie Jacks, then, had to be the one dragging behind like a reluctant caboose at the end of a slow train. Eric tried not to imagine what might be happening to Ethel Wilson. He hoped Hoyt Hurst was safely on the outside.

"Keep 'em moving, Mean Boy!" Jeffries shouted from behind.

Loss of vision, restrained mobility, and the complete absence of control over his own condition inspired in Eric the most intense terror he'd ever known. Unable to respond either by running or by fighting, he fought to channel the raging waves of adrenaline hitting his system, to block out distractions, step outside himself, and create a sort of mental movie of their progress. The cacophony seemed to increase logarithmically as the group shuffled down the hall and began descending the stairs.

Smoke tore viciously at the mucous membranes in Eric's sinuses and throat until they felt as though they, too, had caught fire. He could picture his surroundings. The stairwell was acting like a chimney, funneling smoke up from the inferno below. He gagged as sour bile rose into his mouth and then coughed until his head pounded and his legs felt like rubber.

Eric's knees nearly buckled when, expecting another step down, his foot encountered the flat cement floor. At the bottom of the stairs the air seemed thinner and the quality and quantity of sounds and their reflected echoes changed. What had once been a dull, undifferentiated roar burst open and revealed itself as a complex, high-volume, full-bodied symphony of terror, swirling with discordant screams, shouts, laughter, and constant, varied crashing noises. Eric knew then that they'd entered the rotunda.

From somewhere outside himself, he viewed himself and the other board members as captive animals in some fantastic, prehistoric ceremony of sacrifice, staged in slow motion for the appreciation of the masses. John Jeffries filled the role of high priest.

"Hold it! Move that table!" he shouted.

The parade rattled and lurched to an awkward halt and, to take his mind off the chafing weight of the manacles around his body and limbs, Eric again indulged in his self-protective mind game. Now he envisioned himself as one of several two-dimensional figures in a modernistic mural, part of a symbolic representation of "Society in Chains," his Brooks Brothers slacks and Ascot Chang dress shirt shining like garish beacons against the depressing gloom of a Gothic background, a chiaroscuro vision of civilization's futile, ongoing war with barbarism.

There, in the superheated center of hell's round room, the fully irony of his condition fell upon Eric like a calved glacier. The bound board members were being forced to journey blind, to humble themselves, abandon their individual identities, and travel as a single entity, confessing to and doing penance for the once-powerful and unequal advantage they had held over the souls of others.

"Hey, Jeffries!" a disembodied voice sounded from nearby. "Who're your homeys?"

"Never you mind, Harvey," John shouted back, "they're in good hands."

Laughter sounded, and the bitter, rancid odor produced by hundreds, maybe thousands of men sweating pure hate from every pore filled Eric's lungs. Then a deep voice exhaling homemade brew near his ear sent a powerful message of promised pain.

"Goddamn scum!"

A wad of spittle hit his cheek and slid down his face into the collar of his shirt, and Eric's testicles drew up like prunes into his gut.

"Hang on, cowboy," Earl whispered. "Try to relax. We're gonna be okay. Jeffries ain't gonna let loose of us. He's got something else in mind."

Before he could respond, Eric was jerked forward and, once more, herded with the others down a hallway. They rounded a corner, keys jangled, a heavy, rusty gate shrieked open, and the descent down yet another stairway began.

The noise in the rotunda seemed to recede as the line of shackled men passed into damper, cooler, deeper recesses of the prison. The floor beneath his feet no longer felt or sounded like smooth concrete. It was rough, uneven—like the old-fashioned streets in the preserved areas of the capital. Brick. Eric struggled to remain calm and not give in to hysteria as the falling sensation of the Dream took on a new, terrible sense of reality.

It was as though he were disappearing into a bottomless well, the walls of which were rapidly, silently shrinking around him. As vertigo threatened to overtake him, Eric concentrated on his breathing and automatically began to draw on his diver's spatial senses. As a kid learning to do double twists, flips, and somersaults off the high board, he had learned to intuit the position of his body in space during free fall. To remain constantly aware of the displacement of air and water created by his movements. To shut his eyes, gauge the distances between his body, the board, and the water, and adjust his movements to the effects of air density and the passage of time. Just dive, he told himself. Just breathe and dive.

Gradually, stored memories of successful dives began to nourish his courage. He remembered coming up from the bottom of the pool, lungs nearly bursting, swimming up, up through the cool water, and finally breaking the surface and gasping, gratefully drawing in the moist air. As though the memories were lifelines, he clung to them, wove them into nets, and then cast them out to gather sensory information that would help him envision where he was being taken. To do this, he found himself battling fears that threatened to tear his nets and render them useless. His revived, refined senses told him he and the others were being led down a narrow passage. The slightly cooler air flowing off the surfaces of damp walls nearby made the skin on his forearms prickle.

"Why did I ever get involved with this fucking board?" Willie Jacks whimpered again and again.

Chairman Wyndott muttered, "You should have thought of that, Senator, before you had your picture taken with your favorite hooker."

"I didn't know she was a hooker!" Willie Jacks whined.

"Shut the fuck up, you!" Al growled. A rush of air, a groan, and a sudden jerk on the chains let Eric know Willie Jacks had been hit. Hard.

"Keep moving, come on!" John shouted from behind.
"You can have your fun later, Al."

A minute or so passed before the group regained its balance and moved on.

Something or someone brushed past Eric and back into the space through which they'd just passed. Two heavy, metal doors clanged shut somewhere behind them.

Then Eric sensed that they had entered and were standing in a rather large room. The sweaty, oily rag was jerked from his eyes and he stood, blinded again. This time by light.

Through open half windows, Eric watched the brilliant sun tip on the horizon like a soup plate and flood the room with the molten, blood red light of a fiery sunset. He turned his head, blinked rapidly, and stood in stunned silence.

Before him was an old, oaken chair with straps attached to its stocky arms and legs. A metal skullcap studded with wires lay on its broad seat. In the far corner, beyond the chair, a guard slumped with his hands and feet bound, his eyes covered by a blindfold. His chest, Eric noticed with relief, was slowly rising and falling.

George Davis, who had apparently been waiting for them in the room, removed the connecting chains and tossed them into the corner. Earl stared at him until George nudged his arm.

Still hobbled and cuffed, all but Wyndott were forced to stand with their backs against the wall. Eric watched as John Jeffries strutted over, stood directly in front of the chairman, and gestured grandly toward the chair.

"Mr. Chester Wyndott," the con intoned, "your richly deserved throne. In a minute, we're gonna let you take your rightful place in society. But first, a little coronation ceremony is in order. Don't you agree?"

Mean Boy laughed and licked his lips. John signaled Al, who opened the door and then leaned against the wall, his arms folded, with the .357 Magnum clutched in his right hand. Mean Boy slid into the room and was gone for a few seconds.

Eric watched in horror as a motley crew of cons, led by Mean Boy, entered the room and gathered in front of the chairman.

Some were weight lifters, huge men whose bulging biceps were decorated with poorly executed, homegrown tattoos proclaiming them STUD OF CRAZY. Others were young, excruciatingly thin, and beardless. All were primed, pumped, and ready for some kind of action.

Then, as the crowd parted to allow passage, Eric's glance fell on the familiar face of a young blond male walking resolutely toward Chester. Eric flashed on the humiliating scene that had occurred during his first board meeting and searched his memory for a name. Jeffrey. No, Jeremy. Jeremy Slade.

As the young man strolled over to stand directly in front of Wyndott, his eyes were lit by a strange brightness that went beyond humiliation and anger, even beyond normal hatred. Eric felt sure Jeremy Slade was higher than he'd ever been before, inside or outside of the walls. And yet, when he mocked Chester, his inflection matched Eric's memory of the chairman's own tone of voice.

"How do you think you'll like it in here, Mr. Wyndott?" Slade said, sneering. "Think you'd like to have a little fun with the boys, do you?"

As though responding to cue, two huge inmates stepped forward on either side of Wyndott and a shank appeared. Its glittering blade sliced cleanly through the chairman's alligator belt and down through his pinstriped, Hickey Freeman slacks and red plaid boxer shorts. The men jerked and ripped Chester's shredded clothing off him, revealing

the bloated fish belly, white thighs, and buttocks beneath.
One quick shove sent him sprawling onto the dusty floor.

"Jesus!" Earl whispered through his clenched teeth.

Wyndott, his pristine oxford shirt, Rockports, socks, and silk tie still in place, struggled to pull himself up off the floor. He'd only made it as far as his hands and knees when Slade crouched down beside him, grabbed a handful of hair, and jerked his head up and back. Peering into the chairman's eyes, he gently placed the blade of a pearl-handled straight razor between two of Wyndott's numerous, trembling chins.

"Now, you don't wanna go anywhere, do you, Mr. Chairman?" Slade rasped. "This is your party. You do want to get your presents, don't you?" The young man bared his teeth and jerked Wyndott's head further back. The chairman grunted and the young man asked, "Ah, does piggy want to squeal?"

Meanwhile, Eric, who had been aware of movement among the crowd of inmates, was nevertheless shocked to realize that two burly men had unzipped their pants and were now preparing themselves for the festivities.

One by one, the rest of the crew followed suit. A beefy inmate, his head shaved and shining in the glare of the bare bulb hanging from the ceiling at the center of the room, approached and stood directly in front of Wyndott's upraised face, waving his purple, swollen member like a bludgeon before the chairman's bulging, glassy eyes and slack, open mouth.

"Yes, sir!" Slade crooned. "We've all brought presents, and all we ask in return is some sign that you're enjoying yourself. You know, of course, that what we're doing here is in your best interest." He jerked the chairman's head back further. "After all, you've always been very interested in our welfare. Haven't you, pig?" The young's man's voice spiraled upward. "Haven't you, pig?!"

A thin line of blood bubbled up from within the wrinkled flesh of Wyndott's neck, staining the handle of the straight razor.

The crowd closed in around Wyndott's supplicant form. Although Eric could only see flashes of his white body between the milling feet and legs of the crowd, he knew by the sounds filling the room, the heavy, musky odors permeating the damp air, and the movements and cheers of the crowd, that inmates of every size and race were taking turns sodomizing and degrading the once-powerful chairman.

"Christ," Earl said under his breath, perspiration rolling down his face. He stared murderously at John Jeffries and muttered, "Evil, filthy bastard!"

Gradually, after about half the group had finished, Wyndott's groans turned to hoarse whimpers, his whimpers turned to screams, and, finally, the man's screams gave way to high-pitched wailing.

Eric tried to shut his eyes, tried to block out the sound. But darkness only increased his disgust and terror. Mind games utterly failed him. Frantic, he pleaded silently with George Davis. This would-be writer only shrugged his shoulders and looked away.

All the while, the pale young man held the knife to the chairman's throat, occasionally drawing a few more drops of blood and repeating his questions. "How do you like it here? Been havin' a little fun with the boys, have you?"

Only when Wyndott ceased to struggle, when his eyes rolled back into his head and he could no longer even wail, did the terror end. The last hulk finished with him, grunted, let the chairman's body drop to the floor, and kicked him in the groin. Eric watched as Wyndott curled slowly within himself, streams of dark blood running from the folds of his wrinkled neck and from between his buttocks into two thick, red, dusty pools. Black bruises began appearing on his back and dozens of superficial slashes and cuts trickled bright red. Wyndott's face shone blue-white, slick, and puffy. His breathing was labored.

"Whooeee!" Mean Boy shouted, jumping up and down like a wild man on his first hunt. John and Al looked on dispassionately.

His stomach heaving, Eric couldn't stand any more and turned to face the wall. "For God's sake," he gasped, "help the man!"

Startled, Jeffries wheeled, grabbed Eric's arm, and glared into his face. "Jealous, Williams? You want some of this, too?"

Fear and revulsion gnawed at Eric's guts like unseen monsters frantic to get out, get away.

John Jeffries laughed. "Sorry, pretty boy," he lisped. "This is Mr. Wyndott's special moment. He's queen for a day, right boys?"

The motley crew erupted in coarse laughter.

"So," John said with a shrug, "let's just set him on his throne and give him his crown, shall we?"

He nodded to Mean Boy and one of the larger men. Both stepped forward, grabbed Wyndott by both arms, hauled his immense bulk upright, and slammed it into the big oaken chair. Mean Boy fastened the leather thongs securely around Wyndott's wrists and ankles.

"Looky here, John!" he called out when he saw that the chair's leather belt would not reach around the fat man's belly. More laughter.

Even if he'd been able to save him, Eric knew the chairman could not have stood on his own, let alone walk. His bleeding continued, and his breathing grew more ragged. Eric prayed the man would die soon.

Jeffries approached Wyndott, placed his hands on the arms of the chair, and leaned in close to speak to the dying man. "Now, Mr. Chairman, this is a special occasion," he said. "You graciously allowed many of us in this room to ride you, so we are going to let you ride the lightning." Wyndott's eyes were barely open. He shook his head weakly from side to side and soundlessly mouthed protests.

"But first," John Jeffries said, turning to face the audience, his arms raised and spread like a ringmaster, "allow me to introduce to you all Mr. Chavez Ramirez."

The crowd turned as a young, disheveled Latino swaggered unsteadily out of the shadows and entered the pool of light near the chair.

"Mr. Ramirez here is our glue and screwdriver expert."

No one laughed. Eric shivered as he gazed into the dead eyes of the muscular young inmate.

"Mr. Ramirez here," Jeffries continued, "is going to show you his version of 'riding the lightning.' "

The Latino moved quickly over to the chair, turned the chairman's face to one side against the back of the chair, and placed the tip of an oversized industrial screwdriver in the chairman's right ear. With a quick, powerful slap of his open palm against the handle, Ramirez drove the blade of the tool through Wyndott's head and into the chair with a dull thud.

Like an enraged bull, Earl bellowed in outrage and, head down, charged John Jeffries with a speed that surprised Eric. His massive head caught Jeffries in the stomach, knocking the pistol out of his hands. One of the large inmates quickly reached down and jerked Earl's leg chain upward, throwing him off balance and sending him crashing to the floor. The crowd kicked at Earl as he rolled on the floor.

"Stop!" Jeffries yelled, then sauntered over to where Earl lay half curled in the dust. "Mighty goddamn protective, ain't you, big fella?" He rubbed his gut, smiled, and aimed a vicious kick at Earl's chest. "You wouldn't kill your old buddy John, would you, Earl?"

Eric flinched as Jeffries landed yet another kick, this time to Earl's face.

Earl spat blood and gasped. "Take the chains off for two fuckin' minutes, you worthless son of a bitch," he growled, "and I'll show you what I can do to your bad ass."

John merely smiled and said, "I really wanted to save you for something special, Earl. But you're gummin' up the works, boy." Jeffries bent down and picked up the .357 Magnum, weighed it in his hands, and put it back in his belt. Then he grabbed the scattergun from Mean Boy.

"Now I'm gonna make you suffer just a little bit."

"No!" Eric screamed. Then he pleaded. "No, John, no. Please. Don't do it. We can work something out. I'll guarantee your safe passage out of here. But leave Earl alone."

At a nod from John Jeffries, one of the inmates picked up a length of chain and slipped it through Earl's belt. He stood there, grinning toothlessly at the huge man.

Then Jeffries turned slowly and gazed at Eric. "Mr. Williams," he said smoothly, "you're a little late on that. You see, I'd already planned for you to get us out of here. Your friend here is creating just way too much of a problem. But . . . " Jeffries paused to scratch his groin, "I will do you a favor, just because it's you, Mr. Williams. I won't let him suffer."

Jeffries wheeled quickly, holding the scattergun at chest level.

Earl kicked sideways and made contact with the knee of the inmate holding him. The con fell backward, pulling Earl down with him just as Jeffries fired.

The shot caught Earl just above belt level, tearing away fat and some muscle from his side, but apparently missing vital organs and arteries. He lay writhing on the floor, clutching the seeping wound, and sucking air through his teeth.

John turned to Eric with a pleasant smile. "Oops. Missed. Sorry, Mr. Williams," he said, "I reckon I lied. I did make him suffer some, didn't I, Earl?"

"Jeffries," Earl gasped, "you're a gutless asshole."

John Jeffries brought the scattergun up once more, strode closer to Earl and laid the muzzle of the gun squarely between Earl's eyes.

A deafening roar from above shook the walls and floor of the room. The crowd of inmates was in immediate disarray.

John shouted, "We'll continue this little game later. Go on boys, it's time to move. Fireworks have started in the yard."

The crowd ran up the passageway. Mean Boy was stationed in the doorway shouting questions and getting orders from Al and John.

In the excitement, Earl was forgotten. Eric crouched low, ran over, and helped him stagger to his feet. Eric began to speak, but Earl shook his head vigorously and, together, the two men staggered into a dark corner and collapsed. Eric ripped off one of his shirt sleeves and stuffed it into Earl's belt, desperate to stop the bleeding. "My God," Eric breathed, wiping sweat from his face, "there truly is pure evil in the world."

Earl nodded painfully and managed a grin. "Son," he said, "at least you're learnin'. Most folks go through life ignorant of that fact."

Watching Earl's suffering, and gazing at the grotesque form of the chairman still sprawled in the chair, Eric resolved to keep his mouth shut and watch for an opportunity to escape. Whether he went alone or tried to take Earl and Willie Jacks out with him, his chances seemed slim. Yet survival, among the wolves, seemed even less likely.

19

TAKING CARE OF BUSINESS

While Eric monitored Earl's wound, John attended to business. He handed an envelope to Al and carefully gave instructions.

"Take this list of demands," he said, "and let the boys out front pass them on to one of the soldier boys or a smoky. Get Culiver and Van to be spokesmen. They talk the best and love attention. While the state jerks mull the list over, have the boys put on a little show in the yard. That way, we can tell what their orders have been, whether or not they plan to move in. If they make no moves, we're set. We'll have plenty of time to get out of here. Got it?"

Al nodded.

"We also need to get the word to Chili at that community treatment center." He pointed to the corner where Al and Mean Boy had dumped the guard before the board members had been brought down. "We can still release him if we need a show of good faith. You take care of that when the time comes, right?"

"Right. Jesus, John, you sure as hell got this all planned out, don't ya?" his partner enthused. "Back in a flash." Al trotted down the passageway.

John watched Al leave with a smile on his face that told Eric he took as much pleasure in his ability to take care of business as any corporate executive might. Standing in the doorway to the executive room, John whistled "Love Me Tender" once more. With feeling.

At the governor's office, soft starlight filtered through the large windows. Horton and Attorney General Barry Morris were alone. The serene setting and utter silence masked the tension in the air.

"Barry," Horton said, "you've always been a loyal friend to me over the years."

"I've tried to be, Governor," Morris answered, his heart beating like a boom box inside his chest.

"Tobias is really making it rough on me," Horton said, shaking his head morosely. "Had you come up with anything on him before the riot started?"

"No, sir," the attorney general said, and breathed a sigh. "We were thinking of convening a grand jury to investigate his cattle operation. He raises exotics and recently bought several shipments, totaling about a thousand head, and put them out to graze. Even for a big ranch, that's an awful lot of cows put to pasture in such a short period of time. We might be able to raise some question as to where the money for those cows came from."

"Takes too long," Horton said, fighting the temptation to bite his nails. He thought for a moment. Slowly, his face brightened. "But I have an idea. Is there any way to search around and make it look like Tobias had anything to do with starting this riot?"

Barry Morris looked up from the drink in his hand, surprise written on his usually placid face. "I don't think Tobias would so something that stupid, do you?"

Horton shrugged.

"I mean," Morris continued, "he'd have to deal with inmates who don't know the truth from a lie and don't care. They're all unreliable weasels. I can't imagine he'd be able to pull off something as massive as this riot. Besides, there's all sorts of real reasons for a riot to occur." Morris set down his drink and ticked them off on his slender fingers. "Overcrowding, hot summer nights, inadequate and poorly trained security. All that."

"Morris, you aren't listening," Horton said, a note of impatience entering his voice. "I'm not saying he'd actually be stupid enough to try to engineer it. I'm simply asking whether there might be anything that could point toward his involvement. For example, he represented Jeffries and has been seen visiting him in the pen lately. Rumors of possible collusion between these two could give me an opportunity to neutralize his ability to use this riot against me." Horton paused to sip his drink. "Particularly if some bad shit happens. And we might as well figure it will, given who we're dealing with."

Morris stood and set his empty glass on the antique sideboard that doubled as a bar. He looked at the governor and shook his head hopelessly. "I'll see what I can do, Governor," he said. "But don't hold your breath. You know, one must be very careful dealing with these types of accusations. Inmates are notorious for telling one story to someone one day and another story to someone else the very next day."

"Well, then, be careful," Horton said, reaching out to shake his attorney general's hand. "But remember, any help you can be will be much appreciated. Besides, you owe me after giving that ridiculous speech on overcrowding two weeks ago. You should have consulted me. But what the hell, we're in the briar patch now. See what you can do."

Morris nodded. "I'll do my best, sir."

After closing the heavy door behind him, Morris paused for a moment in the broad hallway. Then he grinned, shook his head, and slap-footed his way up the hall, into the rotunda, and then down the stairway to the back door where his car stood waiting. His driver, a middle-aged highway patrolman, opened the door for him and, once Morris was settled behind the wheel, asked, "Where to, sir?"

Morris replied without meeting the man's gaze, his voice sounding, even to himself, as though he were a million miles away. "I need to get down to McHenry, Dwayne. But first I want to spend about an hour in my office making a few phone calls."

The attorney general settled into the deep cushions of the back seat, closed his eyes, and let a slight smile spread across his face.

III In the yard at the prison, the attention of law enforcement officers and guardsmen were riveted on an inmate who had just collapsed after being raped continuously for a period of over two hours. Only a limited number of inmates had actually been involved in the rape itself. The rest had stood by, cheering. Now guardsmen, who had only a few hours before sat down with their families to eat a quiet, home-cooked meal, watched in horror as two inmates dragged their unfortunate victim over to hastily erected scaffolding at the base of a flagpole they'd uprooted from the rodeo arena.

Two inmates standing on top of the scaffold hauled the man up by a rope that went around his chest and under his arms while others boosted him up from below. A huge crowd of inmates gathered around, shouting and screaming their blood lust as the two men slipped the noose from around the man's chest and up over his raised arms. Then they placed it around his neck and tightened it. One of the two persecutors patiently threaded the rope through the flagpole's heavy-duty pulley, designed to withstand the hurricane-force winds that often ripped without warning across the bare, open prairie. The other stood with the barrel of a homemade handgun shoved into the victim's ribcage.

Because of the governor's order not to fire on the rioting inmates, the troopers and guardsmen were helpless to stop the activity in the yard. The guardsmen carried no ammunition at all. One by one guardsmen and troopers turned away from the scene, frustration revealing itself clearly in their tense postures and still, anxious faces. Watching the scene, one of them said later, was like attending a party in hell that had spun completely out of control and from which no one could snag a ride home. The violent orgy went on and on as everyone checked their watches in disbelief.

Few of the men watching had ever seen violence escalate to such a pitch and sustain itself for so long, and those who had seen military action were fighting the inevitable string of emotional explosions psychologists call flashbacks. A few were forced to retreat from the scene to calm themselves alone or in small, two- to three-man informal support groups. Medics and local ambulance crews were trying, unsuccessfully, to deal with the effects of the emotional and mental stress on military and law enforcement personnel as it occurred, but were woefully unprepared to do much more than give aspirin.

Half-naked, drunk, and drugged-up inmates danced and strutted around the scaffolding, firing weapons into the air and chanting, "Kill! Kill! Kill!" The raped and terrorized inmate desperately tried to maintain his precarious balance on the board at the top of the scaffolding. Finally, the two other inmates on the scaffolding jumped to the ground. All eyes turned in that direction and, for a moment, everyone inside and outside the walls was silent. The victim stood shaking, his head bent as though in prayer. Then he raised his head and stared down into the crowd now milling like bees in an active hive.

The crowd parted in waves that radiated away from a bald, ebony inmate, his bare chest, back, and arm muscles rippling as he bore toward the scaffolding a sledge hammer held high above his head in both massive fists.

The chanting increased in volume and the rhythm became constant, provided a cadence to which the inmate began swinging his hammer at the legs of the scaffolding. Even from a distance, the executioner's broad, gleaming smile contrasted starkly with the darkness of his face. The scaffolding groaned and tilted crazily as first one and then two of its four legs were knocked out from under the platform on which the hapless inmate stood.

Finally, his legs spread wide for balance, the destroyer raised his head and smiled at his victim. The doomed man bent at the waist, shouted down, and pleaded for mercy from his executioner as, with one last expansion of his shining chest, he heaved the immense hammer against the third leg of four. The roar of the crowd mingled with the sound of wrenching metal as the scaffold collapsed. Observers gazing at the scene with binoculars watched silent screams leave the man's throat just before his body swung free and the force of his own weight snapped his neck.

It was this distraction, the clamor created when the metal scaffold made contact with the concrete of the yard and the accompanying explosion of cheers from the audience, that had saved Earl from certain death in the dank basement of the prison.

The heads of the highway patrol and the National Guard militia had received John Jeffries's list of demands through the released guard about thirty minutes later. Following an hour of debriefing regarding the conditions and locations of inmates and officials inside the prison, the guard was excused and told to go home. On the way home, he pulled his Mazda into the parking lot of a Stop and Shop along the highway and made a hurried call from the pay phone outside. The recipient of that call made yet another call to a cheerful, disembodied voice, who then made a call of his own.

That afternoon Gloria Benning, a.k.a. Chili, left the work release center with a weekend pass clutched in her hand.

Her first stop, coincidentally, was at the same convenience store from which the guard had made his call earlier. She spoke only briefly into the receiver, then hurried back to the van that was transporting her to her destination. Thirty minutes later, in a frame shop across town, Kim Whitlock signed out from the work center where she had been placed on Eric Williams's recommendation. She was whisked off in a cab she had not called to pick her up. The driver smiled at the attractive woman in his rearview mirror, wishing he hadn't been paid quite so well to get her to her destination in such a hurry. Gravel flew from beneath his rear tires as he pulled away from the center parking lot and out onto the highway.

III Two hours after the ritual execution in the yard, Al hurried down the corridor and into the electrocution room. "Okay," he said, wiping the perspiration from his brow with one of the rags that had earlier been used as gags. "The word's out, John. Thing's set for tomorrow night. Also, we received a reply from the governor. Our demands will not be met until we release the hostages.

"Well then," Jeffries drawled, turning to stare at Willie Jacks, "I guess we'll just have to send them a message. Senator, it looks like it's your turn to take the spotlight."

Eric watched as a dark stain spread across the front of Willie Jacks's trousers. The evidence of his fear permeated the layers of other odors in the room.

"Please! I haven't done anything to you guys," the once-dignified older man whimpered.

"Whether you have or not, Senator, doesn't make any

 difference. See, you're disposable." John chuckled. "Kind of like shitty diapers, you know? Look at it this way. No one will have to put up with you growing any more senile than you already are." John nodded at Mean Boy. "Take him upstairs and give him over to the boys. When they're done, have 'em pin this note to his chest."

Mean Boy smiled, put the note in his pocket, and swaggered up to Willie Jacks.

"Senator, it's been a pleasure knowing you," Jeffries shouted over the man's screams as he was pushed, shoved, and dragged from the room. "Tell the boys howdy for me and tell 'em I said to make it quick."

Thirty minutes later, a young National Guardsman—who only hours ago had been sitting in an English class at a local community college—decided to sneak a smoke near McHenry's main gate. Leaning against the wall, he lit up and took a deep, satisfying drag on a slightly crooked, unfiltered Camel. Then he froze, held his breath, and nearly gagged trying not to cough.

Someone was speaking just inside the gate beside him. The young man tried to peer through the thick smoke and twilight, strained to see the gate itself or the owner of the voice that now seemed to be calling to him, whispering in a singsong cadence. He could barely make out the words:

"Come here, boy, come on. We gonna make you a hero, boy."

The weekend warrior dropped his cigarette, burning his finger in the process, and scrambled for a hold on his weapon. He fumbled, sucked his burned finger, and slapped in a frenzied panic at the sparks threatening to set his sweaty fatigues on fire. Disoriented by the smoke and darkness, he turned around quickly, ready to bolt, then stopped abruptly.

He listened closely. The voices had gone. He shook his head. Had he actually heard them? The young man sighed, chuckled to himself, and once more reached shakily into his pocket for a smoke. As the flame from his disposable lighter flicked at the end of the fluttering cigarette, something in his peripheral vision caught his eye. He turned slowly, then screamed in horror at the head protruding through the gate next to him, its lifeless eyes staring from beneath a white mane of blood-matted hair into the beginnings of a beautiful, starlit night. Laughter rang out from behind the wall.

III The telephone rang in the governor's office. Horton snatched it up and listened for a few minutes, then slowly nodded and said, "Yes, I heard you. Thanks for letting me know."

He hung up the phone and turned to the expectant faces of his assembled staff members. "That," Horton said, then cleared his throat. "That was our people at McHenry. They've executed Willie Jacks."

The shocked murmurs in the room rose and then sank when Horton gestured for them to listen. "We're going to have to make a statement to the press. A note left on the body said, 'This is the first.' It looks as though we're going to have to deal with them. Either that or storm the Bastille. If we do that, there will be no hostages to recover."

Horton heaved a huge sigh. He looked up at Reardon. "Give me the damn contingency plan. We've got eight hours to negotiate. Get your estimates back to me in eight hours, gentlemen."

III Ethel Wilson's mind raced as she continued her verbal barrage against her abductor. She had known her protests would not alter the relentless progress of the tall man's trek through the nightmarish maze of the prison. Nevertheless, she had continued them for her own sake, in hopes that by doing so she could bolster her courage and push back the tide of terror that had raced through her since the Muslims had entered the boardroom.

Suddenly, John C. Calhoun had stopped before an empty, abandoned cell. His bodyguard had dumped her unceremoniously onto a filthy, trash-strewn bunk.

"Sister Wilson," Calhoun had murmured, "I must leave you here for a moment and attend to some council business. I'll be back." Then he had turned and walked through the door, preparing to shut it behind him. Ethel had run to the door.

"Wait!" she had shouted, "You have no right to do this to me!"

Calhoun had simply smiled and spoke softly. "As a devout Southern Baptist who has vociferously, if ignorantly, attacked the cause of her Black Muslim brothers within the walls of this prison, I can readily understand your fear. However, I assure you, we were not the ones who started this fireball rolling. It is pseudo-Christians, Sister Wilson—white, red-necked, so-called Christians—who are to blame, not only here, but everywhere. They, Sister Wilson, are the enemy. Not us. Not your own." Then he had touched his fingers lightly to his forehead, turned, walked outside the cell, and shut and locked the barred door firmly behind him. "None of this," he had told her, staring into her eyes, "would be necessary if you had ever truly been one of us. Besides, for a faithful follower, your Lord always provides, remember?" Then the tall man had smirked and added, "Chill, sistah." He had pulled a .38 from his belt, checked it, grinned, and said, "Praise Allah and pass the ammunition."

Ethel Wilson stood with her slender hands wrapped around the bars, remembering how Calhoun's back had looked as he had receded down the run. Then, as though the bars had burned her, she drew back her hands and, after a moment, walked toward the far wall of the cell and began to pray.

She had been in the cell for hours. At first she had at least been able to see by the light of the windows in the dome of the rotunda. Now the only light came from the fires burning throughout the prison, which cast weird, glowing shadows on the wall and did nothing to soothe her.

Ethel realized that, although as a rule she found Muslims both aloof and cold, Calhoun certainly had been clever enough to guess the worst of all possible tortures he might inflict upon her. She hated the dark almost as much as she hated confinement of any kind. As an only, lonely child, she had despised being forced to wait in the silent darkness of night for either blessed sleep or morning. Most especially, she dreaded the overwhelming feeling of powerlessness, the total loss of control over her own destiny that imposed solitude was now causing her to feel. Prayer, as always, had helped some.

Still, she had trouble remaining calm inside knowing how much some of these men must hate her not only for the stands she had sometimes taken as a member of the board or because of her faith. She was realistic, and honest enough, to admit that much of her acceptance by the white community, and her effectiveness in the black community, had come about because she was "high yella," as they used to say in the old days, and not because she was well educated. Before, she had never felt ashamed of the fact.

Ethel felt frustrated. These men had to know that, even as a black woman who could have passed for white, she had struggled hard to overcome the subtle racism in this state that was, in some ways, more soul killing than the obvious racism of the Deep South. Blatant, visible, tangible hatred was so much easier to fight than that which was sugarcoated, couched in politically correct modes of behavior and communication—the kind of hatred that was indelibly engraved upon the subconscious thought patterns of those in power.

She had long ago come to grips with racism as it existed between African Americans, whites, Hispanics, and Asians. But she despaired, at times, that she might never come to grips with the racism even now running rampant among members of her own community. Her great-grandfathers had been white, rapist slave masters on both her mother's and father's sides. So had those of many of the men and women she knew.

Still, there was nothing she or anyone could do about the facts but accept herself as, in part, the result of one of the most abominable aspects of American history—slavery. It had taken two hundred years for her people to even begin to be treated as real human beings in this country. It had taken her sixty-eight years of hard work to reach a position from which she felt she could be of help, not only to those of her own race, but to everyone who had never had, or who somehow had lost, a sense of value as a human being. Until now, as a member of the parole board she had felt good about working to see that, by the grace of God, those willing to try to change their lives would receive help in doing so.

Calhoun's parting words had stung her much more than she hoped he realized. During all the many tragedies in her life, her unshakable faith in God had sustained her, nourished her soul, in a way no man, woman, or material possessions ever could.

A sudden, hot anger swelled up inside her, and tears of anger gathered in her eyes. How dare this upstart suggest that she did not know or truly care for her people or for her God! Granted, she knew relatively little about Muslim doctrine. But she had watched too many struggling, disillusioned men and women used by unscrupulous cons like Calhoun, who manipulated for profit. Likewise, she could not forget the lessons her father, a minister and close friend of Dr. Martin Luther King, Jr., had taught her.

As a rebellious young woman she had expressed to him her admiration for the young Malcolm X, before he discovered Elijah Muhammad's true nature and was therefore forced to defect from the Nation of Islam. "At the root of all true religions," her father had said, "is love. Love is what sustains the soul, not hate. Those who preach religious or racial separatism—whether they be black or white, yellow or brown, red or green—those who preach hate between members of the human race are preaching soul death. This, child, is all you need remember."

The sound of footsteps coming near her cell seemed, for a moment, to echo the word "remember" as it ran through her mind.

"Sister Wilson," said the grave, dark-skinned young man standing by holding a torch as another youth opened the cell, "you will come with us, please."

This time she allowed herself to be led up the run on her own two feet. Somehow, it seemed important to take this chance to regain her dignity. *Like a gift*, she thought, *a reward.* "Thank you, Jesus," she whispered.

Calhoun, now as Muhammad, was speaking to an assembly of approximately twenty men gathered around him on the floor of the cell when she entered. Fires burning in trash cans lent a strange, almost ritual air to the proceedings. He did not acknowledge her presence but continued to speak to his rapt audience in a voice that was oddly both comforting and commanding.

"Gentlemen, I believe that for us to ensure our existence we must set up shop here in the east wing. Most of the inmates will avoid it, but we need to make sure that we are completely protected. We will send out groups of three to infiltrate and determine what is taking place. We need to be in position to press out demands and look as good as possible to the administration before this riot inevitably fails. Sister Wilson, here," he said, without glancing up at her, "is our insurance that the administration will not mistakenly find that black men are the easiest to blame and therefore the easiest to kill when blame must be placed for the riot."

Finally he looked up at her, smiling sweetly. "I'm certain Sister Wilson will be happy to carry this message to the administration as soon as this unfortunate event is over."

Ethel Wilson felt confused. Could this all end so easily? Was he serious? Would he actually release her? She fought joy, feared hope, as Calhoun continued speaking.

"Self-discipline is the key to self-preservation. Ultimately, when this riot ends, we will be the ones in charge."

Ethel felt an unwanted stab of admiration. Calhoun, with his excellent command of the language, his intelligence, and his handsome good looks, was a fine example of the sort of African American male who could have done so well had he not gone so bad. He might have made a good politician or, she thought wryly, a minister. In fact, were she younger, she might have been taken in herself.

"And what are your plans?" she asked.

Muhammad El Amin, a.k.a. John C. Calhoun, merely cocked an indolent brow.

"Why don't you tell all your faithful followers what it is, exactly, that you personally plan to do?"

Calhoun the con surfaced briefly from beneath the facade of Muhammad the faithful, and his expression told Ethel Wilson that he had not been prepared for her comment. The answer to her question was not something he had discussed, or planned to discuss, with his followers.

"Sister," he said with only a barely discernible hint of anger behind his feigned shock, "I know that you want to get out of here as quickly as possible. But, please, do not let your anticipation get the better of you. We have no intention of seeing you harmed in any way. We intend to protect you from those who do not respect your womanhood or your years. The faithful," he said, gesturing all around him, "have nothing to fear from anyone. Least of all from their loyal leader."

The men closest to Muhammad turned to gaze upon her with a look of tolerance bordering recklessly close to contempt. Calhoun smiled slyly at her as if to say, "Nice try, old woman, but you have vastly underestimated both me and mine."

"Let's go," he said.

The faithful stood as one and prepared to leave the room.

"Sister Wilson," he said, taking hold of her arm with perhaps a bit more pressure than was warranted, "it is time for us to put you in a safe place so we can observe what is going on outside. Gentlemen," he said to a few men standing near, "begin distributing the printed verses from the Koran. We will meet back here in exactly one hour."

He and his bodyguard hustled Ethel Wilson out onto the run and down a flight of stairs.

"What are you going to do, Calhoun, kill me? Because you know I'm not going to shut up."

"How unfortunate," he said, signaling his bodyguard. The man pulled a six-inch length of tape off a roll and placed the tape over Ethel's mouth.

She began breathing through her nose, inwardly cursing her stupidity. Struggling, as small and frail as she was, had already proven futile. As they emerged into the rotunda, Ethel noticed several of the inmates running into the flame-streaked darkness of the yard, where the noise from outside was steadily increasing in volume. Muhammad dispatched his bodyguard to find out what was going on.

Then, instead of waiting calmly for his minion's return, Calhoun pulled a gun from the belt of his pants and, half dragging her, moved hurriedly outside and down the wall of the canning factory until he found the side door. He held her tight against the wall with one muscular arm as he looked around the corner.

Smoke from the far, north end of the canning factory was blowing directly into her eyes, and they were tearing up. But the fire and smoke only aided her captor. The other inmates seemed too busy trying to put out the fire to notice a young man trying to slip out the back of the building with an old woman in tow. Ethel desperately wanted to cough, but the tape caused her to choke instead. Her legs were weary. She couldn't help stumbling. Finally, she fell. The rough concrete scraped against her knees and hands as she went down.

"Bitch," Calhoun hissed, dragging her up roughly by one arm. As soon as she regained her feet, without really thinking, she kicked him in the shins. He let out an involuntary cry and backhanded her across the mouth. She lost consciousness as she reeled toward the floor.

John C. Calhoun cursed his loss of control as he stood looking down at the dried-up little woman sprawled on the floor. She wasn't dead, though, judging from her soft moans. "Shit," he said, dragging her over behind the machines used to wash cans and place them on the conveyor belt to be filled. Taking a roll of electrician's tape out of his pocket, he taped her thin wrists and ankles, thinking about how much she resembled his grandmother as he wound it around and around. Feisty. Tough. He couldn't help liking her and felt a stab of guilt at leaving her alone here. Still, if his little escape didn't work, under the cover of what was going on in the yard now, he could always come back and retrieve her.

Glancing over his shoulder once more, he hurried down the wall and out the back door of the canning factory into the rodeo arena to a chute where calves were held until their release for the roping events. The old grounds were strangely silent and dark. He crossed the arena floor, flattening himself against the moist stone walls leading up to the gate. Looking up, he noticed that the tower was manned by two highway patrolmen engaged in conversation, their faces turned toward the activity in the yard.

Seizing the moment, Calhoun scrambled under the fence, ran across the utility road, and dived into the brush thirty yards beyond the walls. He waited, breathing heavily and expecting to hear sirens and shouts. When none came, he cautiously rose to his knees, looking over the shrubbery toward the prison. No one was looking in his direction. All the attention was focused on the middle of the yard. Grinning broadly, John C. Calhoun stood, stretched, and slipped gracefully out of his role as Muhammad El Amin and into the darkness.

20

ESCAPE

Attorney General Barry Morris stood like an island in the stream of staff members exiting Governor Horton's office. When the room was empty, he stepped inside and shut the door behind him. David Horton sat with his elbows on the big cedar desk, his head cradled in his hands.

"Governor?" Morris queried softly.

Horton looked up and motioned him toward a chair near his desk.

Morris made his slow way across the tan Berber carpet toward the governor. "I left my office as soon as I received your call. Willie Jacks's death is a tragedy."

Horton seemed not to hear him.

"Ah, David, look," Morris said, stepping behind Horton's desk. He reached out and patted the big man's back. "it will all turn out fine. Whatever decision you make will be the right one, I'm sure."

Horton ran his hands through his hair and sighed. "Thanks, Barry," he replied. "I value your friendship."

Morris looked down into the governor's harried face as he spoke. "I've been called down to the penitentiary, David, to offer legal advice on anything that might happen. But I'll leave word where I can be reached. You've got my mobile number. Don't hesitate to call if you need me."

Horton tried to smile, then gave up and nodded absently. "Of course, Barry," he murmured. "I appreciate that."

Morris turned and left.

III Worried that Earl might go into shock, Eric stayed close to him until, in spite of the pain he was obviously feeling as a result of his injury, the big man was able to doze with his head resting against Eric's shoulder. Even the sound of drywall and boards being torn out of a wall somewhere in the adjoining passageway didn't disturb him. *Guard your strength, buddy,* Eric thought. *Before long, we'll be on the move.* He hated to think about trying to drag his oversize friend to safety somewhere along the way. But he also knew he could not, would not, leave him behind.

Earl groaned in his sleep. Eric shifted so his bulky friend was leaning against the wall. When he was sure Earl was sleeping, Eric stood up, stretched his cuffed hands and legs as best he could, and glanced over at George Davis.

"George?" Eric murmured.

The sandy-haired man turned toward him from the half window. "I, uh, know I asked you this before," Eric said quietly, "but I guess I have a hard time accepting your answer. Why are you doing this? Is three years really that long to wait?"

Davis sighed, smiled slightly, and said, "Well, maybe not for you, Mr. Williams. You have a life. But for me, this place is limbo, a holding pen somewhere between life and death. Inside the walls, nobody grows past a certain point." Davis turned back to the window but continued to speak. "Maybe that's the whole idea, huh? Revoking a man's freedom isn't enough for some folks, Mr. Williams. What they really want is to deprive him of both the joy of living and the peace of death."

"George," Eric whispered hoarsely, "who gives a shit about what they want? What matters is what you want. God, man, you've got such talent! I mean, as a writer, who's gonna care that you're an ex-con? In some ways, your background could even be an asset."

George shook his head.

"But don't you see?" Eric asked. "If you give up now, if you go through with this, you're giving the bastards exactly what they want!" Eric lowered his voice. "After this is over, even if you don't die on the way out, which is highly likely, you won't be able to publish anything under your own name. If you work as hard at it as you seem to want to, your writing will attract the attention it deserves. People will start digging into your past, and your credibility will be shot to hell when they find out who you really are. You'll have to give up writing, man. Or worse, limit yourself to mediocrity. Either way, you won't be able to grow past a certain point, as you say. You'll have created your own limbo! Done to yourself what you claim the system is trying to do."

Eric watched George's face closely, trying to read it as he'd read the faces of countless clients, fellow attorneys, judges, and jury members. The total passivity, the acceptance of fate he read there suddenly enraged him.

"Why go to all this effort to slowly strangle the life force inside you?" he asked Davis coldly. "Why not just kill yourself now, quickly, and get it over with?"

George turned and stepped toward Eric, his fists clenched. "Don't you think I haven't thought of that every goddamn day for the past year? The only thing that's kept me going in here was the thought that, since the gooks hadn't killed me, neither would the joint. I've worked my ass off, and nobody gives a fuck."

"Oh?" Eric said quietly.

George ducked his head and stared for a moment at the toes of his boot. "Okay, man. That was unfair and I'm sorry. But, hey . . . I don't need this." George raised his head and looked sadly into Eric's eyes. "You did your best. You did a good job. We both did. Nothing I do to rehabilitate myself will ever be enough." Davis leaned his forearm against the window and spoke calmly. "I've confessed my sins, I've done penance, I've worked hard, and I'm willing to continue to work hard for the rest of my life on the outside in order to redeem myself. But at some point, men, I need absolution. And someone out there has decided I will never, ever deserve it. That's all. Maybe that somebody is right. I don't know . . . and I'm too damn tired to care."

"Goddamn it, George," Eric whispered angrily, "don't give up!"

"It's too late, Mr. Williams," Davis said, shaking his head and wiping his sleeve across face. "I'll do all I can to help you, but my mind's made up."

Absorbed as they had been in their conversation, neither Eric nor George noticed that the sounds of the wall being torn down had ceased. Or that they had an audience. John Jeffries's applause echoed throughout the room.

"Bravo! What a great scene!" he enthused. "A really dramatic performance, so sweet it makes me want to cry. The heroic, idealistic parole board member tries to con the con into turning himself in. Hell, it's like an old Bogart movie. Williams," Jeffries said, shaking his head in mock sorrow, "I'd have expected something like this from the others, but not from a nice, polite young man like you. Boys always said you gave everybody a fair shake. But counselor, you ain't done nothin' for me, and you sure ain't helpin' Davis here, advisin' him to take action that's against his own best interests."

George Davis flushed and his face set like concrete.

"Nope," John went on, "guess you ain't no more use than the rest of 'em. 'Cept as our insurance policy. Well, gentlemen," he said, checking his watch, "our ride should be pulling up to the curb any time now. Check your powder. Oh, and by the way, Williams, your ugly friend stays here."

Eric's gut contracted. He glanced over at Earl, who was listening, bleary-eyed but awake, in the corner.

"He don't look so good, does he? Probably couldn't run too fast or too far," John said, scratching his stubbly chin. "Sure hope nobody unfriendly comes down here after we leave. But then, I s'pose if somebody don't come by, he might could starve to death. How 'bout it, big guy, you want to take your chances and see if you can sneak by those rowdy boys upstairs?" John snickered.

Earl turned his head away from Eric's sympathetic gaze, his face a picture of pain-filled resignation.

"Well, you boys say your good-byes now 'cause this train leaves in two minutes." John said. He laughed and walked back into the passage.

Eric watched Jeffries leave and, for the first time in his life, thought he could truly find it in himself to kill a man. Earl had shut his eyes. He didn't respond when Eric tried to reassure him that, if he survived, he would get him out. Eric's last few minutes in the room were spent adjusting the packing in his friend's wound and making him as comfortable as possible. Neither dared speak to the other.

III Chili put the paint can and brushes away in a cobwebbed corner of the garage, behind the abandoned farmhouse, ten miles west of the prison. She stood back, admiring the letters she and Kim had just spent three hours stenciling on the van:

DEPARTMENT OF CORRECTIONS

"What a kick!" she said, beaming. "No one will be able to tell it from a real one in the dark!"

Kim smiled and nodded, wiping her hands on the foul-smelling, dark green coveralls that had once hung on the wall.

"John thought of everything, didn't he?" Chili murmured, shaking her head in admiration. She gazed into Kim's dark eyes, and whispered, "Lover, easy street is just around the corner."

It was almost dusk now, but they'd met around three o'clock at the apartment where Kim was supposed to be spending the weekend. From there they'd walked two blocks down an alley to a warehouse where the van was hidden. On the back seat they'd found boxes of food, drink, clothing, lanterns, paint, and stencils. Rifles, shotguns, hand guns and enough ammunition for a ten-day siege had been neatly wrapped in burlap bags and hidden under one of the seats. The keys were in the ignition. Chili cautiously drove down ten miles of backroads to the farmhouse indicated on the map secreted in the glove box.

Ancient smears of white paint clung tenaciously to the gray, weathered walls of the small frame farmhouse staring sightlessly out across the valley from its perch atop a hill. Two or three equally weathered sections of picket fence peeked out from under lush trumpet and honeysuckle vines running rampant along the edges of the small, overgrown lawn.

The house key was on the same ring as the van keys, but Chili had to shove with her shoulder against the door before it finally creaked open. The smell of dust, mildew, and mice had almost overpowered them until they opened a few equally stubborn windows.

After carting the boxes of lanterns, fuel, matches, clothes, liquor, and food inside the house and neatly stacking them along the walls, Chili and Kim had shared a sandwich and set to work on the van.

As soon as they finished their artwork, Chili and Kim walked to the backyard, shucked their overalls, and washed themselves in cool water from an old cistern. Chili made quick work of the process. Then she stood biting her lower lip and staring at Kim's perfect breasts, slim waist, and graceful back as she bent to wash the dry grass off her long, smooth legs with water from a rusty Folger's can. When Kim was done, Chili took her by the hand and led her into the house.

On her way through the living room, Chili snagged one of the Coleman lanterns and a box of wooden matches. Kim silently followed her into a dark, added-on bedroom at the back of the house and stood watching as the lantern flared forth, casting its white glow over their bodies and illuminating a brown painted iron bedstead and striped mattress near the far wall.

"We gotta hurry, baby, but . . ." Chili whispered hoarsely, putting the lantern down on the floor and leading her lover toward the bed. They sat on the edge, and Chili ran her fingers through Kim's hair, her eyes pleading as she crooned, "I just can't wait any longer."

Kim reached, cupped Chili's cool breasts in her slender hands, and rolled the hardening nipples between her fingertips.

"It won't be anything like what we're gonna get used to once we hit Mexico," Chili murmured, "I promise. I want to take care of you, watch you run loose like a pretty, spotted pony on the white sand."

Kim smiled softly as her hand ventured further down Chili's torso, toyed with the damp red curls between her parted thighs.

"Can we maybe get a pony?" Kim's childlike voice asked.

"Sure, baby, sure. But right now," Chili growled, her head tilting back, "I just need a little taste of freedom. It all seems too much like a dream."

Kim, nodded, gently pushed Chili back on the dusty mattress, and buried her face in Chili's warm recesses. Her tongue licked like a flame at the fragrant center of Chili's desire. They rearranged themselves slowly, nibbling, kissing, sliding fluidly into positions of mutual access and activity. It didn't take long. With one hand entangled in Kim's long, raven tresses and the other squeezing her firm, round backside, Chili came with all the sudden, blinding violence of a summer storm. Two seconds later, Kim's back and pelvis arched and she trembled from head to foot. A fine mist of perspiration bathed them both in shining, salty reassurance.

But the afterglow didn't linger. Light was fading quickly in the hallway outside the room. Chili opened her eyes. "Shit!" she exclaimed, taking Kim's hand and helping her up from the mattress. Together they hurried back into the living room.

"If we're late, Jeffries'll kill us," Chili muttered, jerking on a black hooded sweatshirt, slacks, and tennis shoes. As soon as Kim was similarly dressed, they headed outside.

In the gathering darkness, Kim and Chili went back to the garage, loaded the weapons in the van, and checked the map one more time. Kim opened the garage door as Chili slipped behind the wheel of the van and started it. Once Kim was safely in the passenger's seat, Chili turned on the headlights and maneuvered the van out of the garage, down the driveway, and out onto the road where, from a distance, the penitentiary glowed brightly in the night—like a campfire.

III At McHenry, John Jeffries, Al, George Davis, Mean Boy, and Eric entered the tunnel. Not twenty miles away, the private line in Senator Glen Tobias's office rang.

Startled out of his concentration on a press release, Tobias answered the phone. He did not greet the caller but listened for a few minutes without speaking. "How do I know this is a real message?" he asked, then listened for another minute before hanging up the receiver, his expression thoughtful.

An hour later, a uniformed messenger arrived at the office bearing an envelope and instructions that it be opened only by the senator himself. Tobias signed for it and carried the envelope back into his inner office. He shut and locked the door before sitting down, opening it, and reading the brief, handwritten lines. A broad grin lit his handsome face and excitement danced in his dark eyes. "Well, I'll be damned," he whispered. "It *is* for real!" Tobias got up out of his cracked leather chair and hurried straight out the back door. Once behind the wheel of his Allante, he whistled tunelessly as he drove into the night toward a rendezvous he knew would make history.

III The entrance to the utility tunnel was narrow. Eric squeezed through behind John and Mean Boy and then stared in awe at the size of the opening beyond. As tall as he was, Mean Boy was able to walk upright ahead of him, which meant the ceiling had to be at least seven feet high. Judging by the amount of fallen debris, the tunnel had been out of use for some time. Flashlight beams reflected off a stagnant pool of water that appeared to extend along one side of the tunnel's entire length. The cement floor had eroded along both walls.

John and Al had fallen into single file behind Mean Boy. Eric stumbled along behind them, and George Davis took up the rear. Their movement through the tunnel disturbed dozens of rats, which squealed and plopped in and out of the water almost under their feet. *This passage is far worse*, Eric thought, *than the blind walk through the prison had been.* There, at least, he hadn't been alone. Here, the smell was less like danger and more like doom.

He moved steadily forward until the tunnel turned and, quite suddenly, Eric found himself struggling up a forty-five-degree grade. The floor was slick, and he had to steady himself against the wall in order to maintain balance. As

much as he'd hated leaving Earl behind, he had to admit
his friend could not have made it down the tunnel without injuring himself further. Even if he had, it would have taken too much time. Jeffries, no doubt, would have lost patience and ended his struggle for him. Still, Eric had sworn to himself not to leave Earl. Standing in the tunnel, Eric fought the desire to give up and let Jeffries shoot him. Trouble was, he reflected, he might not die quickly enough. He might still end up like Earl.

Suddenly, between the swaying figures of the men ahead, dank concrete gave way to the rich green of vegetation gleaming in the beam of the flashlight. Mean Boy and Al slashed with their knives at the vines and bushes. It was some time before they were finally able to clear a passage.

"Lights off," John whispered hoarsely. He led Mean Boy and Al through the darkness.

George nudged Eric to follow the others, and the next thing he knew, he was standing shoulder to shoulder with four escaped inmates on dry, level ground, staring up at the starlit sky.

The tunnel had muffled the clamor of the riot still going on inside the penitentiary. Now, however, amid cricket chirps and night birds' calls, the hellish sounds drifted back toward them over an open, plowed field. The breeze carried only a hint of smoke from the flames still glowing against the dark horizon.

"There she is!" John shouted. Eric stumbled and righted himself as two of the men took his elbows and hustled him toward a white van parked in a clump of trees about a hundred yards away. Two dim figures, barely visible against the van, waved.

Eric was practically thrown into the back of the van, the doors were closed and locked, and the rest of the group entered through the side doors. As everyone piled in, Eric caught a glimpse of red hair shining against the soft curve of a feminine cheek in the dim lights of the dashboard. The sight tickled his memory. Recognition became complete as his vision focused on the snake slithering up toward the knuckles of the hand that gripped the steering wheel.

"Good evening, Mr. Williams," a familiar voice teased with undisguised glee. "We're so glad you could join us."

"Shut the fuck up and let's go," Jeffries growled.

Chili started the van, revved the engine, and said, "Everything's set up at the house, John. We should be there in fifteen minutes."

As the van bounced and meandered slowly over the furrows, the lights from the fire in the distance periodically lit the faces of the van's occupants. Chili's profile was unmistakable. But Eric had already deduced her identity. The real shock hit Eric when he realized the identity of the woman in the front passenger's seat. "Kim!" Eric exclaimed, involuntarily. As soon as the name left his lips, he thought maybe, just maybe, he'd made a mistake. Surely Kim would have turned around.

"You girls been havin' any fun?" Mean Boy asked, his voice full of vicarious lust.

"Not yet," Chili said, switching on the headlights. "But we will, won't we, sugar? We've got all the time in the world."

In answer, the woman in the passenger's seat leaned toward Chili and kissed her cheek. The lights of the dashboard confirmed his fear. Eric's head reeled and his empty gut lay like an airless balloon against his spine.

The van rolled over a slight hump, and suddenly they were on a flat surface. Chili slammed the van into gear and sped off down the road. The men were all thrown down on the floor as the van made a hard right turn. They sat up and excitement finally overcame the inmates. Shouts, whoops, and hollers echoed around the interior of the vehicle. Mean Boy laughed loudest and longest of all.

"What a piece of cake, John," Al said. "A piece of wonderful, fuckin' cake."

III *Only a little further*, the big man thought, watching the lights blink off ahead. Darkness now lay heavy upon him. In response, he dug raw fingers deeper into the crumbling floor and pulled, dragged himself forward, fighting to retain consciousness. *Only a few more feet*, his spirit told him as he grasped handholds only to feel them slip away, leaving only emptiness and pain behind. At last, white stars spun above his head and closer, to his right, twin red stars blinked on, roared, and danced out into the larger universe.

Earl forced himself to lie still, suck in fresh air and dust, and watch the twin stars. A hundred yards to his right, across the plowed field, the lights of a farmhouse shimmered dimly between the trees.

His senses plotted the vehicle's course for him even as his mind threatened to switch off and let him slip quickly, gratefully into blessed, painless oblivion. When the twin red lights blinked out—about a mile away—he bit hard on his lower lip and, with his left hand holding the packing tightly against his wound, heaved himself up, first to his knees and then onto his unsteady legs. As he headed across the furrows of the field, the reflection of a yard light off of a pickup windshield beckoning to him, anger ignited the adrenaline pumping into his veins and his mind slowly pulled out of neutral.

It had been years since he'd used the tracking skills he'd learned as a boy and honed as a detective. Could he even follow the vehicle he'd seen leaving the field? If he did, would it be a wild goose chase? There was only one way to find out.

21

THE FARMHOUSE

Ten minutes after she had picked up the escapees and their hostage in the dusty field outside the fence surrounding McHenry Penitentiary, Chili steered the white getaway van off the smooth surface of the highway and onto a rutted road. From his cross-legged position on the floor, Eric could see out only by craning his neck and peering between the front seats. Dense trees formed an arch that blotted out the stars above the red clay road. The continuous screening of oak, mulberry, and sand plum branches against the sides and roof of the van frayed much of what remained of Eric's nerves. John Jeffries, however, seemed in high spirits.

"Now, don't roll down your windows, folks," he bellowed. "This here is tick country. I know. They stick to me like flypaper. Have since I was a kid."

George Davis sat silently, leaning his back against the side of the van. He and Eric hadn't spoken to one another since John Jeffries's intrusion into their earlier conversation. While Eric wanted to believe that when a chance to effect his own escape came George would help him, he could not be sure or predict when or how such a chance might occur.

The van had begun to climb a slight hill when Eric noticed a dull glow, nearly hidden from view by foliage, shining ahead and slightly to the right. Eric's pulse raced.

"What the fuck?" John whispered. Then he shouted, "Hit the brake! Hit the goddamn brake!" When Chili responded by slamming her foot down, Jeffries was thrown forward between the driver and passenger seats. The headlights suddenly went out and the van careened toward the ditch on the right side of the road. Half in, half out of the ditch, the van came to an abrupt, in-gear stop as the engine died.

"Jesus, John!" Chili sputtered, "you stupid goddamn—"

"Quiet!" Jeffries whispered hoarsely.

For a moment, everyone sat in silence, listening. Then Chili let out a raucous laugh.

"Christ, honey, relax," she said softly. "It's no big deal. Kim and I got a little . . . carried away before we set out to get y'all. We must have left the lantern burning when we—"

The air inside the van resounded with a loud crack, the sound of flesh and bone on flesh and bone.

"Stupid fuckin' bitch!" Jeffries screamed. Bone and flesh hit heavy glass once, twice. Chili screamed.

"Stop, please! Stop!" Kim shouted.

Someone moved toward the front of the van and the scuffling sounds increased.

"John!" Al said, "Everyone within a hundred miles is gonna hear her. Goddamn it, stop!"

The scuffling noises stopped abruptly.

"Listen," Kim's voice reasoned quietly, "it's okay. Only our tracks showed in the road. No one else has come this way. The lantern light shines only through the window on this side of the house where there's a hall. Coming from the other direction, no one could see it. Nobody lives near here, John. No one would come this way at night."

In the face of her calm reasoning, Jeffries's fury cooled rapidly. "All right," he mumbled, "but you two are going in first. We'll wait till you give us the all clear."

Eric heard Chili and Kim exit the van and listened as their footsteps were absorbed by the silent, velvet night. He'd thought about kicking open the back door of the van when Chili hit the brakes. He might have made a run for it. Then he'd remembered the door had been locked behind him. Besides, trying to make his way, unarmed, in the dark, through dense, tick- and snake-infested undergrowth, with armed murderers right behind him, seemed like the dumbest idea he'd had in years. Still, Eric knew what he needed. John and Al's attention had to be focused elsewhere, as it was now focused on the house.

"There they are!" Mean Boy shouted.

Eric peered into the darkness. A light, suspended and moving back and forth beneath the trees, made Kim's slender, elegant form glow like an apparition.

Then the van's engine roared to life, the headlights came on, and Jeffries drove the short distance up the hill, down a weedy driveway, and into an open garage. He exited on the driver's side and Al on the passenger's side. Eric was about to say something to George, who was bent forward and moving toward the rear of the van, when the back door opened and Mean Boy dragged Eric out by the neck of his shirt onto the dusty concrete floor of the garage.

The group hurried inside, dragging Eric along with them. As soon as they entered, Chili and Kim busily hung blankets over the windows.

"It's going to get a little warm in here tomorrow, boys," Chili chattered amiably. "This place don't have no central heat and air."

John and Al popped tops off cans of cold beer they'd found in the cooler. Mean Boy dug a bottle of Jack Daniel's out of one of the food boxes and began draining its contents. Jeffries frowned at Chili, but Al made an effort at reconciliation.

"You gals sure enough done a nice job in here," he said. "Didn't they, John?"

Jeffries grunted and gazed about at the provisions

stacked around the room. Then he picked up the camp stove and headed for the kitchen.

George, his face partially obscured by the flickering shadows cast by the movements of the others, stood peering carefully around the blanket at the darkness outside. Eric noticed a .38, probably taken from one of the guards, tucked into his belt.

"All right," Jeffries said as he reentered the dining room and snatched the bottle out of Mean Boy's hands, "before you get stupid, we have one more chore to do. Chili, it's payoff time."

"Yippee!" the redhead shouted.

John grinned. "I'm gonna tell you where to go and pick up the money and the new driver's licenses and Social Security cards. Mean Boy and Al, you go along with her. The cuts are gonna be fifty thousand dollars apiece. Bring it all back here, we'll split it up, and I'll tell you the rest of the plan."

"I'll keep an eye on this while we're gone," Al said, taking the whiskey bottle out of Jeffries's hand. "That is, if you don't mind, sir," Al said, grinning.

Jeffries smiled a little crookedly. "Hell, be my guest, friend. It's been a while since you had a little Jack Black." He slapped Al on the back. "You done a good job."

Apparently overcome by relief and excitement, Chili stepped up and tried to hug Jeffries. He pushed her away, but not with the same fury he'd unleashed upon her earlier. "Get back, you fuckin' dyke," he growled good-naturedly. "You might start likin' boys and fuck up yer whole life."

Chili laughed and held out her arms to her lover. Kim walked willingly into her embrace and, over her shoulder, Chili winked at Eric.

"Hey!" Eric shouted. "Go to hell, both of you!"

The men laughed. The two women laughed and walked arm in arm toward the door. Kim, who up until this point had not bothered to acknowledge Eric's presence, turned to wave good-bye to George from the doorway. Her eyes met Eric's for one cool, empty split second. Then she was gone.

Funny, he thought, that seemed to have done it. The pain was gone now. Maybe he was finally learning. Not that he was terribly optimistic about living long enough to use what he'd learned. But he wasn't ready to roll over and die either. Not for love or anything else.

Mean Boy followed the women out the door. But Al hung back. He and John carried on a brief, whispered conversation. When Al left, scraping the door shut behind him, Jeffries popped the top on another beer, sprawled in a broken-down, avocado green recliner, and turned his attention toward Eric.

"Mr. Williams," Jeffries said genially, gesturing toward a straight-backed, chrome and vinyl kitchen chair, "have a seat. You ain't the first man to be de-balled by a pretty bitch."

"Fuck you, Jeffries," Eric growled, more for effect than anything else. And even though Jeffries laughed, he felt strangely good about having said it.

Although his clothes had long since been irretrievably ruined, Eric automatically swept the top layer of dust from the seat and back of the chair before sitting down.

"My, my," Jeffries said sarcastically. "This boy's mama would be real proud. Even under extreme stress, Mr. Williams manages to retain his gentlemanly demeanor. Such a tidy little insurance policy. Right, George?" Jeffries asked.

George, who was leaning against the wall near the window, munched the last of a pair of Twinkies and shrugged noncommittally.

Jeffries drew his .357 from his belt and sat gazing at

Eric as he stroked the barrel. "Hope you don't mind, Mr. Williams, but we decided to extend our policy . . . just in case."

"How long did it take you to plan this, John?" Eric asked.

Jeffries smiled. "Does it matter? The point is, I'm not the idiot some folks like to think I am, even though—sometimes—I let them think that because it suits me. Matter of fact, I'd make one helluva lawyer, don't you think? I never show all my cards and I never do anything half-assed, Mr. Williams."

On the way back out to the van, Al quietly reached behind his back, removed a .357 from his belt, checked the cylinder, and made sure the safety was off. Then he tucked the weapon carefully back in place.

Without speaking, the foursome climbed into the van. Al and Mean Boy sat in back. Chili took the driver's seat. Kim sat next to her in the passenger's seat, her left hand stretched across the space between seats to stroke her lover's thigh.

As they pulled up to the end of the driveway, Al leaned forward between the front seats and rested his hand on Chili's shoulder. "Turn left here and go about two miles, till you see a Phillips 66 lease marker on your right that says Tobias twenty-two," he told her. "You turn in there. Mean Boy, you'll get out and open the gate. Once we drive through, I have to watch for landmarks. So drive slow."

Chili nodded and pulled out onto the dirt road. As she drove, Mean Boy chattered away, punctuating his remarks with long drinks from the half-empty bottle of whiskey.

"Ain't this great?" he hiccupped. "Ain't this just fuckin' wonderful? We done it, right, Al? We really done it. Whooeee!"

No one else could have gotten a word in edgewise if

 they'd tried. Chili and Kim seemed content. Al waited, his mind on the money.

When the red and white lease sign reflected in the headlights, Chili slowed the van and then steered it off the dirt road and onto the neat, graveled entrance.

"Hop out, Boy," Al ordered.

Stumbling only slightly, Mean Boy climbed out of the van and half strutted, half staggered into the bright aura of the headlights aimed at the gate. On his way, he tilted back his head and finished off the last of the whiskey. Then, as he reached the gate, Mean Boy threw the bottle in a high arc. It landed, with a loud crash, somewhere in the darkness.

Chili turned to gaze lovingly at Kim, reached across the space between them, and patted her thigh. "We're almost there, honey," the redhead murmured. Then she turned her attention back to Mean Boy, who was lifting a heavy iron chain from around the heavy, welded pipe gate.

His eyes on Mean Boy, Al, still leaning between the front seats, slid his hand down the back of Chili's seat and down to his waist. As though he might be tucking in his shirt, he reached around his back and inside his belt. The entire series of movements was quiet and deliberate and took less than five seconds. Then Al slid his hand back up to where it had rested before and nestled the deadly business end of his .357 into the soft mass of red hair curling in the slight depression at the base of Chili's skull.

The bullet entered cleanly but expanded on its way through her brain, carrying her frontal lobe, eye sockets, and nose with it when it exited and hit the windshield. Chili died instantly. When her body slumped forward, what was left of her head crunched against the shattered windshield and her breasts rested against the horn on the steering wheel.

As the blast rocked the van, Kim panicked, screamed, and fought like a trapped animal to escape the sight of her lover's lifeless body. But before she could get her right hand on the handle of the door next to her, Al shifted the .357 to his right and fired again.

The force of the shot sent Kim's head crashing against the passenger window and shattered it. Her body slumped grotesquely against the door, the jagged edges of the window forming a faceted halo around what was once her lovely dark head.

When the first shot rang out and the van's horn shrieked into the darkness, Mean Boy threw himself onto the gravel drive and rolled into the weeds alongside the road. After Kim screamed and Al fired the second shot, Mean Boy stood up, crouched low, and ran toward the van. He stopped a few yards away, staring in disbelief at Kim's head.

"What the hell's—"

"Shut up," Al ordered. "We've got work to do." He was already shoving Chili's body into the space between the seats. "Jump in the back, Boy!" he shouted.

With Mean Boy safely inside the van, Al gunned the van's engine and hurried through the gate and onto the lease, the wind from the gaping hole where the windshield had been causing him to squint his eyes.

"Jesus, man," Mean Boy hollered gleefully. "I mean, this is fuckin' outrageous!"

Al ignored him as he drove approximately six hundred feet beyond the gate and down a winding, narrow road. A silent, abandoned oil pump loomed in the headlights like a prehistoric creature encased in rust. Behind the pump, the weed-infested slopes of a slush pit left by the oil company came into view.

Al stomped on the brake, shifted the van into park, and opened the driver's side door.

"Come on, help me with these bitches," he shouted irritably to Mean Boy as he struggled to haul Chili's dead weight over and across the driver's seat.

Mean Boy climbed out the side door, opened the passenger's door, and effortlessly removed Kim's slight body from the van. He carried her in his arms like a bride, one hand cupped around her lifeless breast, to the other side of the van, where Al stood waiting.

"I got it, man," Mean Boy said, unceremoniously dumping Kim's body onto the oil-soaked, red clay road. "John had this planned all along. What a guy, huh?"

Al nodded and motioned for Mean Boy to take Chili's feet. Together they sidestepped over to the edge of the pit, swung her body once, and heaved it out into the shallow sludge. Then they returned to the van for Kim's body and repeated the maneuver. Their work completed, the two men turned away from the pit.

"Well," Mean Boy said, wiping the gore from his hands on his shirt front, "we sure as hell took care of that, didn't we? Huh, Al? All we gotta do now is get the loot."

"'Fraid not," Al murmured, stepping backward down the slope toward the van and slipping his right hand behind his back.

Mean Boy tried to focus his one good eye on his one good friend, but the van headlights made him look like a bewildered rabbit, caught on the center line of a busy highway. "Whatcha mean, man?" Mean Boy asked, trying to shade his eye with one hand.

Al leveled his .357 and fired two quick shots. One bullet entered Mean Boy's gaping mouth and exited through the top of his skull, removing a section about the size of a yarmulke. The other bullet smashed through his Adam's apple and severed his spine. His arms flung wide like a sky diver bailing out of a plane backward, Mean Boy toppled toward the edge of the pit.

Al heard the body hit the sludge at the bottom of the pit but couldn't resist checking to make sure. He jogged back to the van, retrieved a flashlight from the glove box, and returned to the pit.

Kim's hair had fanned out over the murky mixture of oil and water that almost obscured her body from view. Her wide, open eyes staring sightlessly up at the stars. Chili lay face up, spread-eagle, her larger form still mostly visible and, where her face should have been, a gaping black hole as dark as the night sky, surrounded by fringes of red hair. Mean Boy had fallen between them, the remains of his head at a right angle to his body.

Al slid his weapon back into his belt, turned, and was on his way down the slope toward the van when two dark figures stepped out from behind the vehicle.

"That's it, McDougal," a voice rang out. "Put down your weapon."

Al instinctively reached behind his back.

Two shotgun blasts exploded simultaneously. Their loads tore away most of Al's chest. As his body fell back into a clump of weeds, he released his grip on the flashlight. It fell, bounced once, and rolled to the base of the slope.

"Got him, Sheriff," one darkened figure called to a Jeep pulling up the gravel road behind the van.

The Jeep stopped, and a massive figure emerged from the passenger's side, walked past the men at the rear of the van, and headed toward the sludge pit.

"Good work, boys," the big man rumbled. "Looks like that tip we got was straight." His light gray Stetson gleaming, the county sheriff stooped to pick up Al's dropped flashlight. "You hear the other shots?"

"Yes, sir," came the reply. "We were laying low less than a quarter mile away. I almost panicked and went in. Bill, here, had his infrared sight set and saw what was happening." The deputy nodded toward the pit. "Think there's probably a body or two waitin' up there."

A few more striding steps took the sheriff up the slope as far as Albert McDougal's body. He tilted his hat back on his head and glanced down only for a moment before climbing to the top of the slope and shining Al's flashlight down into the pit.

"Can't tell about the women," he called back to his men. "But the big one's probably Mean Boy Miller. Guess ole Albert just wasn't enjoying their company like he thought he would."

As he headed back down the slope, the big man addressed the deputies near the van. "This'll make the boss real happy. I'll get on the phone. Clean up and get plenty of pictures." The sheriff stopped and turned toward the pit. "Make sure you keep your yaps shut, too. Let's wait till we got 'em all. The boss'll want to make the first statement."

The big man climbed back into the car and was soon on his way back down the lease road.

"Yeah," chuckled one of the young deputies who'd remained behind, "I reckon the boss needs this one real bad, after all the shit that's gone down lately. He and the sheriff will come out smellin' like roses, come election time."

III Back at the farmhouse, John was singing his off-key rendition of "Love Me Tender" accompanied by a raucous banging and clanging of pots and pans. The menu wouldn't normally have been all that enticing to Eric. But tonight, when the aroma of canned beans and fried bacon filled his nostrils, his stomach convulsed with longing. George Davis spoke to him from the shadows for the first time since they'd entered the tunnel.

"You can always tell when John's happy," he mumbled. "He sings that miserable fucking song over and over."

John Jeffries entered from the kitchen. "Well, boys," he said, "camp stove works great! It's time for supper. Set the table, George. Five places is all we'll need."

George glanced at Jeffries, shrugged, and set about cleaning off the rickety table and finding plates and forks.

"Yes, sir, we got a visitor comin'," John said cheerfully, "and Al should be back any minute."

Eric heard a vehicle pull into the drive as if on cue. But he knew it wasn't the van. Soon, footsteps sounded on the porch outside. John stood up and walked over to the door, opened it, and extended his hand to the visitor.

"Come on in, Senator, we've been expecting you."

Eric felt a jolt of shock run through him as the immaculate figure of Glen Tobias shook hands with Jeffries as he moved across the threshold and into the farmhouse. John closed the door, moved aside the blanket hanging over the window, and surveyed the area.

"You didn't bring anyone with you, did ya?" John asked smoothly.

Tobias, his hands placed elegantly on his hips, gazed leisurely at Eric, whose still-cuffed hands were clasped together in his lap.

"The message you sent said come alone, John," The Dark Prince answered. Then he grinned. "And you know I always act appropriately."

John laughed. "I suppose you know Mr. Williams, here?"

"Certainly," Tobias responded. "How are you, sir? Pleasure to see you again."

Eric felt bile rise in his throat as he stared at the man's proffered hand. "What the hell are you doing here?" Eric muttered.

 John led Tobias toward one of the chairs that George was busy gathering around the dining table. "Why, Mr. Williams," Jeffries answered, "Perhaps you've forgotten, if you ever knew, that Senator Tobias is my attorney. Always has been. Better treat him nice, son. He's here to help."

George slopped mounds of beans and bacon on the senator's plate and two others. The three men seated themselves and began to eat.

"Don't you worry, Mr. Williams," the senator said around a mouthful of beans, "You're gonna be all right. I guarantee it."

"Just what the hell are you talking about?" Eric said, trying to calm the rising tide of anger and confusion that threatened to overwhelm him.

"Well, you see . . ." the senator said, carefully wiping the corners of his mouth with a handkerchief, "I received a message from John saying that he wanted to give himself up. But only to me. I intend to take him in, make sure he doesn't suffer too much for his actions during the riot, and return you," Tobias gestured at Eric with his fork, "to the loving care of your friend, the soon-to-be ex-governor of this great and glorious state."

Eric noticed that John was listening intently, but not to Tobias. Then he heard them, too. Strange, slapping footsteps sounding against the floorboards of the porch. Jeffries stood up, glanced out the window, and went to the door. "Well, now, George, looks like you better open another can of beans." Jeffries opened the door and said, "Come on in, Mr. Attorney General."

A short, boyish-looking man in jeans, a work shirt, and a canvas hunting jacket entered. His tasteful Cole Haan loafers flapped against the dusty floorboard as though they were oversized clown shoes.

Senator Tobias shoved himself back from the table and

stood up so fast that his chair crashed to the floor behind him. "What the hell are you doing here, Barry?" he said, choking on a half-chewed piece of bacon.

The attorney general smiled. "Don't let me interrupt your meal, Senator," he said smoothly. "You might as well begin readjusting your tastes to the less-sophisticated fare of your boyhood. I doubt you'll be dining at the governor's mansion any time soon. Tsk, tsk. Human greed is such an awful thing, isn't it? But then, it certainly made it easier to get you out here."

"What the hell are you talking about?" Tobias sputtered, his face flushing bright red as his hands formed tight fists at his sides.

John walked behind Tobias, righted his chair, placed his hands on the tall man's shoulders, and pushed him down into it. "Now, Senator," he said soothingly, "don't get your feathers ruffled. Mr. Morris will gladly explain it all to you. Have a seat, Barry."

The attorney general sat down, planted his elbows on the table, and clasped his hands earnestly together over an empty plate.

"You know, Senator," Morris said, "I'm surprised to see that an old country boy like you became so lax about watching the trail behind him. You've been so busy trying to take political advantage of this situation, hoping to ruin Horton's bid for reelection, that you never even considered that John might have resources other than yourself on the outside. In fact, I'm surprised you didn't think about planning a riot yourself."

Tobias's mouth dropped open, and Barry Morris and John Jeffries laughed heartily.

"Well, now, Senator, you didn't think God brought you that good fortune, did you?" Barry asked.

"Guess he's just got too much honesty in his soul for his nickname," John Jeffries smirked.

Barry nodded and smiled. "Of course, there was the little payoff for John here. See, he's always felt you might have done better for him during his last trial. Kind of thought the Dark Prince turned into a pale chicken and didn't give him the kind of representation he deserved."

Jeffries nodded solemnly. "Did you think folks would forget you'd represented me? I, for one, will never forget."

"Well," Morris continued, "after you and he made contact, John called me. Seems he figured he should hedge his bets. Now it appears he was smart to do so. This little affair is my ticket to the governor's mansion and your ticket to oblivion. Mr. Jeffries isn't going to turn himself in, Tobias. But you are going to turn yourself in . . . forever."

The senator managed a trembling laugh and shook his head. "You must be crazy, Morris," he drawled. "You haven't got the balls to pull this off."

"Oh?" Morris asked smoothly. "I wouldn't bet on that." The small man reached into one of his copious jacket pockets. Tobias visibly stiffened. Morris paused with a smile, then withdrew his hand and laid passports, visas, and a thick stack of thousand-dollar bills on the plate in front of him.

"It took hardly any work on my part," Morris said casually. "You did most of it yourself, so we're just gonna leave you here with the evidence. Let's see," Morris said, ticking off his fingers as he went through an imaginary list. "There are the blueprints of the original penitentiary that show the tunnel, Ramirez's stolen rap sheet, your previous involvement with Mr. Jeffries and Mr. McDougal. See? The pieces fit together beautifully."

Tobias sprang up out of his chair, his eyes burning with fury. "You sorry little shit!" he screamed.

A shot rang out, and stunned shock replaced the anger on Tobias's face just seconds before he fell, face first, across the table. One by one, dishes crashed to the floor as the senator's body slid backward, his fingers raking the table's grimy surface. Blood soaked darkly through the back of his light gray jacket and onto the stack of bills.

Eric had instinctively dropped and rolled toward the corner of the room, hoping to stay out of the gunfire. When it ended, he sat up and gazed at the macabre scene. Everything was going wrong. Although most of it made horrible sense, certain pieces of the puzzle were still missing.

Barry Morris stood up and extended his hand to John, who shook it heartily. "Good job, John," he said.

"My pleasure, sir," John Jeffries responded, releasing Morris's hand to reach for the documents lying on the plate.

Morris grabbed his arm. "Not so fast, John, we still have to deal with Williams."

When they turned toward him, Eric spoke off the top of his head, as he sometimes did in court on a bad day, hoping he might accidentally draw the right answers from his subconscious as he asked questions designed to buy time.

"Wait a second, John," he said lightly. Jeffries turned to look at him. "Something puzzles me. I mean, you've planned all this so carefully. Have you ever thought about what the attorney general will do if you . . . accidentally . . . get caught?"

Jeffries's eyes narrowed.

"And you, Barry," Eric continued, this time addressing the attorney general. "What are you going to do once old John here leaves the state? If he's arrested in, say, California, why shouldn't he spill his guts to save himself?"

Barry's face was impassive, but he took one fateful, involuntary step away from his partner. His small, seemingly insignificant movement was all the evidence Jeffries needed. The former inmate raised his .357 and pointed it at the center of Barry Morris's chest.

But the shot, when it came, was not fired by Jeffries. It came from the other side of the room, where George Davis had leveled the scattergun and aimed it at Jeffries's right arm. George pumped the weapon once more as Jeffries reeled and staggered. The second blast struck John Jeffries full in the chest and threw him against the dining room wall, where he slid slowly down, leaving a bloody smear behind him as he collapsed.

The attorney general recovered quickly. "Thanks, George," he said, his voice only slightly shaky. "I was starting to get a little nervous."

Eric's mind swam, trying to gather floating bits of debris and keep them together. Then he remembered. George had served with Barry's brother in Vietnam.

Barry was watching him.

"I suppose," the attorney general said, "you've begun to guess that George and I go way back. In fact, we planned the whole thing months ago. I made sure George was transferred, first. We agreed that John was the only one with the guts and the influence to pull off a riot and an escape. George, here, helped engineer the whole thing. Even delivered the blueprints and the rap sheet on Ramirez."

"We knew John wanted to involve Tobias in order to exact his revenge," George added, "so at the proper moment, we sent the senator an invitation to the party."

Eric looked at George. "Then the interview, the hearing, it was all just cover?"

George nodded. "Morris felt from the outset that I would never make parole. The governor would never go for that. He'd have overridden a favorable recommendation on political grounds. So I agreed to work on the inside, making sure everything went as planned. Jeffries was smart, but unpredictable as hell."

Eric wondered if George realized he'd just described himself. He felt dumber than he'd ever felt in his life. How, he wondered, could he have forgotten that Horton had prosecuted George and would have felt compelled to see him serve out his term?

"But what about the others?" he asked finally. "How did Chili and Kim get from prison to the freedom end of the tunnel?"

"That was easy," Morris said. "The guard John released to talk to the authorities made a phone call. He also arranged for the weekend pass for Chili and left directions and provisions stowed in the van."

Eric considered all the pieces carefully. "But Barry," he asked, "don't you have a few more little loose ends? What about Al, Mean Boy, Chili, and Kim? What if George decides to talk? And George, aren't you going to worry a bit, for the rest of your life, that your buddy here might get his ass in a crack or get nervous? I mean, to old Barry here, you're kind of like a loose cannon, rolling around, just waiting to go off. Aren't you?"

George grinned, shrugged, and reached for the stack of bills and documents still lying on the empty plate. He counted out the cash and gazed fondly at the attorney general. "Fifty thousand, just like you promised, man," he said. "Sorry, Williams. Al, Mean Boy, and the chicks have all been taken care of. Thought you'd have figured that out by now. Your little psychological trick's not gonna work. Barry and I discussed all this long ago. I know the risks and I've agreed to take them."

"His new Social Security number and driver's license will get him a good start," Morris said. "All that's left is a little staging of the evidence." He nodded toward Eric and headed toward the kitchen as George loaded a cartridge into the scattergun, pumped it, and raised the barrel in Eric's direction. Eric felt his heart pound in his ears. So it was going to end now. Like this. He braced himself and fought the urge to shut his eyes.

"Hey, Barry!" George shouted. Barry stepped back into the dining room with a puzzled look that disappeared as soon as the blast hit his face.

The attorney general fell to the floor with a thud and lay next to the body of the inmate he'd helped to escape. Their blood mingled thickly.

George walked up to Eric, took a key out of his jeans pocket, and undid his cuffs.

"All I ask, Mr. Williams," he said, "is a head start. I'll disable the cars on the way out, so it'll take you a while to go for help." George turned toward the door.

"George?" Eric said softly.

George stopped in front of the window, tore down the blanket, and turned toward Eric. The sky was beginning to lighten in the east. The lush landscape was awash in peaceful, misty predawn light. George loaded a cartridge in the scattergun.

"Why in hell did you let yourself get in so deep?" Eric whispered.

"The riot would have happened eventually, Mr. Williams," George said. Then he sighed. "Had to, the way things were going. I tried to tell people, but . . ." George shrugged. "This way, maybe a few of the assholes will be out of the way when you go to work to make your changes."

"Don't run, George," Eric pleaded, "We can still set all this straight. It won't be easy, but—"

"Thanks, man," George said, shaking his head, "but no, thanks. We've been over all that before."

Something nagged at Eric's senses, made them tingle.

He blamed it on the fresh air blowing in from the open window.

"I'm gonna see how it feels to live clean for a while in places that don't have bars on the windows," George Davis said. "Good luck, Mr. Williams." The veteran stepped to the door and opened it.

With a rush, Eric realized that all sound outside the house had ceased. No crickets chirped, no owls hooted from the trees, no frogs croaked in the backyard, and the birds . . . George seemed to sense Eric's sudden concern and turned to look at him.

A quick pistol shot rang out. George Davis spun around in slow motion, grabbing at his right shoulder with his left hand. A second shot caught him in the chest. He sat heavily on the floor, like a puppet whose strings had snapped.

"No!" Eric shouted, *"No!"*

Davis struggled to rise from the floor, blood gushing from his chest wound. His legs wobbled as though they had turned to rubber, and he fell, striking his head hard against the floor.

Eric crawled over to where the inmate lay dying in spreading pools of his own blood. One look told him that any help he might have given was already too late.

The door slammed inward, and Eric, prepared to see a farmer, a county sheriff, or maybe Al, stared in total surprise.

The big man hobbled into the room with a smile as broad as Texas and stood shaking, his back against the wall. Around his midsection was tied a blood-soaked burlap bag. He'd aged ten years. But he was still the most beautiful sight Eric had ever seen.

"I seen it all, cowboy," Earl muttered deliriously as he lowered himself awkwardly to the floor. "I seen he was gonna shoot ya." Dry heaves shook the man's huge frame.

 He cleared his throat painfully. "Glad I made it to the party in time."

"Earl, you goddamn crazy son of a bitch," Eric murmured. Tears flowed freely now down his face as he watched the big man slide sideways onto the floor, a .38 still clutched in his hands.

EPILOGUE

Eric spent three days in the hospital, where he was treated for shock, given sedatives, and allowed to sleep for twenty-four hours straight. After three days he was released and sent home for a much-deserved two-week rest. Jolene drove down to pick him up and stayed with him for a few days until he felt strong enough to be on his own.

Lying by the pool in the backyard, he began jotting down the details of his experience, mostly out of habit. He'd been taking trial notes for so many years that committing information and events to paper was a habit. Now, however, doing so became therapeutic. He found himself getting off track, taking side trips into trauma. As he wrote objectively about the torture he'd endured and the deaths he had witnessed, all the painful losses he'd experienced prior to the riot—his father's death, his mother's death, abandonment by Mary Jane—came flooding back. The darkness of his depression was mirrored by new nightmares that took him back to the blindfolded walk through the prison and his passage through the tunnel.

After a while, however, the nightmares became less frequent, and one bright sunny morning, Eric stared at the stack of legal pads on his desk and thought it was time he took stock of what he'd learned and made his experience count for something. He knew he would probably never be as good a writer as George might have been. But he, not George, was alive to tell the tale.

He was thankful to Earl, even though George had not actually been a threat, by then, to anyone but himself. He was grateful for and amazed by Earl's dogged determination. How many men, in such excruciating pain, Eric wondered, could or would track murderers for miles through the dark, hot-wire a pickup from a farmhouse, and save a friend from what had been, in his own feverish, terrified mind, imminent danger. When Earl had talked to Eric in the hospital, he had told him that even in his feverish state he had remembered from his days of quail hunting with other guards around the penitentiary that Senator Tobias had had an old home place, a farmhouse near the penitentiary, where they would sometimes stop during their hunt. He took a guess, knowing the direction that they were proceeding when he had last seen the taillights. Unfortunately, his guess was right. He was also surprised to discover that George Davis did not pose a threat to Eric. It saddened him that one more had to die.

As he sat by the pool, trying to reconstruct events, Eric found he had no idea how long he had sat crying in the old farmhouse. He vaguely remembered crawling over to check on Earl and his relief when he discovered the man was not dead but only unconscious. He also remembered trying to pack torn, bloody strips from George's shirt around the oozing wound in Earl's side. The drive in Barry Morris's four-wheel drive vehicle to a nearby farm, his conversation with an old man about calling the sheriff, both were events he believed only because they'd been reported to him by reliable sources.

During his stay in the hospital, the riot had petered out to its inevitable end. Governor Horton negotiated a settlement when the inmates ran out of food and water and began fighting among themselves concerning who would represent their interests at the bargaining table.

Although the media had left him alone as long as he was in the hospital, reporters descended upon Eric as soon as he was released. ABC, CBS, NBC, and CNN showed up at his door, and representatives from various production companies called both his home and his office offering huge sums for nationwide talk show appearances. Jolene read his prepared statements and turned down all requests for appearance and interviews.

The governor, however, was not so shy. After all, his television appearances made for incomparable free political publicity. No doubt on Reardon's advice, he refused to appear on *Geraldo*, opting instead for the Larry King Show, whose statewide ratings jumped sky high the day the show aired.

Shock over Barry Morris's involvement in the events wiped out all opposition to Horton's reelection. No one remembered, once the riot ended, that the governor's refusal to appropriate money for the expansion and modernization of the prisons had created an environment that bred the violence that eventually gave birth to tragedy. The public would only remember that a handful of civilians had died in the riot compared to the hundreds of inmates who had killed one another. Churchgoers across the state praised God and condemned the rioters to rot in hell. If they didn't rot in prison first, that is.

Oddly enough, Senator Tobias, dead, accomplished more, in terms of ensuring his own immortality, than he had while he was alive. It seemed to Eric that before Tobias was six feet beneath his old stomping grounds, he was already being hailed as a homegrown hero who had bravely given his life during negotiations over the release of a hostage.

John Jeffries was celebrated as the kingpin of the riot, a fact that Eric knew would have pleased him enormously. His body was claimed and buried by an aunt. Mean Boy was laid to rest in a small rural cemetery. Chili and Kim were buried side by side in a small cemetery for female inmates behind the McHenry women's facility. A support group composed of paroled female inmates, headed by Lydia Steele, was allowed to attend the ceremony. Earl called one day to tell Eric that he'd seen a report that indicated John C. Calhoun, a.k.a. Muhammad El Amin, had been busted in Chicago on charges of distributing huge quantities of cocaine.

Ethel Wilson, who'd been picked up and cared for by one of Calhoun's followers, stopped by one day and treated Eric to the best sweet potato pie he'd ever tasted. Eric wasn't really surprised to hear she'd decided to continue serving on the board. "That fiasco," she told him, "just reaffirmed my belief that what I'm doing is what God intends for me to do. How about you?" she asked him.

Eric smiled and shook his head.

"God always has a plan," she murmured, smiling. "Just sometimes it takes a while for some of us to see his reasons."

Eric's only reply was a hug, but that seemed sufficient.

Jolene called to tell him that the electric chair in the basement of the prison had been destroyed. The legislature, she said, had passed a more humane bill for the carrying out of the death penalty—lethal drug injections.

By the end of his two-week vacation, Eric's mind was made up. He resigned from the parole board, sold his house, and sold his firm to his brightest, best associate for a reasonable sum. Armed with his journals and dozens of filled yellow legal pads, he moved to a small town in Colorado, determined to live alone and write his book.

Eric still swims, still dreams. But now, instead of diving into pools he cannot reach, or struggling through dark tunnels toward a vague, distant light, he reminds himself that he can now control his dream activities in ways he could never totally control before.

On occasional visits back to the state he once served as a member of the pardon and parole board, Eric makes a

point of visiting Earl at his office in McHenry Penitentiary.
Earl grabs his cane, and the two friends walk to the McHenry's men's cemetery, fifty feet outside the whitewashed walls, atop Peckerwood Hill, where the unclaimed bodies of dead inmates are buried. There they remember a man whose death both witnessed, whose funeral both missed, and whose soul they know lives on in the rehabilitation programs that occasionally rise, however briefly, above the state's political quagmire. George Davis's body lies buried in a grave next to that of Larry Baker, the last man in the state ever to ride the lightning.